Alien Legacy: The Shapeshifter

A SciFi Romance (Ancient Aliens
Descendants Book 2)

Keri Kruspe

StarChance Productions

Contents

Glossary

Adapa (a-dap-a) father to Raiden, Zamush, Michel, Pete, and Ben. Hero in The Day Behind Tomorrow.

Akurn (ack-urn) rogue planet in an elliptical orbit around the sun every 3600 years.

Alaingar (al-lain-gar) Akurn Warlord (The Shapeshifter).

Anbu (an-boo) Captain of Murduk's guard

Arammu (are-moo) "love"

Azadi (ah-zaa-dee) Hidden city under the moon's surface.

Bahadur (bah-a-door) Akurn guard (The Shapeshifter)

Ben Duncan: Hero of Alien Legacy: The Empath. Birth name: Ibru-Um (eye-bru uhm)

Commander Kud (cud) Loyal follower of sub-Prince Murduk. Commander of Far Deep Base.

Damkina (dam-kee-na) Akurn nobility – undercover spy for sub-Prince Murduk

Damuzi (dam-oo-zee) Co-ruler of Azadi

Dhasa (Dah-ash-a) "asshole"

Eengurra (Ee-gu-ra) Capital city of Akurn

Edinni (in-din-ee) Co-ruler of Azadi

Ennugi (in-you-gee) Akurn Warlord (The Shapeshifter)

Ereshkigal (eres-ki-gal) Sumerian goddess of the dead or underworld.

Goraxag (gore-axe-ag) Semi-sentient creature used by the Akurns to track prey (The Shapeshifter)

Inanna Azneas (ah-za-nas), Princess of Akurn – mother to Raiden, Zamush, Michael, Pete, and Ben. Heroine in The Day Behind Tomorrow

I'lati (eye-la-tee) "Goddess".

Jazmi-Tiamat (tia-maat) "Maiden of Life" Heroine of Alien Legacy: The Mage

Jaragua (jar-a-goo-a) The world's smallest lizard - a dwarf gecko.

Jelena Aqru (ack-ru) Heroine of Alien Legacy: The Vampire

Jena King McFarlane - Heroine of Alien Legacy: The Shapeshifter

Jordyn Lamont – Heroine of Alien Legacy: The Psychic

Julienne King – Heroine of Alien Legacy: The Empath

Kahu (kah-oo) prison/holding cell/interrogation room

Katr (kat-are) Akurn mouth gag – expands to cover the mouth

Khoshgel (kosh-gel) Akurn endearment. Means "beautiful".

King Du-Uru (doo-are-you) King of Akurn, father to Princess Inanna and sub-Prince Murduk

La'um (lay-um) Akurn guard for Naram-Sin

Lukurra (luke-you-ra) Ancient Akurn word for enemy.

Mattaki-bunu (mat-ta-kee bun-you) An Akurn warlord killed by Murduk

Meskim xul (mesh-kim zool) Akurn curse for evil fiend.

Michael Johnson – Birth name Sandu Etlu (san-dooet-loo) Hero of Alien Legacy: The Psychic

Nabalkuta (naa-bal-koo-ta) Official process to overturn the Akurn monarchy.

Namatar (nam-a-tar) "Lady of the Great Akurn" – The goddess of death and birth. Rules the underworld.

Ngish (n-gish) "penis"

Ninmah (nen-mah) Early goddess of Akurn in charge of pregnancy and birth

Nisba (nes-baa), High Priestess of Temple Namatar

Nungal (nun-gul) Murduk personal guard

Nutesh snare (nut-ish) Akurn slave collar

Pete Hayes: Birth name Ara-Riyad (a-ra ree-yad) Hero of Alien Legacy: The Shapeshifter.

Puzur-Assur (pu-zoor Ah-sir) Akurn Warlord. Damkina's father.

Queen Asta (ah-stah) Akurn. Mother to Princess Inanna

Raiden (Ray-den) Birth name: Domuzi (dom-oo-see) "Son who is life" Hero of Alien Legacy: The Mage

Rappu (rap-oo) iridescent bridle/gag

Rearith, House of (ree-earth). Noble house of Warlord Alalngar from Akurn.

Sahu (saw-hoo) "pig"

Sub-Prince Murduk Utuk Xul (mur-duck u-tuck zool) Series villain

Transkip (trans-skip) transporter device used with mirrors

Uruk (you-rick) sub-Prince Murduk's personal guard

Wapiti (whap-eye-tee) An Akurn domesticated animal - usually used to swear "*wapiti* shit"

Yetu (yet-oo) "shit"

Zamush (zaa-mush) Birth name: Nasaku-Kan (nas-a-koo kahn) Hero of Alien Legacy: The Vampire

Ziyatum (sigh-ya-tum) Akurn warlord

Zikia (zee-kee-a) The Akurn spaceship hidden in the mountains of the Himalayas. It was the vehicle that Inanna and Adapa used to escape the great flood before their sons were born.

Chapter One

~Pete~

Okay, what sick asshole sucked all the oxygen off the planet?

Pete snorted. Someone might as well have wrapped his happy ass in cellophane, shoved him into an air-tight container, and then dumped him into a deep ocean under thousands of pounds of water. He was a drowning man, dying to be anywhere else so he could breathe the sweet taste of freedom.

Oh sure, stopping an alien invasion he could handle. Finding an elusive woman created to find and kill him he could handle. But watching his baby brother fall hard and fast for Julienne, a woman he just met, was hard to stomach.

No way was Pete going to stay while his brother made the same stupid mistake he had eons ago. The piercing squeeze between his shoulders made his head pound. Time to let it all go and find release.

And the only way to do that was to sneak... er, take some unofficial, unexpected vacay time. Before he snapped.

See, he was a thoughtful guy. He'd be doing the family he loved a huge favor by taking off before his uncharacteristic surliness took over. It would be for their protection, of course. Besides, he'd only take off for a couple of days. If anyone needed him, he was only a thought away.

Yeah, now this was what he was talking about. All his cares and worries faded more the farther he drove his classic '68 cherry-red Shelby Mustang away from ground zero. The rumbling purr of his baby was like a lioness on the prowl, zooming up Route 50 high in the Sierra Mountains. Next stop, South Lake Tahoe, California, in the good 'ole U. S. of A.

The white convertible top was down as the stereo blasted Led Zeppelin's Rock and Roll. The pinch between his shoulders melted away with each mile. The ride through the nippy summer mountain air gyrated his thick hair, making the sable strands whip around his eyes. With his sight glued to the road, he reached to the glove box, pulled out a ball cap, and slapped it on. The band was tight, so no worries the thing would fly off.

He rested his elbow on the open shelf of the window while his other hand gripped the leather-covered steering wheel. The car responded with little coaxing as he sped through the twists and turns on the steep mountain incline.

Yeah, he needed this. He snorted, picturing his brother's mindless joy. Pete wasn't the same naïve twenty-something he used to be, and he'd never again give the supposed love of his life a chance to betray him.

Leaving would give him a chance to control his careening emotions before any of his psychic brothers noticed the pain he still carried. Sometimes living with a bunch of psychic jerks who not only read your mind but experienced your emotions was an enormous pain in the ass. Not sure which would be worse. Them trying to help, or them harassing the shit out of him. Or both.

Enough. He glanced at the picturesque towering mountains covered in tall, scruffy pines flanked by prickly manzanita shrubs and small trees. With a deep breath, he welcomed the fresh aroma of crisp, unpolluted air. With his shapeshifter ability to distinguish each scent, he savored the tsunami of the surrounding wildlife. Plenty of big game—deer, bear, and coyotes, to name a few. It was the smaller prey, like rabbits and raccoons, that he wanted to pursue. And he wouldn't wait until nightfall either. As soon as he got to the house, he'd let loose and hunt.

Yeah. His wolf was itching to come out and play.

Pete expelled a heartfelt sigh with a smirk. Even though the family was making plans to thwart an alien invasion, they didn't need him right now. They were too busy trying to figure out how to find Julienne's identical quintuplet sisters. Once they did that, his chance for fun time would come to a screeching halt. They'd order him back, and he'd have to go to fetch one. But until that happened, his life was his own.

He snorted. Like those women were some kind of threat. Oh sure, his older brother, Raiden, more than likely went over in mind-numbing detail all the logical reasons those women were essential. When his brother talked in his dry, monotone way, Pete had a tendency to tune him out. Why didn't his family just wait for Michael, their middle brother, to have a vision?

That was how this whole damn thing started, anyway.

Michael's precog vision was all about Julienne and her sisters and how they were the key in defeating the alien Akurn invasion. No reason to think the man wouldn't have another one. And if he didn't, Michael's other talent would get them what they needed. For shit's sake, the man was a hacker extraordinaire—wanted in five different countries, no less. He could find anyone or anything on that damn computer of his.

Thinking of the pretty Julienne made Pete's frown deepen. Just because Ben fell for the woman didn't mean Pete would be doing the same thing with one of those sisters. No way would he get caught up in any romantic crap again. He shuddered. Watching the pair acting googly-eyed left a sour taste in his mouth.

Eh, what a crock! The only genuine love in existence was between him and his family. Outsiders had their own agenda, and you couldn't trust them. End of story. Even though the deep and abiding feelings his parents had for each other was the real deal, not for a second did he believe his brother experienced the same phenomenon with Julienne. Hell, she was attractive and all, but come on...

The important thing to remember was Julienne and her sisters were genetically engineered as catalysts to attract the sons of his mother—the alien princess Inanna. They could somehow drain him and his brothers of their psychic powers. It had to be dumb luck that Julienne had fallen in love with his brother before she realized what they'd created her for. Instead of killing Ben's powers, she did some damn woo-woo thing, and she now mirrored his empathic talents.

Pete suspected their psychic talents were getting stronger with each passing day. Not that he understood that ridiculous fairytale. How could their "love" override genetic programming?

A large RV plugging ahead slowed him down. No biggie, he'd just cruise by. Not like he had to worry about an overzealous cop pulling him over. No better time to try out the illegal high-tech radar detector his brother Michael had installed last week. He sped past the senior-mobile with a casual wave and grinned as the cool wind whipped around him.

Whistling, he continued up the mountain to Echo pass before entering the small city of South Lake Tahoe. Squinting behind his Maui Jim sunglasses, he basked in the change of scenery as he slowed down. He passed the more-populated area on the California side and headed to Stateline on the Nevada border.

While it would be nice to crash at one of the bigger hotel/casinos, staying at the small cabin he'd built around the late seventies would give him more freedom. That way he could run in the forest without worrying about anyone seeing. He shivered and smacked his lips. Time to run wild as a wolf in the pristine landscape of the surrounding mountains.

The two-lane highway expanded into four.

He eased up on the gas as he approached a red light at the end of the casino corridor. With a forefinger, he pushed his cap up. Nice, look at all the bountiful beauties walking around in skimpy bikini tops and short shorts. Off in the distance, a unique shade of red hair caught his eye and made his breath catch. Whenever he saw that color on a woman, he rubbed a fist over his heart to soothe the ever-present ache.

Son-of-a-bitch! Qamra hadn't crossed his mind in decades, and here he was thinking of her twice in one day. Unbelievable how her betrayal still stung after all this time. You think he'd be over the whole friggin' thing by now.

A curvy blonde in the middle of a female entourage strolled by and caught his eye. She glided across the crosswalk, each sway a mesmerizing dance of feminine grace as she passed the front of his car. Here was his chance to get rid of the painful memories plaguing him. Slim round hips swung in mouthwatering invitation. The lovely creature might barely be in her twenties, but with her experienced hard glance at every man around her, she was a far cry from a naïve debutante.

"Hey, love," he called over the rumble of his muscle car. "Could you tell me where the Lake is?"

Even though the tall buildings hid the clear alpine body of water from where he sat, he damn well knew it was on the left while the lofty peak of Heavenly Ski Resort was on the right. He wanted to check how open she'd be to spend the weekend with him.

The blonde stopped, and so did her friends. They all looked him over as if sizing up a prized bull.

His habitual smile widened as he returned the favor.

She leaned on the metal railing separating the road from the sidewalk. Her delectable cleavage swung as she moved.

He pursed his lips and gave a low whistle.

"Well, that depends." She straightened with a narrow glare. Her friends hung back with varying degrees of smirks.

Okay, he'd play along. "On what?"

"On whether it's old fart day at the beach or not."

With an expert flick, she flung her long flaxen hair over her shoulder. Turning to her companions, she giggled. They walked away laughing with the words "old dude" ringing.

Pete jerked when an angry honk blasted from the car behind him. With a wave of acknowledgment, he pushed the gas pedal. Blondie and her friends made condescending gestures and blew kisses as he drove by.

With a sheepish grin, he had to laugh. Although he and his brothers stopped aging when they hit their mid-thirties, if that girl knew how old he really was, she'd run for the hills in terror.

Singing along with the classic rock blasting from his stereo, Pete rolled up Kingsbury grade and turned off the main street and headed down a beaten trail. The car climbed with ease over the unpaved dirt road, and it didn't take him long to reach the cabin. He parked in the attached garage, turned the motor off, then grabbed two small overnight cases and the sack of groceries he'd stopped to get. As the garage door closed behind him, he put his thumb on the biometric security panel to let himself into the house.

A sense of homecoming made him warm. He loved this place, especially since he was the one who designed it. It boasted three primary rooms—living, bedroom, and kitchen. Nine hundred square feet of delicious freedom for a shape-shifter. Here, he didn't have to worry about any family matters, including those annoying aliens planning to attack. Not to say he didn't love his family and remained committed to the upcoming battle against the Akurns. But it had been way too long since he last roamed unfettered in his favorite animal shape. While he could, and did, morph into other animal forms—and people occasionally—he preferred the wild nature of a wolf.

He tossed his overnight bags onto the leather couch and went to the kitchen to put the groceries away. Whistling, he headed to the bathroom to take his contacts off. His vision was perfect; the brown lenses hid the exotic appearance of his irises. He opened the silver mirror cabinet and grabbed the case to put in his contacts.

When he shut the mirror, he stared at his larger-than-normal, dual-colored oval irises. Bright turquoise was the backdrop to the sunny yellow that surrounded his pupils. The yellow was jagged and sharp-edged, like a sunrise in some kid's drawing.

His reflection showed his habitual smirk was in place, which highlighted the bane of his existence, two deep dimples. He flicked a hand through the strands of his scruffy hair; the brunette mixed with several light streaks was a testament to his active lifestyle. Maybe he'd get a haircut sometime this weekend. He shrugged. Maybe not.

Attached to the lobe of his right ear, a 10K square sapphire stud winked in the low light. The prized possession was won in a duel in the 17th century, and he'd hate to lose it. He pulled the stud out and put it in the special case he kept in the medicine cabinet.

The comment from the young blonde rang in his ears, and he examined his reflection closer. He might look human on the outside, but he wasn't. He was the son of an Akurn woman and her hybrid husband who was part alien and part ancient hominid native to Earth.

Human misconceptions about extraterrestrials were many and varied, but the theory that aliens had the superpowers was all wrong. Actually, the ancient Earth inhabitants were responsible for the psychic abilities he and his family possessed. When the Akurns mixed their DNA with Earth's semi-sentient life forms, they created a strong hybrid with unimaginable powers.

Lucky for him, one of those hybrids was his father. Pete and his four brothers, a set of quintuplets, all carried the paranormal abilities their father did. But each one had their own special strength.

Pete could shape-shift and had the ability to manipulate his DNA at the molecular level. When he was younger, he'd been a little careless, and some humans in ancient Sumer had seen him shift into a wolf. That thoughtless action turned out to be one of the bases of the earliest werewolf legends 4000 years ago. Several cultures had sighted him over the centuries and created their own wolfman tales. Now that practically everyone in the world carried a cell phone with a camera, he had to put a tight rein on his urge to shift and run wild.

Not to mention how the precious wilderness was shrinking at an alarming rate.

He straightened his shoulders. The cabin sat on a coveted twenty acres, which was more than enough room for him to shift and roam around this afternoon.

As he sauntered out of the bathroom into the living room, he kicked off his shoes and tossed the footwear under the coffee table. He tugged his clothes off and dropped them onto the tan cushions of the couch. They'd be easy enough to grab when he came home later.

Once outside in all his naked glory, he closed his eyes and threw his arms up to bask in the warm sunshine. He let loose a gigantic smile and soaked up the rays while the door swung shut. The click of the biometric lock sounded behind him. Not for the first time, he appreciated using his thumbprint to open it rather than worrying about carrying keys when in wolf form.

He had no trouble visualizing his favorite animal, a silver-and-black wolf, as he transformed. When he opened his eyes, his perception was altered. Gone were the colors of his humanity and in its place was a spectrum of gray as he glanced about with wolf eyes.

He lowered his attention to the ground. Various animal scents were easy to separate so he could hunt the prey he wanted. He trotted around the cabin, taking his time to evaluate all the surrounding aromas to familiarize himself with the distinct smells. Satisfied, he took off in a joyous run.

In addition to the abundance of tall pine trees, towering aspens, cedar, and mountain hemlock graced the area. Small shrubbery dotted the thick landscape, along with various wildflowers still in bloom—larkspur, monkey flower, and tiger lily, to name a few. The air was fragrant, and his lupine nose reveled in it.

His heart thundered in response to the bouquet of different animals he picked up. The bear, mountain lion, and bobcat he avoided. He focused on the deer, marmots, and rabbits in vigorous abundance. With an eager growl, he followed the fresh scent of a marmot just ahead. His stomach rumbled as he visualized eating in style this afternoon.

Before he broke into a powerful run, he stepped on something cold with his right paw. Confused, he lowered his snout to see what it could be. With a snap, biting steel gripped his leg near the carpal pad of his wrist.

With an instinctive howl, he yanked back. Blinding, searing pain froze every thought. The metallic smell of blood filled the air. Blackness stole his consciousness.

~Jena~

Oh, for God's sake, Jena. Stop this crap and get your shit together.

Ha! First time Jena had used the words crap and shit in the same sentence without referring to the real thing. She frowned. Stupid unwarranted humor aside, there was no reason for her to suffer constant nausea, headaches, and fatigue. Not to mention the inability to enjoy a full night's sleep for months. At first, she worried she had something physically wrong with her. But according to her doctor, she was in peak health for a thirty-one-year-old woman.

So, on to a therapist. Big mistake. That man was as unhelpful as they came. The daffy doc offered empty platitudes that didn't apply to her. She threw away his prescription for Prozac and doubted she'd ever see his tiresome butt again.

The only useful suggestion he gave was for her to commune with nature. That she could embrace. She used to hike religiously before her adoptive parents died. Taking a deep breath, she adjusted the backpack across her shoulders and enjoyed the sharp, refreshing pine smell of the Sierra Nevada mountains in the Lake Tahoe National Forest.

Summer was in full swing, and the high mountain ravine was dotted with statuesque trees playing peekaboo with the bright rays of the sun overhead.

She detached the water bottle at the end of her knapsack.

A snap of an animal trap being released echoed.

Her breath stalled.

An unguarded howl tore through the air.

Not moving, she strained to locate where the noise came from. There, to the right, just over that small hill. She snapped the jug back onto the heavy backpack and shrugged to adjust it between her shoulders. Without a second thought, she scrambled toward that horrible, familiar sound.

An avid hiker and accredited veterinarian, she treated animals captured in inhumane steel contraptions all the time. No matter how much she fought them legally, it didn't stop the poachers from hunting and trapping wildlife in the forest.

When silence followed the howl, she stopped to listen. Nothing. With a grunt, she pulled her pack off and searched for her high-powered binoculars. When she found them, she dropped the bundle on the dry ground and scanned the immediate area.

Nothing... nothing... wait... there, just ahead. A flash of silver and black on the green-and-brown forest floor. She tossed the binoculars into the pack and slipped the strap over one shoulder, then hurried to where she hoped the animal was. Her heavy Doc Martin boots ate up the slanted, mountainous terrain.

When she caught sight of the enormous unconscious beast, she stopped dead in her tracks.

A wolf? There were fewer than a dozen known wolves in this area of the Sierra Mountains. With careful steps, she approached the still form. The creature was breathtaking. Its body was a midnight black with an underbelly of black and silver. On the front chest was a gray star shape, the same color held in the lengthy, coarse tail.

Dang, the creature was enormous. The average wolf was around five to seven feet, usually under two hundred pounds. This one had to be at least eight feet and two-fifty easy.

The animal was panting heavily. Its mouth slacked open, the tongue lolling out the side.

She carefully dropped the backpack behind her and sank to her hands and knees. Slowly she crawled closer, ready to bolt if the creature showed any signs of waking up. She put plenty of space between her and its massive fang-filled jaw. When the wolf didn't move, she relaxed. A quick glance past the head, and her eyes widened. The mangled wrist joint was caught in the jagged teeth of a steel trap.

Heat flooded her cheeks. Damn them all to hell! All the unnecessary pain the beast suffered because some asshole trapped and killed wild animals in the forest.

She settled on her heels. No way could she take care of this poor animal on her own. Without taking her eyes off the prone wolf, she pulled her cell phone from the side pocket of her pack and hit the speed dial.

"Wa' up?" A muffled masculine voice mumbled.

Nice, the boy was talking with his mouth full. Jena wasn't sure which twin brother answered, but it didn't matter. She needed both of them.

"You and Nick have to come and help me with an animal caught in another trap."

A loud groan. "Man, I just woke up! I'm not ready to help you with your dumb projects this early in the morning." His voice was clear.

Thank God he'd swallowed whatever he'd been chewing on.

"Besides, I'm Nick."

Jena rolled her eyes at her seventeen-year-old brother's whining. "I don't care if you're Thing One or Thing Two. I need both your butts now. Where's Nate?"

A deep snort. "Where do you think he is? He's in his room playing video games with Chris."

"Good." Jena feathered the tips of her fingers through the soft hair of the wolf's head. "Bring him too. We'll need all the help we can get."

"Why?" Nick almost sounded interested. If the conversation didn't involve music, sports, or girls, he'd normally tune her out.

"Nicky, it's a wolf."

"No freakin' way!"

Nick's whoop made her yank the phone away with a grimace.

"A wolf? Are ya sure?"

Oh, for Pete's sake. Not only was she a Doctor of Veterinary Medicine, she also had an obsession about wolves. Her brothers teased her about how she lived and breathed the animals. She'd decorated their home in a variety of wolf motifs. From the kitchen, to the living room, and the guest bed and bath. Scattered throughout were valuable works of art mixed with tacky tourist trinkets featuring a wolf or a pack of wolves.

The only relief was in each of the twin's rooms. They promised her pain and humiliation if she dared enter their sacred retreats. As if she'd ever step in their private domains other than to see if they were alive or not.

Since the death of their adoptive parents due to a drunk driver two years ago, Jena had been both mother and father to her brothers. She didn't hesitate to sell her condo in South Lake and move back home to be with them.

"Of course I'm sure it's a wolf."

She fisted her hand to stop from petting the wolf's head. Damn, only an idiot would pet a wild creature, unconscious or not.

"Grab Nate and Chris and meet me here as soon as possible." She eyed the sleeping giant. "Get a dolly and the animal tranquillizer kit I have in my home office. This is one big critter. He's gotta be over two hundred pounds."

"Woo-boy! No problemo, sis. Tell me where you're at and we'll be right there."

Jena gave him directions, satisfied they'd be there in less than fifteen minutes. She backed up and sat on a fallen log to monitor the unconscious animal.

The right thing to do would be to call animal control, but that wasn't something she'd seriously consider. Their policy was to kill the wild beasts instead of relocating them. Their insane logic was, the creature would find its way back and they'd have to do it all over again.

As she watched the animal pant, a wave of protectiveness made her wrap her arms around her waist to keep from touching it again.

The Blazer her brothers shared rumbled near. After a quick glance at the wolf, she met the truck as it pulled to a stop. Scrambling out of the front and passenger doors came the gangly forms of the twins and their friend, Chris.

Jena smiled at Chris. The contrast between him and her brothers couldn't be more amusing.

Chris was small in stature, barely five foot five, with the taut features of his Filipino ancestry.

The seventeen-year-old twins were poster boys for the next beach movie. Both over six-feet tall, with bright-blond hair and the sky-blue eyes to match. They each had lean, packed muscles on their tanned, wiry frames. Even though they were identical twins, their personalities couldn't be more different.

Nick, the eldest by two minutes, was the sports fanatic of the family. All sports were his passion, whether in school or enjoying the outdoor life in the rugged Sierra Nevada mountains. Snowboarding, waterskiing, and hiking were a few pastimes the extrovert teen loved.

Not to mention the many and varied girlfriends he juggled.

Nate's personality was the complete opposite. An introvert by nature, his obsessions were video games, playing guitar, and writing mysterious thoughts in a private journal. Nate had a steady girlfriend through most of high school, but after they broke up a couple of months ago, he remained single.

The one thing they both shared was their love of sarcasm. Something they practiced on Jena every chance they got.

"Where is it?" Nate's tone came out breathless. He clutched the tranquilizer kit to his stomach. "Is it all right?"

Jena grinned. The boy always had a soft spot for animals, just as she and their mother did. She hoped one day he'd become a vet like her. The only thing holding him back was he refused to put an animal to sleep. Even when necessary.

"It's over there."

She led the way, traipsing through the parched forest foliage. With the warm summer days and the lack of rain, the ongoing drought was in full swing. She coughed as dry dust floated with each step.

When they reached the vulnerable wolf, the guys let out low whistles in unison.

"Man, oh man, is it ever big!" Chris knelt by the snout that boasted a healthy expanse of sharp fang.

The passed-out animal hyperventilated. The right front paw bled while bent in an unnatural position.

Nate opened the medical kit and drew out a large hypodermic syringe and two vials. One vial held ketamine and the other diazepam. Poking the needle into the rubber tops, she created a mixture that would work with the animal's weight and keep the creature out while they transported him.

Jena shuffled close to the unconscious canid, stabbed the needle into the fleshy part of its hind leg, and injected the medication. She smiled when the animal's breathing became steady and the tense muscles relaxed.

"Great." She glanced at the fixated boys. "Now comes the fun part. How are we going to get it into the truck?" Thank God the old Blazer was big enough to hold the animal.

"Let's get the dolly. We'll grab the old beach blanket in the back. All we gotta do is lay him on it." Nate pulled Chris's sleeve. They scrambled down the small incline to the truck, taking the medicine kit with them.

Nick stayed and petted the wolf's head.

Jena checked the animal before putting the cap on the needle. She slid the syringe into a side pocket of the backpack. Back at the clinic, she'd dispose of it properly. "Nick, help me take its paw out of the trap."

He squatted next to her.

"When I open this up, pull it out."

She dragged the levers of the trap toward her in a continuous motion. The pressure was enough to widen the steel teeth for Nick to remove the mangled paw. She released the lever when the wolf was clear.

The steel teeth snapped shut with a dull clang.

"I hate these damn things." With a hard tug, she ripped it out of its anchor in the ground and dangled the monstrosity at her brother. "Here, take this and put it in the truck."

He grabbed it with a nod and scurried after his twin and Chris.

She slipped the bandanna off her neck and carefully covered the wolf's bloody wrist. First chance, she'd examine the damage closer.

The boys climbed back with the clunky dolly trailing behind Nick.

Nate carried a ratty old blanket and spread it beside the animal while Nick pulled the dolly next to it.

As only three young, healthy teens could, they picked up the enormous animal and placed him gently on the blanket before putting the heavy burden on the dolly frame. Nick grabbed the head of the dolly while Nate and Chris gripped the sides of the blanket to keep the animal level.

Jena walked in front, tossing rocks, sticks, and pinecones out of the way.

They made it to the Blazer with little difficulty.

She reached the pickup first and opened the back gate. "Think you guys can get it up here?"

"No sweat." Chris grinned.

The twins grunted.

"Here, move the dolly when we lift him. I'll hold the head." Nick scrambled until the three of them lifted the corners of the blanket and carried the wolf to the shelf of the tailgate, careful not the jostle the injury.

Jena yanked the dolly out of the way.

Nick got in the truck first and dragged the edge to the end as far as he could. He crawled to the side and helped the others push the wolf the rest of the way in. The animal was so long, the tailgate couldn't shut.

"Chris, sit here on the tailgate with me while Nick drives." Nate took his brother's place. Chris nodded and crawled to the other side. He glanced at Jena. "Did you walk or drive here?"

"I hiked, so I'll ride up front with Nick." She frowned at their precarious positions on the open gate. "You guys going to be okay there?"

Chris's broad smile had plenty of teeth. "You're kidding, right? You should have seen the time we..."

"Shut up, Chris." Nate narrowed his glare before sending Jena a wide-eyed look of innocence. "No worries. We'll be fine if Nick doesn't think we're drag racing. Right, Nick?" He aimed a sneer at the back of his brother's head.

"Whatever you say, hoss." Nick snorted.

Jena scooted in on the passenger side and turned to watch behind them.

Nick expertly drove through the rough mountain terrain and took them home.

By the time they reached their ranch-style home, Jena had made her decision on the best place to put the animal.

Nate and Chris jumped off before Nick completely stopped the truck.

"Take it to the kitchen," she commanded. "I've got a new momma German Shepard in the clinic and I don't want to upset her."

"'K." They said in unison as the three tugged the blanket edges and pulled the animal out. The weight of the wolf turned the fabric into a hammock.

Jena joined them, and together they made it to the kitchen.

Slowly, the boys lowered the unconscious animal to the linoleum floor.

Jena knelt to examine the injured paw. She twisted to look at Nate. "Get me a bowl of warm water with some antiseptic soap." She gestured to Chris, who leaned with his hands on his thighs. "Would you mind getting me that medical bag out of the truck?"

"On it!" Chris sprinted.

"What do you want me to do with this?" Nick held up the bloody steel trap and twirled it around. "Looks like one of Pumpkin Head's." That was the nickname the twins came up with to describe their annoying neighbor, Buzz Peabody.

"Put it with the others." She nodded at the locked cabinet containing the other traps. One of these days she'd take her collection to the Sheriff's department and file a complaint.

Chris came in and handed her the bag she asked for. Jena turned to the injured wolf and grabbed what she needed. Now to check the animal's vitals. Heart rate and rhythm, blood pressure, temp, oxygen levels... all good.

Nate stumble-walked with a full pail of water that he plonked upright beside her. The water spilled and made a puddle under the steel base, spreading and soaking her knees.

Ignoring the mess, she put on some latex gloves and took a sterilized rag and cleaned the wound. The teeth of the trap had cut through the muscle, but thank God, it missed the tendons. The animal needed sutures and antibiotics.

"I think it's going to be okay." She finished her ministrations. The boys surrounded her while she worked.

"He." Nate informed her.

"What?" Her mind was preoccupied with the best way to stitch the injury.

"The wolf." Nate gestured to the prone animal. "It's a 'he', not an 'it'."

Well, hell. She should have thought of that. What if it... um... he had been a female with pups? She shuddered. Thank God they don't have to look for a litter of wolf pups.

"Help me stitch him up." She rummaged in her medical bag. Pulling equipment out, she glanced at Nick and Chris. "Would you two go to the clinic and get me the extra-large portable kennel? Nick, you know where it is."

Jena finished the sutures when Nick and Chris came back with the commercial-quality steel pen for a large animal. She showed them where to set it up against the wall that connected to an outside kennel.

The three boys put the cage together, and Nate put a clean, old blanket on the bottom.

While they did that, she placed a medicinal sock around the wrapped bandage that covered the paw, and taped it. If the wolf tried to bite through that, she'd take other measures to prevent that from happening.

Satisfied the gauze was the best she could do, the four of them lifted the limp animal to lie in the pen. His large muzzle was open, and his limp pink tongue hung out the side.

Jena rattled the cage to make sure it was secure. When the steel didn't move, she gave a nod of satisfaction. The reinforced contraption would hold the wild beast while he healed.

Jena and the other three stepped back to examine the sleeping wolf.

"He's a beautiful animal." She bit her bottom lip. "I wonder how he got here."

Nick shrugged and glanced at the animal. "Who knows? How long do you think he'll be out?"

"With any luck, he'll be out until tomorrow." She tested the crate door one more time. "I'll check on him on and off tonight to make sure he doesn't wake up before he should."

"So, what'cha gonna do with him when he's better?" Nate asked.

Jena sighed. "We'll cross that bridge when we get to it." She caressed the top of the enclosure and stared into space. "I've got a feeling he's going to be a handful."

Chapter Two

~Special Agent Claude Reese~

C IA Headquarters, Langley, Virginia.

"Special Agent Stygian, please report to the operations center."

The command came through the earpiece Claude Reese habitually wore. At fifty-six and counting, he was the top special agent assigned to F.E.A.R., the First Encounter Alien Resistance division within the CIA. The original Men In Black. Apparently, the powers-that-be who created his team had a ridiculous sense of humor and assigned their agent designations based on the color black.

He snorted.

The click of his footsteps echoed as he walked down the white marble halls over the famous CIA seal on the floor. Keeping his mirrored sunglasses on, he strode to the private elevator that would take him to the operations center designated for his division.

Once he arrived, he acknowledged the three male and two female agents seated around the conference table.

"Gentlemen and ladies. Apparently we're here to meet with the deputy director." He settled at the head of the table and activated the communication screen floating in the middle. "Deputy Director Obsidian, all present. Please begin."

The outline of the division director remained blurred, the voice disguised electronically.

Claude had never met the man in person, only communicated through encrypted means.

"Very good, Special Agent Stygian."

The video changed to a satellite view of the dark side of the moon.

"We've already analyzed the intel you brought back from the alien's base on the moon," the director's metallic tone was without inflection. "Using NASA's classified Deep Space Climate Observatory feed, we've pinpointed the location of where we believe their secret base is."

The screen expanded and displayed a holographic image of the side of the moon few humans had ever seen.

"These are the pictures of the South Pole-Aiken basin, home to the largest crater in the solar system. Here there is a chunk of metal embedded a hundred miles under the lunar surface. It's estimated to be as large as the Big Island of Hawaii."

Claude sat back with steepled fingers.

Seventy years ago, F. E. A. R was created when a scout ship from Akurn crashed in a remote farmer's field in New Mexico. Until now, it had been a mystery how that alien scout ship could have been so far from its home. It had to have come from the moon base.

Claude twirled the gold band around his left ring finger. Although his wife passed away from breast cancer more than a decade ago, he was loath to take it off.

"Are we sure that's where the aliens are?" Agent Coal flexed his thick fingers. The Latino man was an ex-lieutenant colonel of the Air Force.

"Yes," came the response from the director. "The area is extensive enough to house several thousand Akurns and their laboratories."

"Boy, I'd sure love to explore that place." Special Agent Night, ex-Navy, spoke in a low baritone. The African-American man had prior aspirations for the space program.

The video changed to include the small oval device Claude had recently liberated while undercover.

"This is a portable Transkip activator they used to travel back and forth from Earth."

"You mean those assholes can come and go around here as they please?" This came from Special Agent Ebony in a no-nonsense tone. The Asian-American beauty was a former lieutenant colonel in the Army and served as the team's para-military ops officer.

"Yes, unfortunately." Claude cleared his throat.

"Agent Stygian, brief the team on how you retrieved this intel." The distorted voice of the director commanded.

"Yes, Director." Claude gave a brief nod. "While working with the aliens, I not only discovered that device while un-dercover at that insignificant bank, but I also found out what the aliens have planned once their rogue planet gets within transportation range of Earth. Their intention is to plunge our global economy into total chaos, giving them the opportunity to strip us of our precious planetary resources."

He quieted the hard murmurs by raising his hand. "Not only that, but once they finish ravaging as many resources as possible, their aim is to blow up Earth. According to their calculations, the shock waves from will hit their planet and propel them out of the sun's gravitational pull."

He took a deep breath and ignored the gasps and muttered curses.

"Once free of our solar system, they'll roam and pillage the galaxy, just as they'd done thousands of millennia ago."

"Wait, let's circle back and discuss that device you cap-tured. Why can't we use it to stop the aliens from invading?" Agent Raven crossed her arms. The African-American former New York detective in her early thirties was now their key Analytic Methodologist.

"I agree. We should use it to infiltrate their base." The last member of the team, Agent Onyx, was a hazel-eyed Caucasian-American nearing the end of his forties. The man was CIA through and through, and one of the top weapons analysts for the agency.

"That will be one of your top priorities, Agent Onyx. Examine this device so we don't end up jumping into something we can't control." Claude addressed the room. "I don't know about you, but I don't want to find myself stranded on the moon with no way back. Besides, bigger issues have come up that need our attention. For now, you're all assigned to investigate several unusual anomalies worldwide that have cropped up. Your debriefings are in your agency database. You have less than two days to ready your teams and head out."

Claude sat back and admired the professional acceptance from his team.

"In the meantime, my assignment is to locate those women the alien scientist, Thoth, was eager to find. Too bad I had no idea one of them worked for me at that bank. Since my undercover work with the aliens is at a standstill because of Thoth's disappearance, finding that woman, Julienne, or one of her sisters, is the only lead we have right now. I have to know why she and her identical quintuplet sisters are so important!" He banged a sweaty fist on the table.

"Do you have a way to find them?" Agent Ebony raised an elegant eyebrow.

"With the CIA's advanced database, we've located several promising candidates." Claude changed the screen, showing the pristine visage of South Lake Tahoe, California. "This is where I'm off to first thing in the morning."

"What will you do with those women once you find them?" Agent Coal grunted.

"Why, I'll bring them back here." Claude sat back and twisted the gold ring. "For safekeeping, of course."

~Pete~

A sharp, icy pain throbbed through Pete. Awareness came in spurts as he fought for control. His skin crawled with each suffocating inhalation. Or maybe it was just hard to breathe through the pungent smell of sour halitosis from a dog panting right into his nose.

It was a struggle, but his eyes gave the go-ahead to open. He blinked, trying to clear his vision. When he raised a palm to swipe across his face, nothing happened.

Well, hell. No can do when you don't have a hand to swipe with. Blurry eyes cleared as he lifted a *paw* instead. *Son-of-a-bitch!* He was still in wolf form. He jerked at the sight of the steel bars in front of him. Perfect. He was in a fucking cage.

A low, threatening growl from Dog Breath caught his attention.

Behind the gray steel bars, deep brown eyes glared above a short snout covered in fur as the animal snarled louder. Sharp, foxlike ears were stiff above bared fangs pointed in Pete's direction.

He whipped back to take in the rest of the animal. Ah, it was a medium-size dog, a red-and-blue Australian Heeler—a breed notorious for its herding abilities and its fierce safe-guarding nature.

And just his luck, this one was in full protective mode.

Growling, barking, and hissing with its hair raised as it bounced with each bark.

Pete sneezed through his long snout. Stupid dog didn't stand a chance against a two-hundred-pound wolf. Even with his injury.

While Pete was by nature an easygoing guy, in wolf form, his animal instincts kicked in. Which he wrestled for control more than he cared to admit. Right now, he'd better let this annoying mutt know who was the alpha from the get-go.

He returned the animal's growl with a deep, threatening one of his own.

The compact dog didn't flinch. Its bark increased. Large puddles of spittle flew as the smaller body quivered. The stubby tail swung back-and-forth as its stumpy legs bounced with each antagonistic woof.

Okay, buddy. Time to show this little monster who was boss. Pete jumped to his feet, only to crash in an undignified heap when his right wrist gave out. Shit, now he was pissed. He blasted an angry roar at the foe in front of him.

Which only caused the deranged dog to bark harder and faster, still hopping.

"Doggett!"

A feminine squeal startled Pete.

A woman grabbed the bouncing mutt by the collar and pulled it to a different door than the one she entered by. Her back was to him as she struggled with the ferocious hound. Wiry black and silver fur flew in every direction as the woman and dog battled for supremacy. After several tussles, she dragged the furiously yapping dog to a door and yanked it open.

A spectacular view of the forest on the other side showed he was still in Tahoe.

The woman pulled the dog up under the forelegs and dropped it outside. She shut the door before the mutt could rush back in.

It howled like a loon.

"Doggett, be quiet!" The woman smacked an open palm on the closed door. "Now!"

With her back to him, Pete ignored the throb of pain jumping to his feet caused. He licked his drooling snout and enjoyed the lovely view of her bent feminine backside on glorious display for his pleasure.

Lush, chestnut hair was confined to a ponytail, the heavy strands reaching a trim waist. Her body was athletic; solid muscles adorned her calves and her arms were toned. The khaki shorts she wore below a peach-colored tank top revealed tanned legs that led up to the firm, round globes of her ass. On her feet were sturdy hiking boots with heavy socks.

When she turned around to face him, his eyes widened. Holy shit! It was Julienne King. His brother Ben's mate.

Wait, that wasn't Julienne. While the two women might look identical at first, in reality they weren't. He shook his head.

The woman took tentative steps closer. The pupils in her eyes expanded.

She was only a few inches from the cage when her scent hit him. Lush, earthy, spicy, with a hint of sensual feminine musk that slammed into him.

Savage instinct gripped him. MINE!

Whoa, where in the hell did that come from? He sneezed. Licking his snout again, he drank in the image of the beautiful woman. She was absolutely breathtaking. Rich brown eyes crinkled at the corners as her warm, open smile made his heart thunder. A hint of a cute dimple graced the side of her full, sumptuous lips. After a sharp, satisfying breath, he imprinted her scent into his psyche. Now she'd never escape him. He'd be able to find her anywhere.

Her mouth held him mesmerized. Full lips with a light, glossy pout. In one corner, a modest brown mole teased.

He couldn't help it, his tongue hung out.

She knelt in front of the cage, just out of reach.

He whimpered. His tail thumped.

"Hey, baby." She crouched at eye level and cooed. "You're all right now, yes you are."

She might croon at him in baby talk, but she was smart enough to stay out of his grasp. Yeah, he loved an intelligent woman.

"How are you feeling, hmm? How's that nasty widdle paw of yours?" Her smile widened. "Are you hungry? I bet you'd like something to eat." She went to the counter beside the cage and pulled out a large measuring cup from a bottom cabinet.

With quick efficiency, she scooped chucks of dry dog food in an enormous silver bowl.

She came back, gripping it in both hands. "I know this isn't what you need or want, but it's all I've got." She gave a sheepish smile that matched her sheepish tone. "Eat up so you can get your strength back." Then she brought over a full dish of water and slid both between a slot at the bottom on the cage.

Holy shit! She's got to be kidding, right?

It might be a natural, meat-based dry food, but he'd be damned if he put that harsh, tasteless cardboard crap in his mouth. He'd probably choke on it. He'd rather starve. He refused to dignify the offering with a glance.

Besides, he'd rather feast his eyes on her.

She frowned and nodded to the bowl. "Come on, buddy. Try to eat."

His eyes narrowed. He sent her an image of a plump rabbit.

She glared back. "No rabbits for you, buster." Her brow furrowed as she bit her bottom lip.

Well, hell. Did she get a mental picture of a hare from him?

A loud commotion jerked his attention to the closed door between the kitchen and rest of the house. The ruckus was loud enough to be a proverbial herd of elephants heading straight for them. His gaze skittered to the woman. She acted like the massive clamor was an everyday thing.

She stared at him, frowning, arms crossed.

A deafening bang caused the door to fly open. The assault began. Three gangling teenage boys trampled over each other, laughing and jostling as they charged into the room at the same time. Then they did what all teenage boys did the minute they stormed a kitchen. They headed for the fridge.

Pete watched the boisterous trio. Hey, he was in someone's personal kitchen. Complete with all the homey touches of a well-lived-in room. Various scents fought for dominance as the woman stepped back. The lingering scent of past cooked meals struggled with the aroma of a garbage can that needed to go out. Added to the mixture were several animal odors. While not unpleasant, the sharp smells made him sneeze.

"Oh, cool!" one boy exclaimed, rushing to the cage.

The woman put a hand out to stop him. "Don't get too close." She moved to block the boy. "He's not drugged anymore, and being wounded, he might try to bite you."

Pete gave an internal snort. He had no intention of biting anyone. No matter how badly his paw throbbed.

"Eh, Jena, you worry too much." The boy shook off her restraining hand. "I'm not going to get too close."

He got too close.

Pete resisted the urge to snarl a short warning at the child to teach him a lesson. He instead rolled to his haunches and favored his injured paw. He did his best to be as nonthreatening as he could—tongue out, eyes wide, and tail wagging.

"Bro, look at his eyes!"

The youngster pointed at him. His companions crowded in front of the cage. In unison, the three put hands on their thighs and gawked with open mouths.

"Cool."

"Awesome."

As the boys watched him, Pete watched them right back. It didn't take a genius to figure out the first youth was an identical twin to his companion at the end. A shorter Asian-American male stood in-between. They all seemed to be in their mid-teens.

The twins were bright blond with shiny blue eyes. One twin was a touch more muscular with an outgoing, bold stare that reminded him of... himself. The other twin wasn't as toned and held himself back with a tense purse to his lips.

"Hey, sis! Why are his eyeballs so big and two different colors?" This came from the reticent twin. His brows furrowed as he scratched his flat stomach.

What did that kid call her? Oh yeah, Jena. Pretty name.

She replied with her hands on her slim hips. "Hmm, that's a good question. I've never seen anything like that before."

Pete narrowed his gaze at the rapturous expressions from everyone in the room. Well, shit. He couldn't change his eye color now. He settled his head between his paws. No matter. He'd be gone before it became a problem.

He glanced at the woman. Damn, look at him finding Julienne's sister without even trying. In less than a day, too. He checked around the kitchen before focusing on the appreciative grins from the teenage boys. Yep, best to stay as a wolf for now. Find out what he could about the woman and then shift when the time was right.

With her arms and legs crossed, Jena leaned on the edge of the kitchen counter and focused on him. With a loud sigh, she pushed from the counter and herded the boys away from the cage. "Okay, guys. Time to eat breakfast. Chores don't get done by themselves."

The three boys rolled their eyes in unison and groaned exaggeratedly.

"Shit, Jena. It's the middle of the summer..." The muscular blond groused.

Jena smacked him upside the back of his head. "What'd I tell you about cussing?" She poked him in the chest and tilted her head to glare at his advanced height.

The boy had to be at least six-one or two to her five-and-a-half feet.

"Why do we have to have this same conversation every day? Just for that, clean out the cages in the clinic before you go to work later."

The other twin hooted with a raised fist. "Yeah! Better you than me, Nick. Come on, Chris. Let's grab some chow."

"Right behind ya, Nate."

They bumped elbows before whooping and scrambling to the refrigerator.

Watching the antics of the teenagers reminded Pete of how he and his brothers were at that young age. While that had been a long time ago, there were some things you never forgot.

"Damn it!" Nick crossed his arms and glared at Jena.

She, in return, mirrored his stance with narrowed eyes and a tapping foot.

When she didn't back down, the boy huffed and ran a hand through his scruffy hair. "Fine, sis. You win."

Jena's bright-brown eyes twinkled when she motioned to a large see-through plastic jug on the counter tucked in a corner. Taped to the side was a crumpled, stained piece of lined paper with Cursing College Fund written in block letters. The thing was almost full.

"Put what ya got in your wallet right there, buddy." Her smile was wide.

"Left it upstairs," Nick mumbled as he headed to the fridge and peered over his brother's shoulder. "Whatcha' cookin' for break...?" The last word was bitten off when Nate shoved a container of eggs at him, along with a jug of milk and a carton of orange juice.

"Put these on the counter and get that big frying pan out." Nate pulled out a slab of bacon and some pre-cut potatoes and handed them to Chris.

With boisterous teasing and playful shoving, the three teenagers moved with a coordination that didn't surprise Pete. He and his brothers worked together in the same seamless way.

While the boys were busy creating the biggest mess possible while making something to eat, Jena squatted in front of his cage.

He licked his snout, ignoring the urge to gnaw and bite the bandage around his paw. The damn thing throbbed like a mother.

~Jena~

Jena couldn't believe how calm the beautiful wolf was. His thick silver-and-midnight pelt shone with health, except where the gauze wrapped around his paw.

It was his eyes that held her spellbound. The oval wide irises were bright turquoise with a black pupil surrounded by a jagged burst of sun-yellow. It reminded her of an eclipse of the sun when the moon blocked it. She'd never read of any animal having eyes that shape or color, much less a wolf. What was also weird was the animal acted as if he understood everything going on around him.

The boisterous antics of the teenagers caught her attention. Her stomach sank. All too soon silence would replace the noise. The twins and their friend were about to head for a two-week summer camp expedition in North Tahoe. While she looked forward to some alone time, her chest still squeezed at the thought. With a forced smile, she turned from the wolf to check out the damage the kids created. "Are you guys sticking around for dinner tonight?"

The three of them having supper together was a rare occurrence. The boys were usually busy with typical summer activity. If they were home, they'd hole up in their rooms to play video games or pound away on a computer.

With brisk efficiency, the food was prepared.

The boys took plates piled high to the table before going back for their milk and juice. Then they plopped around the table, and dug into the mountains of scrambled eggs, skillet potatoes, and strips of bacon on their plates. All the while they teased and tried to outdo each other.

"We've got to help at my family's restaurant tonight," Chris suddenly announced.

His family owned one of the popular Thai restaurants in town. He and Nate worked there on and off all season, waiting on tables and making sushi. "We won't get off until after midnight." His dark gaze focused on Jena with eyes wide as he bit his bottom lip.

Damn it! They both knew she didn't like her brother out that late.

Jena glared at them. "Okay, for tonight only. Let's not make this a habit of coming home so late."

She turned to Nick before he left the room. "What about you? Home for dinner?"

"Nah. I'm gonna meet a bunch of guys at Hidden Beach." Nick spoke through a mouth full of his last bite before jumping off his chair. He raced to cram his food-free plate into a crammed dishwasher. "Then I'm meeting Kimberly at the casino corridor later. We're going to the movies."

Kimberly must be his latest girlfriend. The four casinos/hotels crammed at Stateline had the only movie theater around. Most of the teenagers in South Tahoe hung out there at the casino corridor, doing whatever teenagers did when they hung out.

Nick fished out the Blazer's keys from his pocket and shook them in front of his brother and Chris. "You guys need a ride? I can drop you off on my way."

"Sure, take us to Chris's."

Nate and Chris plopped their empty plates into the machine.

"Let me grab my work clothes and we'll go." Nate poked his twin's chest. "You'd better not make us be late like you did last time."

"Chill, little bro." Nick swiped the accusatory finger away from him. "Jeez, no need for hostilities, dude!"

The three of them left with the topic still under discussion.

Jena sighed and glanced at the quiet creature in the cage. "Sometimes I understand why certain animals eat their young." The smart phone on her wrist vibrated. "Damn, I've just enough time to get ready for my lunch date with Claude."

She wasn't sure why she'd accepted a dinner invitation from the older man. The only reason had to be the interval since she had a personal adult conversation with someone. She met the man when he brought in a stray cat with a broken back leg to the clinic the previous day. He was charming and attentive, and when he asked her out to lunch, she surprised herself by agreeing. In hindsight, maybe that wasn't the brightest thing to do. But what the heck. It was only lunch. What could it hurt?

Jena carefully approached the wolf's pen.

He lay on his stomach with his head between his paws. His exotic eyes glanced up at her.

She crouched and scooted as close to the cage as she dared. "You going to be okay, boy?"

The animal tilted his head as if he understood her.

"I have to go. Try to get some sleep, hmm? I'll check on you when I get back."

With one last wistful look at the stoic animal, she headed to her bedroom to dress for her lunch date.

~Pete~

Pete watched Jena walk away. What's a Claude? It never occurred to him that Julienne's sister would have a man in her life. *Shit!* His teeth snapped when he swallowed, a rumble threatening to escape. The image of some guy touching her set the growl loose.

What in the hell was wrong with him? Damn! He'd better get his head out of his ass. And what better way to do that than to talk to someone annoying. Someone with no personality or imagination. And that someone would be none other than his eldest brother, Mr. Prig of the Year, Raiden.

The man took his status as eldest of the quintuplets to a ridiculous, serious level.

Pete doubted humor ever poked its head into Raiden's miserable life. Yeah, teasing his reserved brother was a favorite pastime.

Pete closed his eyes and relaxed. Visualizing Raiden, he formed a mental picture that cooled his urge to find some stupid human named Claude to pound on. He started with Raiden's long white hair that was usually pulled over his slightly pointed ears, worn in either a man-bun or a tail that reached the bottom of his waist. Raiden's angular face, complete with high cheekbones and a strong masculine nose that topped a full mouth, rarely smiled. The only resemblances he and his brother shared were the unusual shape and dual color of their eyes and the deep cleft in their chins.

To connect mentally with his brothers, Pete had to concentrate on their unique scents

Each brother carried a particular combination of their quintuplet's signature with a little extra. Raiden's scent had a sharp astringent mixture.

Pete dubbed him "the hangover".

Raiden? Pete mentally nudged his brother. *Come out, come out, wherever you are!*

An echoing silence was his answer. Now that was odd. Even if Raiden didn't answer right away, he should be able to "feel" his brother. He tried again.

Raiden?

Nothing.

What the hell? An irritated growl rumbled low in his throat. He'd never been unable to reach his eldest brother before. Was he hurt? Dammit! Why wouldn't someone tell him if there was something wrong with Raiden?

RAIDEN! Son-of-a-bitch. How embarrassing was it to yell like a lunatic?

What do you want? You're supposed to contact Ben for your insignificant problems. I don't have time to talk to you right now. Radian's usual calm tone had a tinge of exasperation all over it.

Pete bristled. He'd done nothing to make his brother talk to him like that. He sucked in a breath to blast his snotty brother when he hesitated. Even he might be smart enough not to tease if the timing wasn't right.

Are you all right?

Of course I'm all right.

Raiden's stern reply came across absent-minded. It didn't take a genius to figure out his brother's attention wasn't on their conversation.

What do you want?

Even in wolf form, his eyebrows rose. *Are you sure you're okay? You sound funny. Why did it take so long for you to answer?*

I'm fine.

The man sounded anything but fine. One advantage of being in wolf form was the ability to hear nuances and inflections he normally wouldn't pick up. Raiden's irritability couldn't be about Pete. Shit, he'd done nothing wrong. Lately.

Last thing he wanted was to delve into his brother's wacky behavior, so he went straight to the point. *Well, I've got some good news and some bad news. The good news is I found one of Julienne's sisters. The bad news is I did it by getting severely damaged while in wolf form, which is how she found me.*

Good, good.

Pete clenched his jaw. It was one thing for Raiden to ignore him on a normal day, but it was quite another when he said he was injured. The asshole's attention deficit was getting on his last damn nerve.

Yeah, you see, a bear chased me, and I got caught in a steel trap. Damn thing snapped my paw clean off! Then that stupid bear nabbed it and ran off with it in its mouth. The last I saw of my paw was the beast gnawing on it before swallowing it in one gulp!

Well, that's fine... fine. I've got to go.

The last word came out clipped as the mental barrier between them slammed shut.

Fuck you, you sanctimonious prick! Wait 'til I see you again, I'm gonna kick your pale ass! Yelling mentally into a blank space where his brother had been might be stupid, but it made him feel better.

He snorted and glanced around the barren kitchen. The savory aroma left by the teenagers' devoured breakfast made his stomach rumble. After a final halfhearted growl, he laid his head between his paws. Good thing he wasn't in any danger where he was. He could try contacting one of his other brothers, but sometimes communicating with them was sporadic after using his limited telepathic abilities. No matter. Once everyone in the house left, he'd get out of this cage and make some calls. Plus, when he turned back into his human form, he'd heal his throbbing paw... hand, whatever. Maybe he'd snoop around and find out what he could about this particular sister.

Speaking of Jena, her mentioning some guy named Claude made him snort through a closed snout. When the time was right, he'd make sure this Claude had other things to do besides hang around Jena.

Until then, might as well indulge in a quick nap.

Chapter Three

~Pete~

The clicking of sharp heels on the linoleum floor jerked Pete awake. Jena breezed into the kitchen, bringing with her the aroma he'd now associate with her. A spicy combination of cracked pepper and a hint of cinnamon with an underlying element of clean, healthy female.

Holy God, was there a more gorgeous woman who ever lived? Covering her taut frame was a thin-strapped peach-colored sundress with a bodice tight enough for the tops of her luscious, full breasts to be on glorious display. Toned, tanned legs ended with cross-tied heeled sandals. Cute little pink manicured toes peeked out.

He drooled and his tongue hung out. She leaned to his cage with her hands on her thighs and cooed something inane he couldn't catch. He was too busy ogling her cleavage that was thoughtfully perched in his line of sight. He whimpered when she straightened and left the room. In her wake, the alluring, feminine scent remained.

After the click of the front door being locked, Pete plopped onto his wolf forearms. What in the world just happened? One minute he was a cool, self-contained man who had been with hundreds of beautiful women throughout his long life. And now this. None of the other women had affected him as much as Jena did just by walking into a room. She took his breath away. Encased in his animal body, the instinct to claim her about overrode any higher consciousness he might have.

My, aren't you a civilized creature?

Pete jerked at a purring male voice echoing in his mind. He lifted his head and glanced around. No one there. Head back between his paws. Ok, he'd pretend he wasn't delusional.

What's the matter? Cat got your tongue?

Again, that condescending male tone. This time a chuckle followed the words.

Pete skimmed the room. Great, nothing.

An echoing purr sounded from above.

There, on top of the refrigerator, lay one of the fattest Siamese cats he'd ever seen.

The feline lounged on a soft bed that covered the top of the appliance. With agonizingly slow precision, the cat cleaned his paw and twirled it around his dark triangle of an ear.

Lick, twirl, repeat.

Pete frowned. If he didn't know any better, he'd swear the cat spoke. He shook his head. Yep, it was official. He'd finally lost his mind. Well, wouldn't that make Ben happy he was right all along? Ever since they were kids, his younger brother insisted Pete was crazy on a good day.

Of course I talk. A calm, concise reply. *I, however, don't normally converse with inferior life forms.*

The cat stopped grooming. His ice-blue eyes perused Pete with a lip curl that exposed one white fang. As regal as only a cat can be, the feline stood, stretched, and hopped from the fridge to the counter. From the counter, he landed on the floor and sauntered over to the pen. His enormous belly swayed with each movement.

The creature stopped in front of Pete and tilted his chin with a knowing regard. *Well, hybrid Akurn. What do you have to say for yourself?*

His wolf's jaw dropped. *Huh? What did you call me?*

Don't be obtuse. I know it's hard, but pay attention to what's important. The cat licked a raised paw.

Pete glared.

Don't hurt yourself. Even with your immature intellect, I know you can understand me just fine. The feline stopped grooming and gave Pete a steady gaze. *It is necessary for me to talk to you so I may ask a question, Akurn.*

Don't call me that. Pete growled. *I am nothing like them.*

Whatever. The cat narrowed his piercing regard. *Quit thinking you're crazy. Now pay attention, you substandard creature. Are you here to block the other Akurns from taking my pet?*

Pete's eyes widened. *Huh?*

The cat squeezed his eyes closed before opening them with an impatient glare. *It is such a trial to converse with mediocre life-forms.*

The feline might have mumbled that to himself, but Pete had no trouble catching what he said.

Are... you... going... to... stop... the... other... Akurns... from...

I heard you the first time. Pete interrupted the sanctimonious little prick. *What other Akurns? What pet?*

The hybrid female. You know, the one just like you. The cat sneezed. *She is my pet, and I will not allow the Akurns to steal her from me.*

What other Akurns? Pete ground his back molars. Why couldn't the stupid thing be a little clearer? *And how do you know an Akurn wants to take her... wait a minute. How in the hell do you even know what an Akurn is?*

Oh, please. You think you're the only exterrestrial race to inhabit this world? The cat rolled on his butt, raised his right leg, and cleaned his private parts. *We were assigned to watch over this protected habitat million of years before your puny planet Akurn got stuck in the solar system. It's only by our generosity your people have been allowed to stay. I assure you, that hospitality is thin at best. Especially after you tried to destroy Earth with a great flood.*

What? You were alive when that happened?

Pete had never seen a cat roll its eyes before.

The feline finished his grooming, the tip of his pink tongue sticking out. He sent a pointed stare. *Don't be obtuse. My race has a genetic memory for scents, especially for the stench of Akurns.*

I am not an Akurn. Pete's mental voice raised.

Oh, really? The snide remark came as the cat groomed the other thigh. *You smell like one.*

My mother is an Akurn, Pete admitted. *My father is a genetic hybrid of an Akurn and the ancient hominids from this planet.*

He's an Adamou? The leg went down and Pete became the object of the cat's intense study. *Him I would love to meet. Where is he?*

Look, we're getting off track here. He wasn't going to discuss his ailing parent with some damn cat. *What makes you think Akurns are here for Jena?*

Can't you sniff them? The cat snorted. *I haven't seen them, but their recent scent is around the house. At first I thought it was you. Though I admit you do smell slightly different from them.* The cat plopped on his side, legs spread in front as his belly rested heavily on them. *Are you here to protect my pet or not?*

Yes, as a matter of fact I am. Pete glared down his snout. *I intend to take her away from here so they can't get their grubby hands on her. Once we defeat the Akurns, I'll bring her back.*

I suppose you'll come back with her. The smirk on the whiskered muzzle was creepy as hell.

Why would I do that?

Yep, dumber than a bag of dogs.

The cat stood with a flick of his tail. With one last glare, he turned his back on Pete, head and tail held high as he strolled out of the kitchen. His bulbous stomach swayed with each step.

Holy shit, Pete was in the Twilight Zone. Here he was, stuck in a cage in wolf form, having suffered a stupid injury a newborn pup could have avoided, and his normally unflappable brother was distracted as hell. Added to all that weirdness, he just had an insane conversation with a fat Siamese cat. Who not only talked about aliens, but rightly guessed that Pete was one.

Dammit.

The plan to leave was shot all to hell. If what the cat said was true, Pete'd better stay and find out if the Akurns had been around or not. At least as an injured wolf, he had the perfect alibi to hang out.

No time like the present to get things rolling. With a quick sniff to make sure nobody else was near, Pete concentrated on turning his paw into a man's hand to unlatch the crate door. As a bonus, it healed the excruciating injury. Licking his chops at the relief, he crawled out of the cage. After clicking it closed, he eyed the unlatched doggie door and snorted. Good thing one of those twins took the annoying Heeler with them so no worries about tangling with the mutt. He resumed his wolf shape.

He nudged through the flap to the outside. Oh, the indignities one had to endure, but there was no help for it. It would be faster to run as a wolf to his cabin and change back into a man there.

With any luck, he'd find Jena at Heavenly Village and interrupt her lunch with Claude. Then he'd charm the crap out of her.

Yeah, piece of cake.

~Jena~

As Jena sat across from Claude at an outdoor café in Heavenly Village, she choked on the dry lunch. It wasn't the food; it was the company. Oh, the man was handsome enough to turn any girl's head. Plus, he was polite and listened without constant interruptions. But there was just something about him that bugged the crap out of her.

She eyed her lunch date's full head of thick white hair that offset the deep hazel of his eyes.

Clean-shaven, and his casual clothes were expensive and immaculate. He wore a single gold band on his wedding ring finger.

When she'd glanced at it, he explained his wife passed away over ten years prior from cancer.

He was the perfect gentleman. And as phony as hell.

What really weirded her out was his overall scent. It made her itch. She, someone who had never had a sharp sense of smell, had a nose-twitching reaction to the malodor coming off him. While his cologne was light and expensive, an underlying layer stung and brought a sour tinge to the back of her throat. Her imagination ran wild since the only word to describe the smell was deceit. Like he played a role she should be leery of.

Their lunch couldn't be over soon enough. When they parted, she gave a vague response about the next time they'd meet. Not that she had any intention of getting close to him ever again. She told him she had to pick up her brothers and turned down his offer to escort her to her car.

Not giving the man a chance to argue, she turned and left, then rummaged through her purse to grab her keys. Walking along the cobblestone plaza staring into her purse, she didn't watch where she was going. Between one second and the next, her low-heeled sandals got stuck on something. She squealed, her arms flew out, and her purse spun and flipped around and around. While her foot remained stuck in place, the rest of her kept going. The rough ground raced to meet her face-to-face.

Instead of suffering a hard splat on the cobblestone ground, she landed in a pair of warm, strong, masculine arms. A fresh scent of leather and licorice wrapped around her and cradled her senses. With a deep appreciative breath, she glanced up at her savior.

Espresso-brown eyes held her captive. Her heart raced and her stomach fluttered hard enough to make her breathless.

The man holding her smiled, his full lips framed by cavernous dimples as his mischievous eyes crinkled at the corners. The more they stared at each other, the more his face relaxed and his sensual gaze dilated. His mouth pursed as his attention focused on her lips.

Something unexpected happened. All the tension between her shoulders melted away. The consistent headache she suffered from dissipated, along with the restless urge she wasn't doing something she was meant to. There was no doubt she was right where she should be, in this man's arms. Everything in the universe clicked into alignment.

Her heart thundered as he leaned close. For one crazy moment, her lids lowered as she readied for his kiss. Yes... kiss. She needed his kiss... she craved his kiss. Had to have those plump lips touch hers. Had to see if he tasted as good as he smelled. With eyes closed, her mouth parted, welcoming the expected connection...

"Hey lady!"

A quick tug on the end of her skirt made her jump. Jena's eyes flew open with a gasp.

"You want your purse or not?"

A small boy held her purse between his fingers. His front toothless grin was as wide as his brown eyes.

The innocent rasp of the cherub helped settle her racing heart. The man put her on her feet with a firm grip. She faced the youngster and took what he offered. "Oh, thank you so much! I really appreciate you picking this up for me."

"Mateo!" A flushed, wild-eyed young mother raced to the little boy who couldn't be older than six or seven. "Don't you dare run off like that again!" The woman grabbed the boy in a hug tight enough to make the poor child squeak.

"But Mama, the lady dropped her purse!" Little Mateo's lips quivered when his mother stepped back and glared at him with her hands on her slender hips.

Jena squatted to be level with the youngster. "You're my hero." She stood and faced the other woman with a wide grin. "You've got a wonderful boy there. It would have been a fate worse than death if I'd lost my purse! He saved me. Thank you so much."

Mateo's mom gave a relived, grateful smile. "You're welcome." The woman took her son's smaller hand in hers. "Come on, we've got to meet Papa for lunch."

Jena watched them walk away with a grin. She checked her handbag and breathed a sigh. All the pertinent things were still in place.

A man's warmth caressed her at her back. His wide masculine palm rested on her shoulder. She shivered as his gentle breath feathered the side of her neck.

"Are you okay?" His rumbling baritone was low and sensual.

Her womb clenched in response. Biting her lip, she sucked in a fortifying breath and turned around.

Holy God, the man's striking good looks stunned her. Lavish, sable hair that matched the masculine line of his brows brushed the tips of his ears. Thick black lashes surrounded dilated, rich-chocolate eyes as they examined her. A killer smile creased his full lips, framed by two dimples deep enough to drown in. Lightly calloused palms caressed the skin at top of her arms.

Jena tilted her head back to take in his perfect height. He had to be just shy of six feet... not too tall and not too short next to her five foot five. A dark-blue, short-sleeved polo shirt covered his muscular chest. The shirt flowed loose over tight black jeans. On his feet were comfortable, but expensive dark Chukka boots.

What did he ask her? Oh, if she was okay. She gave him a wide smile, full of teeth and everything. "I'm great!" Her face heated. She giggled like a dork. "Thank you for catching me."

The inch separating them became smaller. "I would catch you anytime." His nostrils flared as his gaze locked with hers. "What's your name, lovely lady?"

She inhaled his enticing scent. "Hi... I'm, um, Jena MacFarlane." She itched to touch him.

He must have read her mind. With a gentle smile, he brought her hand up to his mouth for a soft kiss. "Beautiful." His breath caressed her skin before he turned it over and placed a matching peck on her wrist.

"I'm Pete Hayes."

His unblinking stare hypnotized her.

He squeezed her hand and let go. "And I am very happy to meet you, my *I'lati*."

She gaped. "What does that mean?"

His lids dropped. "Goddess."

Jena's stomach fluttered. Woo-boy, this man is a'flirtin' hard. Did that bother her? Nope... nope, it didn't.

"I would love for us to get acquainted. May I buy you lunch?" Those deep dimples peeked out to play. He gestured to the various open cafes behind them.

Jena shook her head and bit her bottom lip. "I just ate. I'm sorry."

"How about a cup of coffee then?" He leaned forward with wide eyes.

Thoughts raced. She should go to the clinic, but she didn't really have to. She'd been slowly giving her clients to the other veterinarian she sold the business to. With her brothers going away to college in the fall, she wanted to be free to do some extensive worldwide traveling to cure the restless urge that plagued her.

She peered at him. No need to go anywhere now. Jena suspected he was everything she'd been looking for.

"Okay. Let me make a phone call."

His open grin made her melt.

Hours later, Jena parked the car in her garage. She pushed the remote to close the door and entered the kitchen with a hand over her heart. How she got home was anyone's guess. It was all a blur. She'd been too busy daydreaming, reliving the soaring, ecstatic response she experienced being with Pete.

Who'd have thought a confident woman like her would act worse than a preteen with a crush?

Mr. Pete Hayes.

Mister sexier than any male model in the universe Pete Hayes.

Holy cow, that man was a walking poster boy for everything she'd ever wanted in a guy. She snickered and sighed all at the same time. Never in the world's history did two people connect as quickly as she did with Pete. It was amazing how much they had in common. They both loved classic rock, muscle cars, and football. Except he had an abominable taste in which football team was the superior unit in the NFC West. They also enjoyed outdoor sports—she was an avid golfer while he argued rock climbing was superior.

Those hours rushed by in a blur. It wasn't until the server asked if they wanted a menu for dinner that Jena admitted she had to go. As they walked to her car, they exchanged phone numbers, thumbs flying on cell phones.

When she stood at the door of her Cherokee and faced him, she quivered, waiting for that kiss she'd been dying for all afternoon.

Instead of giving her what she craved, she received a light peck on the cheek. He promised to call early the next day. The only thing she could do was nod since blabbing anything intelligent was beyond her.

A movement out of the corner of her eye drew her attention to the enormous wolf in the cage.

His black snout twitched as his head raised. He wheezed and licked his jaw.

Why did he pant like he'd been running? His eerie gaze unnerved her. She'd swear there was human intelligence behind those amazing eyes. With caution, she stepped to the cage.

"Will you let me take a look at that paw?" She kept her voice quiet. "I promise I won't hurt you."

The animal gave a regal nod.

She shook off the last images of Pete and inched closer. Eyes wide, she sucked in her bottom lip. She waited and stared at the animal.

The wolf poked the bandaged paw through the cage bars.

Her eyes widened. Did the animal somehow understand her? She put her hand on the paw to gauge his reaction. She settled on her knees and examined the bindings. They were loose and poorly wrapped around the injury. The animal must have been chewing on it. With a tsk, she unwrapped the frayed bandage full of holes. The wolf lowered his muzzle and licked the back of her hand. She shivered as the warm tongue stroked her skin.

The wolf didn't move except to lick between pants.

Jena checked the damage, or at least she examined where the gaping wound had been. She leaned for a closer look. The extensive injury had knitted closed. If she didn't know any better, she'd say it was weeks old instead of hours. She turned the paw over to examine the underside. It too had minimal damage. The pads of his feet were intact, with pink, healthy skin. Her wide eyes jerked to the alien, exotic ones of the animal.

What the deuce?

The wolf tilted his head. Damn, she'd swear he understood what she was thinking.

With a frown, she applied antiseptic ointment on the furry limb. With care, she wrapped a clean bandage around it when an image of raw steak crossed her mind.

She jerked and glanced at the animal. Where did that come from? She was a borderline vegetarian, eating shellfish, tofu, and chicken. She did her best to keep beef off her menu.

With a laugh, she'd swore the wolf had his begging face on.

Those exotic-colored eyes were wide, his snout was high, and his ears were erect. His thick tail thumped.

Again, an image of a big, juicy, raw steak made Jena salivate with an unexpected craving. She swallowed. "I... I don't have any steak."

A large salmon replaced the vision of steak. "Um, in the fridge there might be some trout the boys caught yesterday. Will that do?"

How lame was talking to this animal as if he understood her? Had to be guilt talking since he hadn't touched the dog food she'd given him earlier. Yeah, that's all it was.

Damn if the wolf didn't nod as if he agreed. His pink tongue came out and rolled across his chops.

Okay, it was official. She'd lost her mind. First, she imagined smelling deceit on her lunch date, and now she acted like she could talk with animals. Forget that she was Dr. MacFarlane, DVM. Nope, just call her Dr. Doolittle.

What the hell? Jena got up from the cool linoleum floor and headed to the fridge. She hated taking her eyes off the wolf, but after staring at him for a few seconds, she admitted she had to have imagined the whole thing. With a chuckle and a self-deprecating sigh, she opened the appliance door.

A Mackinaw trout wrapped in thick foil was in a plastic storage bag. Nick had already gutted and beheaded the gray body for a future meal. She was sure the boys wouldn't mind if she shared their booty with the wolf after she told them he hadn't eaten.

And speaking of the little devils, it sounded like one of them was home.

"Yo, sis! Ya here?" Nick called from the other room.

"In the kitchen!" She finished unwrapping the fresh catch.

"Hey, whatch'a gonna do with that? Your lunch date that bad?" He bent his blond head to the exposed fish with a twitching smirk.

"Ha! Not for me." She gestured to the quiet animal in the enclosure. "It's for him." She shrugged. "He hasn't touched the food I gave him, and I don't want him to lose strength."

Nick nodded. "Yeah, you'd better give him something to eat, so he doesn't think we're on the menu." He peered at the animal with narrowed eyes. "But then again, we can always feed him Bubbas." He thumbed to the top of the refrigerator. "Where's 'His Hugeness' anyway?"

On cue, the Siamese cat sauntered through the open door. His laser-blue eyes widened and zeroed in on her. A pitiful, mournful yowl came next.

Jena's heart melted. She never could resist snuggling her precious cat. She scooped the large feline and draped him over her left shoulder. "Quit picking on Bubbas." She stroked the sleek fur and scratched behind his ears.

His loud purr vibrated. The rumbling echoed in the cozy room, and the cat's charcoal tail swished back and forth.

"How's my baby today, hmm?" She couldn't resist petting the prone cat as he draped over her shoulder like a limp bag of rocks. Although she'd never admit it, the overweight cat was heavier than a bag of rocks.

"Hey, Nick. Give the wolf that fish, would you?" She wouldn't tempt fate by getting her cat close to the fishy treat.

"Yeah, can't have Jabba the Cat swallow it whole." Her brother grabbed the beheaded fish and tossed it between the front paws of the wolf in the cage. "Here you go."

The animal didn't hesitate. It only took two bites to devour the trout. With a swipe of a pink tongue across his snout, his dual-colored eyes narrowed.

"Wow! Did you see that?" Nick's jaw dropped. "He almost ate that thing in one bite. How sick is that?" He raced to the fridge. "I bet he wants more."

Jena peered at the wolf as she stroked the flattened frame of Bubbas rumbling away. "Of course he needs more, he's a gigantic animal." She frowned. "But only one more. We can't have him getting the runs or anything."

When Nick tossed in another fish, the animal settled on his bent elbows and took his time devouring the meat. Once he finished, he lapped water from his full bowl.

"So, how was your date with that old guy?" Nick took a glass out of the cabinet. Grabbing a container of juice from the fridge, he filled it before putting the carton back. "You gonna see him again?"

Her shrug wasn't obvious with the weight of the cat. "I doubt it. Something about him bugged me." A dreamy smile escaped before she hid it.

Too late.

Nick's brow creased. "If he bugged you so much, what's with the goofy smile?"

"I met someone!" Jena slapped a hand over her mouth. She tried to keep her love life away from her brothers since she'd taken over their care. A race of giddy adrenaline made her spill her guts.

"You're not gonna believe this, but I met this guy, and he's so wonderful. I can't believe we talked for hours and we had so much in common and he likes the same things I do and..."

Nick's baby blues widened. "Holy crap, sis. Slow down." His brow furrowed. "Where did you meet this paragon of virtue? What's his name? I think Nate and I need to..."

"No, no." She knew that look. If he thought he had to protect her from someone, he wouldn't hesitate to step in. Even though the boy was only seventeen, he'd already achieved a third-degree black belt in tae kwon do.

Jena couldn't help but grin. "His name is Pete. I met him after that crappy lunch I had with Claude." A girly giggle escaped. "I wasn't looking where I was going, and I tripped. He saved me from doing a face-plant at Heavenly Village." A dreamy sigh followed.

Nick squinted. "You know, it's about time you got serious with someone. I've been telling you for months you should do us all a favor and get laid. Maybe that would cure your crabbiness."

Her face heated and she smacked his arm. "My love life is none of your business!" No way would she admit she thought the same thing earlier. Like she hadn't been trying to find someone. But the dating pool in South Tahoe wasn't large to begin with.

"See what I mean? You wouldn't me hit me all the time if you weren't such a crankin-stein."

"Don't you have somewhere else you have to be?" She lifted the rumbling cat from her shoulder and nuzzled his face before she put him on his refrigerator bed.

"Yeah. I'd better get Kimberly." He nudged her and ruffled her hair.

He'd been doing that since he'd become tall enough to get away with it. Good thing the boy was agile enough to duck when she swung to smack him again.

Laughing, Nick skipped away. He air-kissed her cheek and bounced out the kitchen.

Jena glared at the innocent doorway until the wolf sneezed. Jerking her attention to the animal, she gave the door one last disgusted glance and went to him.

The wolf stared with his unusual eyes, the yellow starburst taking over the aquamarine.

She'd swear the wolf grinned as his tongue hung out. A strange, almost familiar masculine voice rang in her head. You think I'm wonderful, eh? Crouched in front of the cage, she plopped on her butt.

The wolf's yellow/turquoise eyes left hers and focused on her exposed upper thighs. His pupils expanded, the black taking over the dual colors.

With a huff, she rolled to her knees. Great, not only was she hearing voices in her head, now she imagined some animal lusted after her.

The wolf poked his snout through the bars to nuzzle the top of her hand. He closed his eyes and swiped the pink tongue across her skin.

It was an automatic response for her to stroke the silky fur. "You are one beautiful animal." She smiled and lightly scratched the tip of his snout. If she didn't know any better, she'd swear the wolf was going to purr like Bubbas any second.

The animal crept closer.

Her smile widened as she stroked an ear. The velvet fur was silky under her fingertips.

His eyes closed as he preened under her touch.

"Do you belong to somebody? He had to be a domesticated animal. He was too calm around humans to be born in the wild. "Maybe I should check the USDA database and see if anybody has put an alert out for a missing wolf in this area." She kneaded his ear one last time before scooting backward and wrapping her arms around her raised knees.

The wolf opened his eyes, the bright yellow/turquoise colors mesmerizing. He rolled his head and his body followed, exposing his belly. His thick, furry tail thumped as he looked up at her with his tongue rolling out the side.

"You silly thing. I will not rub your belly, so behave yourself."

The wolf sneezed and rolled back on his stomach. He put his head between his paws.

"Well, I've got to get going. I've a short shift in the clinic this evening. I hope you'll be okay by yourself for a while."

She glanced around the room. "Since Nick brought Dogget home, I'd better let that dumb dog in. If I leave her outside, she'll dig a hole to China." She went to the back door and opened it. "Doggett? Where are you, girl?"

The Queensland Heeler came barreling in and made a beeline for the cage. This time, instead of barking, she growled with bared teeth and a lowered head.

The wolf returned the growl with a low rumble.

Doggett stopped and stared with wide eyes at the bigger animal, her head cocked as she sat on her haunches.

That's right, mutt. Back off before you become dessert.

Jena blinked when that masculine voice echoed in her head. "Someone there?" She glanced around the room... no one, just her. What the hell? Why was she hearing some guy's voice in her head? Heart thundering, she put hands on her hips and glowered at the wolf. "Why do I feel like me losing my mind is your fault?"

The wolf's wide-eyed, innocent stare didn't fool her one bit. She narrowed her gaze. "Yeah, well, you're lucky I've got to go to work. Behave and I'll check on you when I get back. Then I'll figure out what to do with you."

She patted the side of her thigh. "Come on, Doggett. It's your turn to be the clinic mascot."

After she changed into some comfortable scrubs, she headed out. Before leaving, she couldn't resist checking in on the animal.

He lay with his head resting between his paws. His exotic eyes rolled to look at her.

With a thoughtful frown, she left.

~Pete~

Pete watched the Australian Heeler amble out the door behind Jena, her stubby tail raised high. He snorted. The mutt wasn't the least bit intimidated by him. He admired the dog's bravery. He would never hurt the pooch, but she didn't need to know that.

Alpha status aside, he wanted... needed more from Jena. When he first touched her as a man, a firestorm raced through him, never letting up. The profound yearning to keep the fascinating, beautiful woman at his side was hard to shake.

When he sat with Jena at that outdoor café, it shocked him how intense his emotions grew around her. Any other relationship, including the one with Qamara the betrayer, paled in comparison. This quick-witted woman was, without a doubt, meant for him and him alone.

But he'd better play it safe and do the right thing that his family expected of him. Even though Jena looked like Julienne, he had to make absolutely sure she was one of the hybrid sisters. Before leaving San Francisco, his brother Michael briefed him on a characteristic he suspected Julienne's sisters had—a small birthmark in the shape of a tiered crown, used by the Akurns to identify their creations.

A happy sigh rumbled through his snout as he imagined examining the luscious Jena. Savoring his full belly, he closed his heavy eyes. Nothing he could to do right now. Late tonight, with everyone asleep, he'd snoop around. After that, the "wolf" would escape, and he'd be free to waltz back into her life as a man.

Drifting asleep, he dreamed of various ways to woo the delectable Jena.

Long after midnight, Pete listened to the quiet sounds in the house. Three steady heartbeats thumped in slow, deep rhythms that matched the soft snores floating in the air.

By habit, he closed his eyes and visualized his human form. The change wasn't painful, just disorienting. The ability to morph from one shape to another was as comfortable as putting on a pair of pants. Of course, he'd been shape-shifting for thousands of years. So, if nothing else, he ought to be good at it by now.

Before opening his eyes, he savored the cool mountain air sliding across his naked body as he crouched in the pen. Yeah, time to get out and look around. Even in human form, he kept most of his animal senses. He had no trouble seeing the latch that held him prisoner. The steel hinges gave a slight squeak as the door crept open. He stopped to make sure no one woke up.

Nothing.

Pete crawled out of the cage. He stretched and uttered a slow groan of satisfaction. His muscles and tendons settled with minor pops. He strained to get that nagging kink out of his lower back. While he could spend days as an animal, his normal practice was to stop after a couple of hours. Once he was finished, he blew out a grateful breath.

A low growl rumbled from his stomach and echoed in the small kitchen. Shape-shifting took a lot of energy, and he was starving. One twin had brought home leftover pizza and put it in the fridge. That treasure now belonged to him. He grabbed the box and opened the lid. Inside was a mountain of meat smothered in a nest of cheese. With a wide smile, he devoured cold what the boy had thoughtfully left.

He shut the fridge and patted his belly. On the counter sat a batch of bananas that would be the perfect ending to his meal. He peeled one and plopped it in his mouth, throwing the skin into the trashcan.

He left the kitchen and entered the rest of the house. With his keen sense of smell, he determined which room was Jena's. Her unique fragrance captured him and led him like a beacon in the dark. Her door was partially open. He stopped to make sure she was asleep.

Satisfied all was well, he poked his head in.

Jena silently snored on her back, one hand over her head and one resting on her stomach. She had on a wispy baby-doll top with a strap rolling down her shoulder. The blankets gathered at her waist, exposing her hard nipples beaded beneath the satiny material.

His body reacted.

Down, boy. Now wasn't the time.

Bubbas lay next to Jena and jerked in his direction. Ice-blue eyes widened before they narrowed. *What are you doing in here?*

Doggett, at the foot of the bed, raised her head and opened her snout.

Pete tensed and waited for the dog's loud bark.

Knock it off, dog. Bubbas snapped. *Get out and go sleep with the boys.*

Doggett's slobbery tongue hung as a line of drool pooled between her paws. She tilted her muzzle in the cat's direction. With a quiet dog sneeze, Doggett jumped off the bed. Before she passed through the door, she peered at Pete and gave him a low growl.

Now. The cat commanded.

Pete crossed his arms as he watched the dog obey without a sound. He stared at the feline.

Is there a reason you're in her room naked, Adamou? The ice-blue eyes narrowed. *If you think I'm going to leave you alone with you looking like that, think again.*

Please, I'm not stupid enough to get physical with her. Pete uncrossed his arms and put his hands on his hips. *I'm not an animal who can't control himself, ya know.*

Then what are your intentions? The steely blue eyes never lost their focus.

I just have to make sure she's the person I'm looking for.

He glanced around the room, then sat on the end of the bed opposite the cat. He made sure he didn't wake Jena before taking her hand off her stomach. When she didn't move, he brought it up and inhaled her intoxicating essence. Something about her spicy cinnamon scent dazzled him. He couldn't get enough.

His stomach dropped. Well, hell. Look at him turning into a friggin' stalker.

Carefully he turned her hand over and examined it. No birthmark. He put her hand back on her stomach and watched her sleep. The wrist over her head caught his eye and he leaned in closer to study it. Again, nothing

What are you searching for? Bubbas cocked his head. *Does she have a birthmark somewhere?*

Pete picked up the blanket and sucked in a breath at the sight of her slightly splayed legs. He gritted his teeth and ignored his member as it grew harder the more he watched the warm, sleeping woman.

A birthmark? Why are you searching for something like that? The Siamese raised a paw and licked.

I told you I have to make sure she's the right one. He shrugged. *We suspect the Akurns track these women through a birthmark.*

Visually, he searched every inch of Jena's exposed flesh. No birthmark. He put the blanket back. What a tremendous waste of time. On the one hand, he struggled to stay detached and maintain a cynical air, while on the other, his instincts fought for him to get close. Skin to skin close. Which wasn't as easy to do as he pretended. Especially with the painful, swollen part of his lower anatomy he struggled to ignore.

Bubbas stopped licking his paw and gave him an unblinking gaze. *You need a birthmark to tell you if you have the right female or not? Can't you tell by her scent or the way you react to her?* The last sentence came out with a dose of superior disgust.

Well, um, yeah. But doesn't hurt to be sure. He straightened with a snort. *How do I turn her over without waking her up?* He said this more to himself than to the cat making fun of him.

Jena sighed and rolled on her side, facing away from Pete. When the thick curtain of her hair parted, a dark shape became clear at the juncture between her neck and shoulder.

Pete sucked in a breath and bent for a better look. There it was. A strawberry mark in the shape of a crown. He was just about to touch it when a loud *'MRROW'* yanked him back.

What do you think you're doing? Bubbas demanded. He lifted his hefty body and waddled to Pete. *You'll wake her up!*

Oops, sorry. He sent the cat a sheepish smile. Damn, almost lost it there. He scooted away and watched the sleeping woman. She's really quite exquisite, isn't she? He fought the pressing need to crawl into bed with her so he could touch all that soft skin.

Well, of course you'd think so. The smug voice of the cat answered his rhetorical question. *After all, she's your mate.*

Chapter Four

~Sub-Prince Murduk~

The rogue planet Akurn, five months from transportation range of FarDeep base on Earth's moon.

Sub-Prince Murduk, supreme co-ruler and sovereign of Akurn, Governor of the capital city of Eengurra, experienced something he never had before. At first, the way his body reacted confused him. His hands were shaking, and waves of dizziness caused black spots to swim across his vision. His heart raced hard enough to drown out any noise outside of himself.

He held his breath. Was that... fear?

Unrelenting, a tsunami of terror threatened to suck him under. Emotions and he had parted ways long ago, so who could blame him if he didn't know how to handle situations he rarely experienced?

After seeing Inanna alive for the first time since she escaped all those millennia ago, he immediately cloistered himself in his private quarters to get hold of his careening emotions. Speaking to her shifted something deep inside him. While he once believed she might not have survived the ancient world-wide flood, he had received various reports over the years that she lived. Not only lived, but she bred with one of those disgusting Adamou and produced five sons.

It was absurd how those offspring became the foundations of some of Earth's legends. They, along with other Adamou who'd escaped separately from Inanna, had dominated Earth's past. These beings could not only read minds, but they could manipulate and create matter while controlling anyone they chose. See, this was the reason the Akurn monarchy had made it unlawful to mix their genetics with any alien species. It was fortunate that as the abominations bred, the Akurn DNA became dominant and the powers dissipated with each subsequent generation.

His eyes narrowed. He'd give anything to have a tenth of what those disguising atrocities so carelessly possessed.

Now after this first conversation with Inanna, Murduk sprawled on a plush couch. He ignored the humongous window overhead with its blurring colors of interplanetary dust, cosmic rays, and the coronal ejections from the bodies throughout the solar system. With shaking hands, he lit his hookah and inhaled. A ribbon of red narcotic smoke twirled around him. He exhaled and sighed at the smoldering comfort. Soon his hands steadied, and his vision cleared. The tight tension between his shoulders relaxed.

Clarity hit. Those sons of hers shall not continue to live. His gut burned. By Akurn law, since they were the offspring of the only heiress to King Du-Uru and first Queen Asta, they were in line to the monarchy before him. The only solution would be to eliminate them, wed Inanna, and plant a child in her as soon as possible. Only then would his claim to the throne be unbreakable.

Even if it was discovered he wasn't the biological son of King Du-Uru. To say his death would be a public spectacle would put it mildly. Lowborn citizens who tried to better themselves at the expense of the monarchy died horrendous deaths.

Time was running out. The slow-acting poison he'd given the king had finally taken hold.

The monarch now lay in a deep coma, his life fading away.

If Murduk didn't solidify his place as king, the warlords would declare Nabalkuta. Once invoked, each warlord could choose to fight not only him but each other to the death for the coveted position of the monarchy.

He wasn't altruistic enough to say his only goal was to save Akurn from a blood war. But the citizens didn't need to know that. He'd only tell them what they wanted to hear in order to control the populace.

Murduk snorted and sucked in another long drag of the soothing smoke. He leaned back and let the narcotic do its magic.

The red vapor turned gray and twirled above his head.

At the last gathering of the royal court, one of the rival warlords demanded he explain how they'd harvest Earth's reserves with over seven billion humans in the way. The demand for answers heated up. Until that moment in the Royal chamber, the populace of Akurn were not aware how dire their situation was. Without Earth's resources, the people would die a horrible, lingering death once the shield protecting their planet collapsed.

A low ping echoed in his ear. It was his personal channel despite the "Do not disturb" toggle in place. He blinked to open the internal communication.

The craggy face of one of his closest guards, Uruk, appeared with downcast solemn eyes.

"Yes, Uruk,".

"Your Royal Highness, you asked me to advise you as soon as FarDeep Base conducted their analysis of Thoth's whereabouts." The man did not glance up. "They report they are unable to locate the scientist. They believe he is either deceased or held somewhere on Earth we do not have access to."

The acid in Murduk's throat left a bitter taste in his mouth. "What does Commander Kud recommend?" Kud was the commanding officer of FarDeep Base, whose fanatical loyalty to Murduk was priceless.

"He has regrouped with Thoth's assistants and is conducting a search not only for the physicist, but for those female Adamou he created to neutralize the abominable children of Princess Inanna." For the first time Uruk looked up, his light-turquoise eyes direct. "He expects we will discover them any day now. Once located, we will use them to find the princess's offspring. Do you have any further orders, Lord?"

Murduk brought the solid-gold tip of the hookah to his mouth and breathed an unexpected dose of the fiery smoke. Resisting the urge to choke, he squinted with pinched lips. "Not at this time. Make sure Kud keeps us updated regularly."

Uruk bowed with a slight nod, putting his hand over his heart. "Yes, sire."

"In the meantime—" Murduk laid the hookah arm on the table next to him. He leaned back with his fingers in a steeple. "—I need you and Nungal to meet me in my chambers. There is a certain warlord who has to answer for the alarm he revealed to the people earlier today. He had no right to discuss any difficulties we might experience from Earth because of the human population." He relaxed; a sardonic smile creased his lips. "I believe an unfortunate accident is about to happen to him."

"Your will as always, Highness."

~Pete~

Pete froze at the cat's stark words. *Well, aren't you just a bundle of unhelpful crap? You have no idea what you're talking about. I think I'd know if she was my mate before you did.* Denial was his second language, right behind sarcasm. While his reaction to Jena caught him off guard, he'd never admit she could be something more. Even to himself.

He was a proud love-and-leave-'em kinda guy. But he always made sure he didn't break his partner's heart. The memory of the emotional pain Qamar inflicted on him remained fresh to this day. He made sure he never got close enough to anyone to cause that in someone else.

Pete stumbled off the bed and put distance between him and the annoying cat.

Jena stirred and rolled over onto her stomach before she settled with a soft snore.

He froze. Phew, she didn't wake up. He glared at the fat feline.

Protest much? Bubba sniffed and raised his snooty snout. *Just so you know, Adamou, my only concern is for my pet. I want her safe and happy. And if I have to knock some sense into you to get your head out of your ass, I'm just the cat to do it.* The cat shook with a silent sneeze. *So, finish finding what you are looking for and be done with it.*

Pete bristled as he rubbed the bridge of his nose. He caught himself peeking at her sleeping form and jerked his glance away. The image of her baby doll top bunched in the middle of her back and her shorts riding up the edge of her bottom was seared into his brain. The sight of all that succulent flesh made him swallow. His neck heated and his breath deepened.

His lips tightened at the haughty cat. *Let's focus on what's important here, cat, and put the whole "mate" thing on the back burner.* He pushed the vision of Qamar's taunting face aside. *So try not to bring it up again, hmm?*

The cat's answer was an unblinking stare.

Pete refused to believe a cat could smirk.

When the feline said nothing else, Pete relaxed. Ha! Looks like he got through to the annoying creature. He tore his gaze away from the Siamese and checked out the room. Going over to her closet, he opened it and peeked inside.

Now what are you looking for? Curiosity was definitely this cat's middle name.

Just checking things out. I want to learn as much about her as I can. That way, when I have to convince her to come with me to San Francisco, I'll know the best way to go about it.

Nothing interesting in the closet or the rest of the area. He put his hands on his hips. Maybe he should explore the house.

A heartfelt sigh from the cat echoed in his mind.

Boy, take a closer look. The answer you seek is all around you.

With arms crossed, Pete glowered at the cat.

In response, Bubbas nodded, gesturing for Pete to turn around.

With a grunt, he played along. He examined the dresser, the nightstand, and a LG TV mounted in the corner. At first, he noticed nothing unusual. It wasn't until Bubbas gave him a low growl that he realized how Jena had decorated the room.

Wolves were everywhere. A couple of miniature sculptures were here and there, a beautiful sizable giclée print of a wolf howling at the moon dominated the far wall. There, on the blanket gathered around her sleeping body, was the outline of a wolf pack.

Mouth open, stepping quietly, he entered the hallway. Along the walls were more wolf pictures, some as photographs and some hand-drawn silhouettes. When he reached the living room, the wolf theme was everywhere. The highlight was a portrait he'd swear was an original Michael Pape depiction of a white wolf. Here was an obsession he was right at home with.

Bubbas had followed him out, the tip of his tail twitching.

The cat turned around with his tail up and head held high. *Now don't hurt yourself trying to figure this out, okay? I'm going back to sleep and I wish to not be disturbed again. He left with a mental huff.*

The damn cat's arrogance was as bad as his older brother, Raiden's. Speaking of I'm-too-important-to-have-a-personality, he should contact his sibling with an update. Nah, what would he tell him? Besides, if Raiden hung up on him again, he'd have no choice but to knock the shit out of the self-important snot when he saw him again.

Not that he'd get away with anything like that. Raiden had frighteningly strong mental powers that would incapacitate Pete without breaking a sweat. Shit, the man could read Tolstoy and compose music while he kept Pete frozen.

Pete snorted. At least he knew how to have fun while big brother remained stuck in the no-fun zone all his life. Come to think of it, when was the last time he saw Raiden with a woman? Like, never. Shit, the man could be a virgin for all he knew.

Well, now wasn't the time to unravel the mystery of his brother's personal life.

Pete checked out the rest of the house. He poked his head into the boys' bedrooms and softly chuckled at the vast differences between their rooms. One twin lived in utter chaos, while the other teen was ridiculously tidy. It didn't surprise him that the neat freak was the jock, while the king of chaos was the more sensitive one.

Nothing new there. Time to go outside and sniff around. To morph into his wolf form, he visualized the shape. Once he'd completed the change, an olfactory explosion of information hit him. Sorting through the cornucopia of extrasensory scents, he trotted to the dog door in the kitchen and squeezed his way out.

Pete investigated the backyard before jumping over the fence to sniff around the rest of the house. The usual pleasant aromas of woodland animals along with the pine-filled forest greeted him. But an underlying alien scent caught his attention. It was human—male, but also faintly familiar. He found a particular spot that must've been where the man stood to observe the house. Pete sat on his haunches to figure out what the guy was so interested in.

Hey, it was the window to Jena's bedroom. His hackles rose as he growled with a low rumble. Some human male was spying on his woman... er, yeah, okay. He sneezed.

Huh. Someone was covertly watching Jena and her family. Swallowing a louder growl, he circled the house, sniffing meticulously.

He ended where he started and sat on his haunches. The scent was stronger in that one spot, except for the trail from the street. The only streetlamp was two houses over, signaling the end of the cul-de-sac where Jena and her brothers lived. The dark street was eerily quiet, which was unusual in the middle of the night in the forest. There were no night sounds, no coyote howling or night creature scurrying about looking for food. There wasn't even a slight breeze to make the trees sway and sing in the shadowy night of a full moon.

He sat still, gathering as much sensory information as he could. Damn, the unnatural silence was getting on his nerves. A small breeze swirled by. It carried a faint scent of humans, small beasts, along with the distinctive scent from the spot in front of Jena's window. The smell was fresh, as if the man just left.

With one last glance down the empty street, Pete jumped the fence and headed back inside through the doggy door. That smell reminded him of his brother Ben. He wasn't sure why, but a strong sense of urgency decided his next move. He'd wake up baby bro and share that scent with him and see if they could figure this out together.

Eying the animal cage, he grimaced, knowing he had to go back in. Shit, the undignified crap he had to put up with...

Pete shifted his paw to a human hand to open the latch and let himself into the cage. After locking the door behind him, he turned his hand back into a paw. He shook it to get the circulation running again. Damn, it freakin' hurt whenever he partially shifted.

He visualized the youngest brother of their quintuplet, Ben—who he'd dubbed Einstein. Concentrating on the man's signature scent of cool peppermint, he pictured Ben's dark-blond short hair, slight overbite, and height just a tad taller than Pete's own 5 foot 11 inches (okay, six foot three was more than a tad). Raiden was the serious one of the group, but Ben was freakishly intelligent, especially with anything mathematical. A small part of Pete had always been envious of Ben's ability to calculate complex equations in his head. Aside from that, he and baby bro shared a variety of interests and a similar sense of humor. To complete the image, he pictured his brother's dual-colored, oval eyes.

With snout between his paws, he opened his minuscule psychic senses. *Ben... oh, Ben! Quit goofing off with your female and talk to me.*

No telling what his brother was doing. Being a psychic was Michael's gig, not Pete's. The effort always gave him a headache.

A garbled *wh'a?* echoed in Pete's brain. Sounded like baby bro had been asleep. Ben maintained a different daily shift than Pete did. Probably all those years he'd done office work and kept regular 9 to 5 hours. Pete preferred a more nocturnal way of life.

Pete, that you?

Ben's mental voice was identical to his physical one, except for one minor difference. Whenever Ben talked mentally, he had a slight lisp, which was hilarious. But as a gesture of unusual goodwill, Pete'd let that go this time.

Ah, you know you miss me.

Ben gave a mental snort. *Like a boil on my ass.*

His brother's loud yawn rambled around Pete's head.

Why are you contacting me at... a brief pause... one o'clock in the morning?

Hey, I'm supposed to contact you when I find something weird. Well, I found something weird. He filled Ben in on what happened to him since he'd left San Francisco. Especially about the weird scent he picked up in front of Jena's house.

I'm not sure whose smell that is, but it reminds me of you.

It was easy to share Ben's startled reaction. Is it similar to an Akurn's?

Pete had to stop and consider that idea. *Yes... but no. It's like a human who's been around an Akurn.*

Hey, wait a minute! I just realized you found Julienne's sister!

Ben's mind whistle made Pete grimace.

Damn, that was fast.

What can I say? When you're good, you're good. No way would he confess Jena found him. By accident, literally. He glanced at his now-healed paw and the remains of the bandage that fell off when he shifted.

So. Pete prodded. *Any suggestions on how I can get her to come with me to SF?* Another stretch of silence made Pete uneasy. *Well?* Asshole better answer.

Hang on! Impatient much? I just told Julienne you met one of her sisters. A mental sigh. *She wants to know all about her, like what's her sister's name? Where does she live? Is she okay? When are you bringing her here?*

Pete closed his wolf eyes. If only he had fingers to pinch the bridge of his nose. Might help lessen the frustration building between his ears. Holy shit, what was with his brother going all emo on him? *Whoa. Dial it down a notch, true?*

Weariness pulled. Whenever he used his limited telepathic ability, he had to keep it short, or he'd pass out from the strain. *Listen, I have little time left. Do you have any suggestions on what I should tell her? I tried to connect with Raiden earlier, but he cut me off. Speaking of tall, pale, and no personality, what's going on with him?*

Nothing as far as I know. Besides, he normally cuts you off. Ben reminded him.

Humph. So true. *Okay, listen. Before I go, here's the name of Julienne's sister. It's Jena MacFarlane. And she lives in Zephyr*

Cove, Nevada. Have Michael run a background check as soon as he can.

That would be child's play for their computer-genius middle brother.

Another mental yawn from Ben. *Sounds good. Later.*

When Ben severed the connection, the tension squeezing Pete's eyes melted away. He yawned. He might as well get some shut-eye. With one eye open, he peered around the outside of his cage one more time. All quiet. He closed his eyes.

Damn. He hated being confined. Sometimes life just sucked.

~Jena~

Jena shuffled into the kitchen, scratching the side of her head, her eyes at half-mast. Brain full of mush and mouth dry as sandpaper, she headed for the refrigerator to get a cool glass of orange juice.

Damn, she hadn't felt this groggy in the morning since her college days. Weird dreams plagued her and kept her half-awake all night. Scenes of running wild through the forest, but not on two legs. It was a continuing dream she'd had on and off for years, of being in a four-legged form. Much like a wolf roaming free in the crisp mountain air.

But this time it was different. This time she dreamed of a companion trotting close beside her. His bigger body would bump and tease as he looped around her in circles, as if laughing and teasing with wolfy joy.

The lingering steamy heat the dream generated made her frown. Why in the world would a dream about wolves be erotic? She poured a glass of juice before putting the jug back in the fridge. Pushing her flyaway hair out of her eyes, she sat at the kitchen table and took a gulp. It wasn't until she put the glass down that she noticed the mess in the kitchen.

Backpacks, sleeping bags, and various fishing gear were scattered all over the table and stacked on the floor. Oh, hell. She'd forgotten the twins were going camping at North Shore with Chris and his family.

To add to the chaos, the counter next to the fridge had a white silky substance spread all around. How in the heck did Bubbas get in the flour again? Distinct cat paw prints pointed the way to where his hiney-butt nestled in his cat bed on top of the refrigerator.

Not that the mess registered with the Siamese royalty. He lay on his side, grooming his front paw with closed-eye ecstasy. His bulbous belly poofed and trembled as he gave a low, rumbling purr.

Jena sighed and finished her orange juice. Thank God it was the weekend. She didn't have to report to the clinic today. Looked like housework was on the menu.

A thumping herd crashed through the kitchen door. With a whooping "good morning" in her direction, Nick and Nate were raring to go. Not for the first time, Jena wished they were this wide-eyed awake during school. Those winter months it was a battle just to get them to wake up and convince them to pull their happy butts out of bed.

Over his shoulder, Nate asked if she wanted anything to eat. The thought of food made her shudder, so she declined. Juice was the only thing she craved in the morning. She sat at the kitchen table and stayed out of their way. With a wistful smile, she watched them create their regular substantial breakfast worthy of any buffet served at the casinos at Stateline.

With messy efficiency, they took their food to the kitchen table. Sitting between the fishing poles and the tackle gear, they devoured their bounty.

"You guys all ready to go?" Her fingers clutched the empty juice class. She swallowed the hard knot in her throat. Damn, what was she going to do when they went to college next year?

An urge to speak to Pete made her shudder. Just yesterday, she was restless and itched to find that elusive *something*. Now all she wanted to do was look at that man's smiling dimples and grab that kiss she'd almost gotten. Hmm, maybe she'd give him a call and see if he'd like to come over for dinner...

"Yeah, just gotta grab Doggett and head out."

She startled at Nate's announcement.

He plopped his empty dishes in the dishwasher before heading to the entrance of the living room and peeking around the doorjamb. "Anyone see psycho mutt anywhere?"

"Oh, right. I let her out earlier." Nick rushed to put his dishes away in the machine before he opened the back door and called the stocky little mutt into the house.

Doggett sharply barked and scrambled inside, making a beeline to Jena for an expected head rub. Putting her front paws on Jena's lap, she wagged her stubby tail so hard her hindquarters vibrated, bobbing her butt up and down.

The animated little dog made Jena smile. Scratching and snuggling her precious pooch, she nuzzled her nose along the dog's snout. She'd miss her pup just as much as she'd miss her brothers.

Doggett scrambled down and her sharp front claws scratched Jena's thighs.

Ouch.

The Heeler turned around and glared at the wolf in the cage. With a lowered head, the dog growled.

The gigantic wolf returned a deep rumble of his own.

Jena jumped out of her chair and pulled the dog by the collar. "Stop it! Honestly, you two are worse than teenagers."

"Hey, I resemble that remark." Nick swung a backpack around his shoulders. He passed Nate and smacked his brother upside the head. "Bro, why ain't you ready yet? Move it, dude."

Nate returned a playful fist bump on Nick's arm. "As usual, you speak with no brain. I was ready last week." He slung a backpack over his shoulder and wiggled Doggett's leash at Jena. "Come on, stumpy, let's go."

Jena took the leash and clicked it onto the dog's collar.

Doggett trembled, and her thick, short fur flew in every direction.

She handed the leash to her brother. "When will you guys be back?" She bit her bottom lip to stop it from quivering. Damn, she was going to miss the chaos twins.

"In about two weeks." Nate scratched Doggett's pointed ears.

Nick grabbed his car keys from the hook by the kitchen door to the garage. "Yeah, make sure you keep your wild parties down to a dull roar. We'd hate to come home and have ta bail ya outta jail or something."

Jena narrowed her eyes and gave a mock sneer. "I'll never get caught, bucko."

"From your lips to God's ear, sis." Nate enfolded her in a quick, awkward hug because of the myriad of camping gear he carried. He let go.

Nick gave her the same encumbered embrace. "See ya!"

"Don't worry, we'll bring back tons of fish for you to eat." Nate threatened and laughed as he followed his brother.

Doggett trotted dutifully behind. Her doggy rump wiggled, and her stumpy tail flicked high in the air.

Jena shuddered. She hated fish. Loved shellfish but couldn't stand fish. She hoped they had a blast catching the nasty creatures. If she was lucky, they'd eat everything before they came home.

She blew a raspberry and took in the scattered mess littering the kitchen. The aftermath of a riot had to look better. Lucky for her, housekeeping was on the menu today along with grocery shopping. A movement caught her eye.

The wolf watched her with dual-colored eyes wide as his tongue slobbered.

She frowned at the animal.

He returned her stare with a calm expression.

As she and the animal gazed into each other's eyes, a slight pull twisted inside. It was as if she was being invited to communicate with him. An image of Pete flashed, making her face heat. With a shake of her head, she stepped backward. At least having the wolf around explained those weird dreams.

"Looks like it's just you and me, boy." She gave the animal a meager smile. "I guess I'd better get dressed so I can tackle the day." With an ache in her heart, she ignored the messy room and headed for the shower.

~Pete~

An adrenaline rush made Pete tremble. With the boys leaving, now was his chance to be alone with Jena for days. That was a stroke of luck he hadn't seen coming. After transforming a paw into a human hand, he unlatched the cage door and exited. Shifting into his human form, he stretched until the crick in his neck popped.

It was safe to come out since Jena left to run some errands after cleaning the kitchen. By the time she sailed out the door, Pete had to get out of the crate for more than one reason. He was starving, and he had to go to the bathroom. He'd be damned if he went to the outside kennel to do his business.

A soft chuckle rumbled in his head. Pete glanced at the refrigerator topped with the world's most irritating creature.

What? He glared at the cat. *You have something to say to me?*

The feline finished his endless grooming to peer down his snout. His cat sigh was as annoying as any human's. Bubbas gave a pointed glance at Pete's growing erection. *Shouldn't you wear clothes as you strut about?*

Yeah, hold that thought. I'll be right back.

He left the room and took care of personal business. After a brisk argument with himself on whether he should take a shower, he jumped into the youngsters' shower and washed away the grime shape-shifting left on his skin.

After a thorough wash, he grabbed a towel and dried himself. Next stop was one of the boys' rooms. While the twins were taller than him, all he needed was a pair of sweats and a T-shirt.

Clean and dressed, he headed back to the kitchen. He prepared a substantial stack of lunch meat into a sandwich and devoured it. Still hungry, he opened the fridge and looked inside.

The huge feline dropped from the top of his perch to the counter that shook under the cat's weight.

I'm not surprised you eat so much, Adamou. Bubbas' silky dark brown tail swooshed as he walked across the counter and jumped to the floor. *If you would be so good as to share your repast with me, I will endeavor to assist you in any way I can.*

Wow, damn nice of you. Well, he was smart enough to use any ally he could. Pete pinched a handful of cooked chicken from a package and put it in a cat dish next to the fridge. He watched the cat inhale the meat. Ah, a chicken sandwich sounded good.

After making and eating two sandwiches, Pete sat on a chair by the kitchen table to reflect. He snorted. Look at him, taking the time to reflect and all. Anyway, he had to figure out what to do next. First things first, he'd call Jena and set a time for them to get together. He spied the phone, but voted against doing it from there. It would freak her out if the caller ID listed her home number.

Good thing he'd brought over a satchel with his wallet and cellphone. Checking the clock on the wall, he estimated she'd be home in less than an hour. He'd better set something up now for them to meet.

The call went better than imagined. With a breathless, sexy tone, she asked him if he wanted to come over for dinner at her house.

Pete was positive his wide, shit-eating grin came through as he replied. She gave him directions (ha!) and they ended the call in an awkward silence. He loathed ending the connection and believed she felt the same.

Keys rattling at the front door jerked him out of his musings. With barely a second to spare, he stripped his clothes off and dove back into the cage. After latching himself inside, he tossed the clothes and phone out the kennel's doggy door that led outside. He'd get them later. With a quick breath, he shifted.

Jena breezed in with her hands full of plastic bags from a nearby grocery store.

The rest of the afternoon passed in agonizing bit-by-bit increments.

Throughout the day she did some various housecleaning duties. Later in the afternoon, she prepared homemade tomato sauce. As she worked, she'd periodically danced around the kitchen to the beat on her iPod station.

He gave a healthy sigh of contentment as Boston's *More Than a Feeling* blasted. Fantastic. A kindred soul who appreciated classic rock is much as he did.

When evening settled, Jena hustled in the kitchen. She was doing something using the sauce she'd made earlier with boiled flat noodles and lots of cheese.

It took a moment for it to dawn on Pete what she was doing. She was making homemade lasagna from scratch. Huh, he never knew it took so much work.

And look at that huge tossed salad, full of healthy crap he'd never dream to include.

She put a loaf of garlic bread in the oven to toast.

The warm, spicy fragrance of home cooking filled the room.

His stomach growled in appreciation.

She set out an expensive bottle of Merlot to let it breathe on the countertop, then she rushed out.

Pete glanced at the cat as if the feline could provide answers.

Bubbas was in the middle of taking his umpteenth nap for the day. No help there.

It didn't take long for Jena to return, wearing a cute strapless dress that exposed the top of her breasts and flared above her knees. Her toned and tanned arms matched the athletic turn of her legs.

Pete's heart raced.

With her sable hair loose around her waist, she had to be one of the most beautiful women he'd ever seen. All that for him. He needed to head out the doggy door to the outside kennel where he'd put some clothes from home earlier. He couldn't wait to be with her again as a man.

Her back to him, she turned off the oven and took out the plate of garlic bread. The doorbell rang. She jerked and clanked the tray on the stovetop. She yanked the protective mitts off and raced out of the room.

Wait... who was at the door? He glanced at the clock. He wasn't due to arrive for another half-hour.

The front door clicked open and a man's voice mixed with Jena's. The voices raised in volume as they neared the kitchen.

Rage clouded Pete's vision. Who was this man Jena let into her house? A hard snarl rumbled as he stood with his head down. Before the man and Jena stepped in the room, the man's scent preceded him. It told Pete everything he needed to know. He growled louder in response.

When the door swung open, Jena came through with fists tight and her face beet red. Right behind her was that man who'd stood outside of Jena's bedroom window in the middle of the night.

Pete's growl roared as he zeroed in on the tight grip the older man had on his woman.

Chapter Five

~Jena~

When Jena swung the front door open, the buoyant lightness in her chest crashed and squeezed tight. Here she was expecting to see the stunning, deep-dimples-to-die for Pete, all ready for a home-cooked supper. She couldn't wait to see if the chemistry-off-the-charts thing was real or if she imagined it. In normal circumstances, she'd never invite a guy she just met to her house for dinner. But for some reason, it never occurred to her that asking Pete over was a bad idea.

Instead of Pete, it was her mediocre lunch date, Claude, standing there. Talk about disappointment. The hair on her neck and arms bristled. She grasped the edge of the door.

"I'm sorry to drop in on you like this." Claude's light-hazel eyes were sharp as he folded his hands behind his back. "But I have something urgent to discuss with you."

Jena's brows furrowed. "Why not call me?" A glint of something bright over his shoulder caught her eye. Not seeing anything, she swung her attention back to the man. "And how did you know where I lived?" While they'd exchanged phone numbers, she never told him her address. She pulled the door closer and gripped the doorknob with a tight fist.

"When we met at the clinic, I heard someone say you lived next door." Claude gestured to the animal clinic next to her house. "What I have to say can't be discussed over the phone." He cocked his head, as if trying to appear nonthreatening.

It didn't work. The tepid way they'd left each other at lunch made every alarm bell in her head ring. "Now is not a good time." She kept a tight hold on the door. "I have other..."

He pushed the door open and crowded her backward. "As I said, I'm sorry. But what I have to say can't wait. I assure you, this won't take long."

Jena gritted her teeth and glared at him. "Hey, what do you think you're..."

Claude grabbed her upper arm. "Let's go inside nice and quiet like." He nudged her in the house and kicked the door closed behind him. "Just cooperate and everything will turn out fine."

His steel grip caused her to suck in a breath. Her heart raced as he spun her around toward the kitchen. She frantically searched for something, anything she could use against him as he pushed her into the other room.

A roaring growl thundered behind the closed door to the kitchen.

If Jena didn't know any better, she'd swear the wolf knew she was in trouble. He must've scented an unknown male and perceived it as a threat.

Smart animal. Hey, maybe if she inched over to the cage, she'd could let the wolf out. Best-case scenario, he'd attack Claude. Huh, he'd probably attack her too, but at least it'd give her a chance to get away.

The older man shoved the kitchen door open and pushed her in, his fiery breath creepy on her exposed neck.

With a quick glance, she checked the wolf.

Sure enough, the animal was in alpha mode, ready to attack. He crouched, the midnight hackles raised. The dual-colored turquoise-and-bright gold eyes narrowed, and his sharp, long fangs were bared. The lengthy, rumbling growl left no doubt of the animal's intention as he glared at Claude.

"What the fuck is that?"

Jena smirked at the fear lacing Claude's voice.

"Sit over there." He gestured to a chair at the kitchen table.

She scowled at him over her shoulder. Come on, come on. There had to be something she could use as a weapon. She must've hesitated a little too long because he gave her a slight push. The unexpected shove made her trip over her own feet. She landed hard on her hands and knees.

All hell broke loose.

Sucking in a sharp breath, she jerked when a large dark-chocolate brown-and-silver blob sailed from the top of the refrigerator.

It landed smack on the back of Claude's neck.

The wolf's howl abruptly cut off.

With wide eyes, Jena watched in stunned disbelief when the wolf vibrated, then morphed into a crouching man. A crouched, naked man. At first all she saw was his bent head, the dark sable strands of his hair obscuring his face.

Then he looked up.

She gasped. It was Pete. But this Pete wasn't the same relaxed, laughing man she'd met earlier. This one was red-faced as he bared his teeth. His oval turquoise/gold eyes focused on Claude.

She tore her gaze from him to watch a struggling Claude. Yeah, she almost felt sorry for the bastard as Bubbas fiercely attacked. The man's face and neck were getting bombarded with scratches and gouges that peppered his exposed skin, now bubbling with blood. Jena put a hand over her mouth as a bark of laughter erupted.

No time to process Claude's fate as the wolf cage slammed open.

Pete raced to the wounded man and pulled the spitting feline away by the neck and dropped him on the floor.

Bubbas didn't let that stop him. The cat renewed his efforts. He clawed and bit through the synthetic blend of Claude's pants.

Jena was positive bits of skin and hair weren't getting much protection from the torn cloth.

While Bubbas attacked below, Pete wrapped a muscular arm around Claude's neck and pulled him backward.

Claude's high-pitched gasps and angry squeals stopped.

Pete turned the older man around and punched him in the face.

Claude crashed to the floor without a sound.

Bubbas leapt away, barely avoiding getting caught under the man's weight.

On her knees, Jena stared at the unconscious man with her mouth open.

A trail of blood trickled out of his nose and down the side of his mouth.

Damn, Pete had one helluva punch if he caused that kind of damage with only one hit.

A pounding shook the front door. "Open the door! Agent Stygian, open the door!" The doorknob rattled.

The door must have automatically locked when Claude kicked it closed.

"Fuck! He brought reinforcements. Come on, let's go." Pete grabbed her by the elbow and pulled her up.

The beating at the front door changed into hard thumps, like someone's body slammed it.

"Hurry, let's go out the back. If we're lucky, they haven't surrounded us."

Pete yanked her to Nate's room.

After grabbing a pair of sweats her messy brother had left on the bed, he put them on.

Jena only had a split-second vision of his round, sexy ass cheeks.

With firm-set lips, he rushed to the window and heaved it open. After a quick jab, the screen flew out. He motioned for her to hustle. "Come on! Through here."

Jena gave a mortified squeal as he swung her over the ledge, dropping her on the backyard grass. Any wild idea to not follow never entered her mind. A loud crack told her the door had crashed open. Okay, that was all the incentive she needed.

Shouts and stomping footsteps filled the bedroom as Pete jumped out.

Her eyes widened as the glint from a streetlamp reflected on raised rifles through the open window. Countless pings hit the tree beside her, splintering the bark. She yelped as Pete grabbed her hand and sprinted through the backyard.

They didn't stop until they reached the wooden fence that blocked them from going any farther.

Without a word, Pete swooped her in his arms and ran the short distance to the looming wooden wall.

She squealed and grasped his neck. "Wait... the fence...!"

From one step to the next, Pete jumped over the six-foot wood fence with her in his arms. He landed on the other side in a crouch, grunted, and raced to the thick forest with her cradled in his embrace.

A zing blasted the trunk of a nearby tree. Several repeating buzzing sounds zapped and hit the ground along the surrounding tree trunks. Bark splintered in the air.

She buried her face in the crook of his neck with a death squeeze. If Pete hadn't been running so fast, those bullets would've found their mark more than once.

Lifting a smidge from the safety of his neck, she bravely took a peek behind. Couldn't see much; hard to focus with her head bouncing up and down. Too bad that didn't stop her from seeing a team of camouflage-clad men fanning out. Even though they were all dressed in black and gray, it was easy to tell they wore combat gear and helmets.

Not to mention the freakin' rifles pointed and firing at them.

"Hang on, arammu. This is going to be, um, uncomfortable."

Before she asked what he was talking about, they became airborne. Her arms loosened around his neck at the same time he tightened his hold. They landed with a thud, making her breath whoosh. She sucked in air to calm her racing heart.

"Don't make a sound." Pete whispered in her ear. "If we're lucky, they won't look up."

Eyes wide, she peered over his shoulder. She gasped at the sight. They were high on a huge rounded limb of a Jeffrey Pine tree. Looking down made her dizzy.

Pete sat, dangling his legs over the branch, and settled her across his lap.

She lessened her grip and twisted to watch the action under them. Those men had enough weaponry to take over a small city. Wow, they were quiet.

They made barely a sound as they walked over the loose leaves and sticks on the forest floor.

One leader stopped and held a fist up before gesturing two fingers to the right and then two to the left. The group broke up and fanned out in opposite directions. The guy's head tilted as if making sure they carried his orders out.

Jena held her breath and prayed the man didn't glance up.

After an eternity, he finally slunk away.

She sighed.

Pete tightened his hold around her. "Ha!" he exclaimed in a low tone. "Stupid humans never look up."

Well, wasn't that a weird thing to say? She pulled away to see him better. Even in the forest's nightly gloom, she had no trouble noticing his dual-colored eyes reflected in the low light.

Now what?

Jena bit her bottom lip and whispered. "Okay, tell me what's going on before I freak the hell out." Her gaze narrowed. "Is your name really Pete Hayes or is everything you told me at lunch a lie?" She stiffened. Those

deep dimples caught her attention as his smile widened.

"I'd never lie to you, Jena." He shrugged with a sheepish grin. "I admit I've omitted some stuff. But hey, it's never good to unload all your secrets on the first date. Don't you think?"

She snorted. "Nice try." She glanced down at the forest floor and didn't see any other combat men wandering around. She swung her attention back to him.

He brushed away the hair in her eyes. "You know, we should stay up here for a little while just to make sure we've given them the slip. It'll give me a chance to fill you in on some things. That okay with you?"

At her nod, he put his back against the tree trunk, and swung a leg back and forth.

She remained snug across his lap and rested her head against his chest. The steady thumping of his heart calmed her.

"A long time ago, in a galaxy far, far away..."

She smacked his arm. "Pete, please be serious."

He chuckled. "I hate to tell you this, but that's how this weird tale begins." Pete outlined an outrageous story filled with ancient aliens, psychic abilities worthy of any Avenger, and finished with an impending alien invasion.

She closed her eyes and kneaded the taut skin at his side. "Okay, that ridiculous story aside, why are those people at my house with guns?"

He snuggled her as his nose nuzzled behind her ear. "I'm afraid you're a key player in this crazy drama."

She pushed away. "How would you know that?"

He at least had the excellent sense to distract her with a sheepish grin that deepened his dimples.

"My family and I only recently came across the aliens' convoluted plan to create hybrids here on Earth." He laced his fingers with hers and tipped his head to the side. "So, tell me, do you have any recollection of your family before you were adopted?"

Her breath caught at the flashes of forgotten memories. Over the years, she'd avoided thinking about her life before her adoption. While most images were hazy, the lingering emotions of terror, love, and belonging remained strong. Since she never understood those conflicting emotions, she decided a long time ago to forget them. Why remember pain when she grew up as a cherished daughter of the MacFarlenes? Even when her parents adopted the twins when she was fourteen, they never wavered in their unconditional love for her.

"Not really, why?" She trembled. She had a bad feeling whatever he said next would change her life forever.

He kneaded the back of her neck as he answered. "I have to give you a full confession here. When I said we learned about the Akurns creating hybrids, I was talking about you and your sisters. In fact, my family and I were trying to figure out how to find you when you rescued me after I was stupid enough to get caught in that trap." He glanced around. "Looks like we found each other in the nick of time." He held her hands in his.

Her mind blanked.

"From what I understand, the Akurns created you and your sisters as a lure for me and my brothers. After we meet, you're somehow programmed to steal our psychic abilities, and we'd end up vulnerable to abduction. Once they have us, they'll torture us and blackmail my mother. They want her back on their planet to force her to marry her bat-shit crazy half-brother so he'll have the legal right to take over the monarchy."

Her face burned as Pete clenched his jaw. Out of everything he said, the one thing that bothered her was he thought she wanted to hurt him. "You know I'd never hurt you." She chuckled a self-deprecating laugh. "Not that I have any idea how I could."

His thick eyebrows rose along with his contagious grin. "Well, that's nice to know." He patted her. "The good news is, one of your sisters has already overridden the genetic programming. So I'm hoping you can too."

Jena's face scrunched. "Wait a minute. You keep mentioning sisters. I don't have sisters... do I?"

Pete's laugh was soft. "Remember when I said we had a lot in common?"

She nodded with a frown.

"Well, we have the unique privilege of being part of a set of quintuplets."

Her eyes widened. "What?"

"Yeah, the only difference is you come from identical quintuplets and my brothers and I are fraternal." His fake sigh was loud. "Something I thank God for every day."

She shivered. Could this be true? Was she some kind of a weird genetic hybrid with four sisters she'd never dreamed existed? How could she not know all of this? Jena grabbed his warm, firm muscled arm and faced him. "Do you have any idea where they are yet? When can I see them?"

He shrugged. "The only one we found so far, besides you, is your sister Julienne, who lived in Vegas. She's now in San Francisco with my brother, Ben." He squeezed the curve of her waist. "Would you like to meet her?"

Jena cleared her throat and searched the forest floor to see if any of those soldiers wandered around. "That'd be better than where we're at right now. Think it's safe to get down yet?"

Pete's eyes closed as he leaned back.

Jena studied his relaxed expression. He was still the same handsome man she met earlier. But after the craziness they'd escaped from, he was something more. She stifled the urge to squirm and run her fingers through the strands of his windswept dark hair. His ski-sloped nose flared, as if he took in the surrounding scents. With those intense eyes closed, it gave her a chance to admire his thickset lash line. No amount of mascara would make her lashes rich like that. Not fair. Those suckers had to be double-rowed. His mouth caught her attention. Those plump lips settled in a loose line, a luxuriant image that fueled her fantasies about suckling the soft skin. She clenched her fists to keep from acting on that stupid urge.

He swallowed and his Adam's apple bobbed. The beginnings of a five o'clock shadow peppered his lower jaw and cheeks. She swallowed a groan. That deep cleft in his chin was another tempting place she'd

love to outline with her tongue. She jumped when his head snapped straight. He opened his eyes and focused on her.

Those eyes. They were the main reason she didn't dismiss his whole bizarre story. No one had larger-than-normal, oval, dual-colored irises like his. A jagged ring of shiny lemon-yellow surrounded the black oval pupils, similar to a burst of sunlight in an eclipse. The yellow swam in a sea of deep turquoise.

His exotic gaze remained fixated on her. The black pupils widened. The tip of his tongue peeked out and licked his bottom lip.

She caught her breath and watched those lips fill her vision. With bated breath, she lowered her eyelids.

He held her jaw as his warm mouth touched hers. His touch was tentative, barely pressing against her as he pulled her close. Then the masterful strokes turned into something stronger. The full length of his lips slanted and dominated across hers.

She breathed in his masculine scent of fresh leather with a hint of spicy licorice. Mmm, a whiff of his heady aroma upped her arousal, making her gasp.

He dove inside. Their tongues danced.

She whimpered and wrapped her arms around his neck.

Without breaking contact, he turned her around to straddle his lap. The kiss deepened. Moans vibrated between them.

Pete broke the connection.

With eyes squeezed shut, she chased after him with pursed lips. When all she met was fresh air, her eyes flew open. Heat flooded her cheeks. She pressed her lips together and waited to see why he stopped their kiss.

His red face twisted as if in pain. "Damn, growl at the moon, woman."

She swallowed a smile of satisfaction.

His solid body shivered. "I have never... I mean... shit. Never mind." His Adam's apple bobbed as he swallowed. "Yeah, um, I think we'd better get going while we can."

Jena resisted the urge to sigh. "Is it possible they're gone from the house by now?"

"Hard to say. But we shouldn't go back there. I have a cabin not too far from here. We'll head there so I can make some phone calls. Okay?"

She gave him a tentative smile and shivered, rubbing her arms. "Yeah, that sounds okay." She gasped as she covered her mouth. She stared, eyes wide. Something just occurred to her. "What about Bubbas? We've got to find him!"

Pete closed his eyes for a moment before he regarded her with a grin. "He's fine. I saw him run out the door after I knocked Claude out. We'll regroup and catch up with him later."

Regroup? Catch up with him later? She didn't get a chance to ask him what he meant when he swept her in his arms and stood steady on the large limb. She squealed. Holy crap! The man was freakishly strong.

"What...?" Before she finished her question, he leapt. When they landed, she bounced, but he held tight and she didn't fall. Gawking at him, she couldn't believe that superhuman move.

"Do you mind if I carry you?"

She glanced at her bare feet before looking at the forest floor. She ran around barefoot a lot, but tromping in the woods with no shoes wasn't something she wanted to do on a good day. Jena examined Pete's face. He didn't seem strained, but she'd hate to wear him out before they got to safety. "You okay with that?"

The fire in his exotic eyes matched his dimpled smile.

She trembled.

"I could walk the ends of the Earth holding you in my arms."

Jena couldn't help it. She laughed. "Holy crap! That cheesy line ever work for you?"

He chuckled with her. "Nah, but you can't blame a guy for trying. Hang on."

Pete took off.

She yelped and wound her arms around his neck. Even in the gloomy evening, she had no trouble seeing the fast pace he set.

He jumped over fallen limbs and ran without tripping or stumbling.

Jena jolted in his arms when he stopped.

He kept her close as he set her on her feet and kept hold of her hand.

She gazed around before she saw a clearing ahead with a small, one-story ranch house. "That your place?" She tightened her fingers on his.

It was an attractive older home, probably built in the seventies or eighties. The pristine appearance boasted a proud owner.

Pete stood taller. "Yeah. I had it built quite some time ago. It's my special place when I want to get away." He lifted his nose, and his nostrils flared before he glanced down at her. "Stay here and let me check things out. I have to make sure no one is around, okay?"

Jena's bare arms pebbled as the cool night air whispered over them. Her bare toes wiggled in the sharp, dried pine needles and dusty ground. She cupped her upper arms, rubbing them for warmth. She nodded. "No worries, sounds good. Just hurry."

With a grin, he gave her a two-fingered salute and sprinted away.

She admired his muscular backside. The sweats he'd put on molded a firm, perfect gluteus maximus. She couldn't help but sigh.

He disappeared around a corner for a moment, then he came back with a smile. Taking her hand, he led her to the front door.

Damn, she was in love with those dimples. Face it, Jena, you're totally infatuated with all of him, not just those seductive dimples. Who cared he was a shape-shifting, half-alien smartass? Not her, that's for sure. Wait, what had she just admitted? Her knees threatened to buckle. Okay, forget the crazy stuff for now. She might have acted cool and collected when Pete told her that wild story, but only because she hadn't had time to think about it. Survival first, funny farm later.

Pete put a thumb on a biometric security panel next to the front door. A green light blinked as a click unlocked it.

She followed him inside.

He closed the door and turned a light on, then took her hand and led her into the room.

The interior warmth was welcome. She gripped her upper arms as her teeth chattered.

Pete examined her with narrow eyes. "Why don't you take a quick shower to warm yourself up?" He led her to a bathroom. "I'll grab some drawstring sweats and a T-shirt for you to wear." He put a set of towels on the edge of the sink.

Her shivers and teeth chattering intensified. Holy crap, she was losing it here.

Pete frowned and encircled her in his arms.

She stiffened as she continued to shake.

"Relax, it's okay," he murmured, stroking the back of her head. "I know it's a lot to take in, but I promise everything will be fine." His warm hands framed the sides of her face with a gentle hold. His turquoise/gold eyes held her spellbound. "I won't let anything happen to you."

Jena searched his expression. His steady, lower-pitched voice matched his set jaw. She relaxed and nodded. "Okay.

Why I trust someone I only met twenty-four hours ago is anyone's guess." She gripped his wrists. "But for some stupid reason I believe and trust you."

Pete hugged her.

His warmth covered her as he chuckled in her ear.

"You're anything but stupid, Jena. And I promise I'll do my best not to make you regret your trust in me." His exotic eyes focused on her lips.

She parted them. When he lowered to her, her eyes closed. The man's addictive kiss did not disappoint.

His tongue swept inside as he possessed her mouth and controlled the contact.

Her nipples hardened and ached. Now she trembled for a whole other reason.

With exaggerated slowness, he pulled away.

The man's dilated eyes and heavy breathing told her their kiss affected him as much as did her.

Pete ran a hand through his tousled hair. "Shit, I promised myself I wouldn't push things with you." He zeroed on her mouth again and cleared his throat. "No matter how much I hate myself for stopping." With a deep breath, he stepped back. "Take your shower, and I'll make some phone calls." His tone was low and ragged.

The door shut behind him with a firm click.

Jena wasn't sure if she was glad he left or not. A big part of her wanted nothing more than to throw whatever sense she had away and jump headfirst into a physical relationship with the gorgeous man. The only thing that stopped her was the damn man being all gallant and such.

Great.

She made the spray as hot as she could stand and got in, letting let her mind go blank. Too bad inspiration didn't pop in and tell her how to navigate through the bizarre twist her life had encountered. Squaring her shoulders, she cut the shower short. After dressing in the clothes he provided, she marched out of the bathroom to meet her destiny with head held high.

"Son of a bitch!"

Hearing Pete curse, Jena ran around the corner into a brightly lit room and skidded to a halt.

Pete stood in front of the kitchen sink, gripping one of his hands as blood gushed between his thumb and forefinger.

Water from the faucet splashed, soaking Pete's dark T-shirt and the lap of his black jeans.

A classic chef's knife lay on the floor by his bare foot. The sharp edge was covered in blood.

"Oh my God, Pete!" She hurried to his side. "What happened?"

His handsome face contorted in a grimace as he muttered through clenched teeth. "I was cutting some veggies when I sliced myself instead." He hissed a breath and squeezed the edges of the injury together.

"Here, let me see."

He threw his shoulders back. "No, that's okay. I've got it." He wrenched the wound away from her but kept it over the sink.

Men.

"Pete, I'm a trained veterinarian. The sight of blood doesn't bother me."

His dark eyebrows rose. "Are you insinuating I'm an animal?" His dangerous dimples deepened.

"Of course you are. Now let me see."

With a rumbling chuckle, he let her examine him.

She gasped as the deep gash knitted itself together. Before her eyes, the gouge became smaller as the skin and muscles merged until only a pink line remained.

"Holy God! Look at that!" She grabbed his hand and yanked it close to examine. I've never seen anything like that before." She caught his sheepish smile. "Do you heal this fast all the time?"

A flush crept across his cheeks. "It depends. This was more of a flesh wound, so it didn't take long to mend." He shrugged and sidled closer as she examined the front and back of his hand. "See? All better now."

The words caressed her in a sensual whisper. His heavy voice and his nearness jerked her out of her musings. She stared into his exotic orbs that expanded the closer he came. The sound of water rushing from the kitchen faucet faded into the background. The only thing filling her vision was the man's heavy-lidded intent.

He pulled his now-uninjured hand out of her grasp and wrapped it around her waist. Closer, ever closer, until nothing separated them.

She zeroed on his mouth as it parted. With a sigh of expectation, she closed her eyes and leaned in to meet him.

He twisted and the noise from the running water cut off.

Enveloped in Pete's warmth as he cradled the back of her head, she was held in place as soft, masculine lips searched and covered hers with a hint of restraint. She craved more. She wrapped her arms around his neck, causing their torsos to connect. With a groan, she thrust her fingers through his thick strands.

The caress deepened as he grabbed her ass, locking them together.

The solid steel of his groin was easily felt through the thin fabric of her sweatpants. In reaction, her clit swelled, and moisture gathered, making her slick. Since she had no underwear on, the liquid lazily cruised down her leg.

"Damn, Jena." Pete broke away to suckle the sensitive skin along her neck and inhaled. "You smell so good."

She grabbed him to resume their kiss. Their tongues met, stroking and petting. His lavish musky aroma had her spellbound. Everywhere they touched, a maelstrom swept through, creating an unrelenting ache that throbbed low. She squirmed. He answered her silent plea by rubbing his hard length where she needed it the most.

A rumble rolled from his chest as he pulled away. "Aw, look. I've gotten your shirt all wet." His lips smacked with a tsk. "Here, let me help you get more comfortable." He reached for the bottom of her shirt, caressing her with callused fingertips.

Her skin pebbled.

"Shall I?"

How sexy was it he assumed nothing but made sure they were on the same page? Her huge grin was so wide it hurt. "Only if I can return the favor." She crept under his soaked shirt to glide her fingers over his inflexible abs.

His answering grin said it all. He grabbed her jersey and whipped it over her head. It landed on the floor with a wet plop.

Once free of the garment, the cool air on her wet skin made her nipples poke to attention. Not one to let a golden opportunity disappear, Jena attempted to mimic what he did by trying to pull his messy shirt off. As the soggy material stuck to his sculpted chest, she struggled to lift it over his head.

With a deep baritone chuckle, Pete flung the offending piece of clothing off, and it joined her shirt on the floor with a solid plonk.

Jena plastered herself to him with a breathy sigh and sought to resume their lip lock. The sensation of the hills and valleys on his chiseled chest with its smattering of hair rubbed against the sensitive tips of her hardened nipples. Blazing feverish need swamped through her. She clawed at the tousled curls at the nape of his neck.

"Skin. I want..." She swallowed hard and narrowed her eyes to glower at him. "What I mean is, you... naked... now."

"Ah, how I love a woman who isn't afraid to demand what she wants."

Jena squealed as Pete lifted her. With a groan, she pressed her lips against his for another burning kiss.

He returned the kiss, his lips firm and demanding, his tongue thrusting and rasping over hers.

She was going to burst into flames any second now.

He hurried them out of the kitchen, holding the globes of her ass in a firm grip.

She wrapped her legs around his trim waist. Each hard step inflamed her desire as the journey to his bedroom was all a blur. One minute she was flush against his firm pecs and the next she landed with her back on a supportive, soft mattress.

Pete wrestled out of his wet pants until he stood before her gloriously naked. Without missing a step, he grabbed the bottom legs of her sweats and yanked them off, throwing them over his shoulder.

Jena giggled.

Pete covered her shivering body and resumed their blistering kiss. There was nothing gentle or soft about his actions. This kiss was a full-blown sex act. It was a hungry devouring of her lips and mouth as he settled. The heat and weight of his body on her added to the intoxicating, white-hot kiss.

Jena gasped when he broke away. With a moan, she nibbled her bottom lip as he laved attention around her neck and shoulder before heading down. Holding her breath, she prayed he found the hard button of her clit dying for his touch. She quivered as he bypassed that ridged flesh and suckled the sensitive skin of her inner thigh. No, not there! For God's sake, she wanted the good stuff. Now.

"Pete, do you need directions? A roadmap perhaps?"

"Hush."

"Freakin' men never ask for directions... ah!"

He licked the indentation behind her knee.

She grabbed the tousled strands of his dark hair that she could reach.

Without looking up, he grasped and encircled her wrists. "Don't touch me. I'm busy exploring uncharted territories."

With a frustrated yelp, she released his hair. Her face heated.

"Yes, my succulent *arammu*." He let go and licked over her belly button. Then he flicked inside.

Her stomach rippled in sharp reaction. She arched as he nipped the sensitive skin on her tummy and resumed his journey south.

Her empty sex burned. The agonizing slowness of his explorations made her quiver. She hungered for this man. Everywhere. Intense lust stormed through her. Yes, there.

His tongue finally found the swollen mound of her sex. With a hard lick, he spread the cocoon of her clitoral hood and exposed the hard button of her clit.

Her eyes popped open as cool air hit her hot skin. "Oh, my holy God! What are you doing to me?" She clawed at the satin bedsheets.

"Hmm, I must not be doing it right if you have to ask."

His rumbling vibrated against her straining sex. He was a master of the tease. The man played and conquered the sensitive pearl before suckling the extended flesh into the blistering cavern of his mouth.

The tension holding her still snapped. Her back arched as fire erupted and a starburst of passion took over. A hedonistic kaleidoscope of pleasure swamped through, and the only thing she could do was

shriek with joy.

After several shuddering breaths, Jena floated back to reality. Lethargic, her legs flopped open as she released her tight grip on the sheets. The tiny licks and kisses he gave her sensitive bud made her quiver. Her eyes widened as a jolt of anticipation rippled through her. She couldn't possibly be ready for more. Could she?

His fiery tongue gave one last swipe before he crawled up her torso.

She shivered as his wide chest covered her, blanketing her with his undeniable heat. The heavy-lidded blaze of his exotic eyes bore into her as his mouth claimed hers. She tightened at the foreign taste of their mixed flavors.

The only thing to do was surrender to the building lust his kiss created. Hunger clawed; an intense sexual tsunami roared into life. Everything faded into the background and the basic need for oxygen became secondary. The only thing she wanted, no needed, was for his hard length to stretch her soaked, empty pussy.

"Do we do this, *arammu*?" His treacherous whisper feathered along her pebbled neck. "Do I make you mine?"

Holy crap. She purred as he talked like a reject from a cheesy romance novel. Damn, she was going to come again just from the enticing words. "You... yes... better... stop... not..."

A growling chuckle. "Ah, I have to be doing something right. I've made you speechless." He used his knees to part her thighs.

The heavy crest of his cock stroked the sensitive flesh at her entrance.

Without giving her a chance to take a breath, he drilled his wide girth in until he settled halfway in.

Her flexing sex, coated with her overabundance of slick juice, welcomed him with minimal resistance.

He drew back and pushed farther inside.

Each stroke of his throbbing erection made Jena suck in a breath at the sharp, pleasure-pain. She hadn't had a lover in a long time. With excruciating slowness, he stroked the walls of her pulsating channel until he was lodged fully.

He lifted himself and studied her.

"Jena, my *arammu*." His oval black pupils dilated under half-lids and his forehead shone beneath ruffled hair. The tan skin of his cheeks flushed, and his dimples flattened when his lips pressed into a tight line. "I confess I've never been consumed by another so deeply in my life." His croaky voice took on an unrecognizable accent. His brows furrowed while his mouth pinched.

She waited for him to continue, but the mulish expression never wavered. Her eyes filled. His confession crept into her heart. This beautiful, thoughtful man acted like she might somehow hurt him.

"I feel the same way, Pete." His tentative smile loosened her burgeoning tension. She stroked the side of his clenched jaw and wrapped her ankles around his firm hips. She squeezed his steel cock inside her.

While discussing the touchy-feely part of making love was something she treasured, right now that wasn't what she wanted. The only thing she needed was him. It didn't matter she'd just found her release. The glide of his heavy, throbbing erection ratcheted her lust to an extreme level. She rolled her hips and squeezed tight to capture him. She swore, if the man ever moved, she'd come after one thrust.

His eyes widened before sliding into a magnetic gleam of possessive intent. Capturing her lips with his, he rocked with shallow thrusts and mimicked the takeover of his kiss. Steady, sure strokes deepened with each plunge. His cock caressed her at just the right angle. The pleasure was brutal. Jena became lost.

Each powerful move created a building firestorm. She lifted to him, craving the friction that would send her flying. "Oh God, Pete! Yes, right there..."

Pleasure took over. It swirled around her, closer and closer as it gathered and increased inside. The climax electrified until it tore and burned. She latched her mouth to his tough shoulder, muffling her whimpers. Pete's grip under her ass held her still, and the broad length of his cock pulsated deep inside. With a jerk of his hips, the heat of his release coated her rippling channel.

With a shudder, Pete relaxed most of his weight on her, his fingers kneading the globes of her butt. "Shit, Jena." He groaned and rolled to the side as his softening dick slid out. "If I died right now, I'd consider myself a lucky man."

She inhaled a deep breath and enjoyed the combined scents of their pleasure. "Oh, yeah." She squirmed as a mini aftershock turned her into jelly. To steady herself, she gripped his forearms that encircled her waist.

Being with this man filled the gaping hole in her soul. The dark, bitter, unknown pain she'd endured her entire life disappeared. It was then it hit her. Being with Pete cured the constant void. She bit her lower lip. The only question, was she brave enough to admit that to him?

Jena grunted. What in the world made her think now was the right time to confess anything? She closed her eyes in blissful mindlessness as she lay side-by-side with Pete. All she wanted to do was to bask in the afterglow of one of the best sexual encounters she'd ever had. She dared anything to budge her from his sheltering embrace.

A heavy rumble from Pete's stomach interrupted the euphoria. Her echoing rumble was equally loud. They both jerked.

Her startled eyes met his and they burst out laughing.

"Well, with that not-so-subtle hint, I guess it's time to get something to eat," Pete quipped.

Her grumbling tummy agreed. She covered her complaining belly with an open hand. Okay, maybe that answered her dare.

Pete rolled and nuzzled her neck. "I know what I'd rather nibble on." He laughed and suckled the skin with loud smacks.

She lightly slapped the top of his arm. "Food first, sexy times later."

Her nudge to move him met no resistance as he sprung off the bed. The cool air of his missing body made her quiver. At his mischievous grin framed by those seductive dimples, she returned the smile.

"As my lady demands." He gave a gallant naked bow worthy of any courtier in the distant past. "I will endeavor to create a repast deserving of your beautiful self." He grabbed a pair of jeans from the nearby dresser.

She hummed when he didn't bother to put on a shirt. Yeah, all that glorious chiseled physique was on display for her to enjoy.

"There's a robe on the back of the bathroom door. Or if you want, just grab some of my sweats from the bottom drawer." He stole a hasty kiss. "First, I'll call my family to let them know what's going on. Then I'll make some sandwiches. Meet me in the kitchen."

Jena nodded. "Okay, I'll be right there."

After a quick trip to the bathroom to freshen up, she found some more sweats and another pullover to put on. As she approached the kitchen, she heard him cussing under his breath. "What's wrong?"

He stared at an old-fashioned rotary phone attached to the wall, the receiver cord dangling from his white-knuckled hold.

She'd never seen a working one before. The dark-green avocado color made her giggle.

Pete glanced at her before looking away. "I can't get hold of anyone." A red flush stained his high cheeks. "There isn't a signal from either my cell phone or the land line." He wiggled the receiver before putting it back.

"Does this happen often?"

His brows furrowed with a snort. "No." He rubbed his slick chest. "I've never had this problem before." His hands fisted. "I've tried to connect with them telepathically but..." He stilled. His head jerked and cocked as his nostrils flared.

Jena's hands fisted as she held her breath.

"Son of a bitch!" Pete grabbed Jena and twisted her to the floor, covering her with his body. The action pushed them flush against the island counter.

A bright light flooded the room as an ear-piercing whine followed.

Then the world around her blew apart.

Chapter Six

~Pete~

The silence was deafening.

Pete struggled to remain conscious as warbled sounds fought to catch his attention. A faint spicy aroma of black pepper with a dose of cinnamon made his nose twitch. The soft ground under his chest moved with a moan.

Jena!

Pete scrambled off. Damn, he'd better not be crushing her with his weight. He pulled the unconscious woman onto his lap and took a tentative glance around.

Glass was everywhere. The kitchen cabinet doors had shattered, along with the glass window over the kitchen sink. Nothing else appeared to be broken.

As his hearing returned, his eyes widened.

The male voices outside shouted in Akurn. Holy fucking hell! Were those damn aliens surrounding his house? And how did they find him... shit, did they know who he was?

Not waiting around to see what happened next, he stood and adjusted the limp Jena in his arms. He ducked his head and strained to make out where the least amount of resistance might be outside.

Jena murmured.

That cinched it. He stepped over the jagged edge of the sliding glass door and strode to the backyard. He gritted his jaw. He hadn't toughened the bottom of his feet before leaving the kitchen with glass strewn everywhere. The sharp shards sliced the bottoms of his feet. The only good thing was that the sting from each step helped to clear his mind. It took a second to create an impenetrable layer under his feet that also cured his injuries. Now his acute eyesight was restored, his nose twitched at the various scents, and his ears opened with a pop.

Pete inhaled to analyze the world around him. An acrid stench rode in the wind and surrounded the house. It carried the distinctive alien smell he associated with Akurns. He tilted his head. If he wasn't mistaken, there had to be at least five of them headed his way.

A quick glance at the unmoving woman made his mind up. He darted to the woods.

The loud shouts from the Akurns were close behind.

Pete gritted his teeth and rushed to put as much distance between them as possible. He ran on instinct. Not for the first time, he admitted having accelerated strength and speed came in handy. He took a linear track, refusing to hike farther up the steep terrain. His best bet would be to find one of the abandoned vacation rentals littered around the mountainside. That would give him a chance to regroup and try again to connect to someone in his family.

His inability to reach them mentally filled him with dread. Even though he wasn't a strong telepath, he'd never had trouble reaching Raiden or Ben before. If only his father, Adapa, wasn't fighting for his life in stasis. His father's psychic abilities were twice as strong as anything Pete or his brothers had.

No time to dwell on something he couldn't control. He stopped and opened his senses once again to take in his surroundings, controlling his breathing to avoid making extra noise.

There, a rustling that disturbed the indigenous animals and the prickly pine needles covering the forest floor. He stilled. Where were they going? His lips pressed as he concentrated. They weren't getting any closer to him and Jena, but it didn't sound like they were leaving either.

Closing his eyes, he focused on discovering any nearby dwellings they might hole up in. A blank void in the natural life force ahead let him know he wasn't too far from a man-made building. He took light steps in that direction, making sure he didn't disturb the natural order surrounding him.

Jena moaned when he held her close to his chest. He'd better get her some place safe before she woke up.

The trees thinned as he neared a clearing. A cursory peek through the thick tree trunks revealed a sprawling old-fashioned motel. It was a rectangle ranch style with about five rooms attached in a long line. The windows were sporadically boarded up.

Perfect. As Pete got closer his nose crinkled. Damn, the place smelled of dry death. Nothing living had been near this place for years, decades probably. Bypassing a door that proclaimed office, he went to the unit next to it. Locked solid. The boarded windows would take too much time to try to get in that way.

He examined the long length of the other motel rooms and didn't see any obvious ways in. Backing up, he checked out the roof. At first, he saw nothing except crumbling tiles, but two units down he noticed an indentation that could be the beginning of a hole.

A quick check at the passed-out Jena decided for him. This might be a good place to lie low for a while, but he had to find help. He stood straight and expanded his senses to take in the surrounding wildlife. Within a mile radius, he sent a plea to the myriad of indigenous animals to send him an alarm if anyone approached the area. His tense shoulders relaxed when he received several confirmations in picture form from the nearby wildlife.

With extra care, he laid Jena on a soft mound of pine needles. A shrug to loosen a kink, he stepped back. Jaw clenched with determination, he sprinted full speed to the end of the motel and jumped. He landed on edge of the roof, his arms pinwheeling to catch his balance.

Heart racing, he took a step to get a steady foothold. After catching his breath, he leaned over to check on Jena. Still unconscious. Pete scrambled to the indentation on the roof. It might look solid, but he doubted it. Only one way to find out.

Pete stomped the center. The crumbling tiles imploded as easily as a sandcastle being kicked by a bully on the beach. He glanced around to make sure the rumbling sound hadn't alerted anyone.

The forest was quiet after the noise he made, but within a few moments the natural rhythm of the woods resumed. Chirps, whistles, coughs, and low growls filled the air.

Pete sent out a mental question to the surrounding animals. Reports came back in pictures, letting him know nothing unusual was around.

With a grunt, he crawled to the side of the hole and looked down. Dust floated, which he waved away with a small cough.

Debris from the roof tumbled to the floor in a dirt-filled cloud.

When the air cleared, he took in a deep breath. Satisfied there were only rat droppings and insect scents, Pete flipped himself over to land feetfirst on the ground inside.

His extraordinary eyesight helped Pete see through the gloom.

The place housed cheap abandoned bedroom furniture left to rot.

An adjoining door to the next room was easy enough to kick open. The same degradation greeted him.

It wasn't until the last unit that his luck changed. This area seemed to have avoided the decay and neglect of the other rooms. Although the room was dusty with an air of abandonment, the furniture inside was intact. There was even an old-fashioned TV complete with rabbit ears, bravely claiming the right to continue its existence atop the dresser.

A hard yank opened the exit to the outside. Keeping his senses open for danger, he strolled over and picked Jena up. Back in the room, he sent out a request for the surrounding animals to keep a vigilant watch.

Their return confirmation was swift.

Pete kicked the door closed, and with extra care, placed Jena on the sagging, dusty mattress.

She moaned and rolled to her side. A light trickle of blood leaked out of her ear.

With a trembling hand, he felt her forehead to check for a fever. She was burning up.

Her lips parted and a slow rattling sound came out. Her breathing was shallow, as if she couldn't catch her breath.

It had been decades since he'd seen something like this. And that was on a battlefield when he watched comrades fight for their lives. A sharp pain squeezed his chest. No, she'd be all right. He had to be overreacting about her condition.

"Jena, my *arammu*," he crooned with a soft voice. "Can you wake up for me, my love?"

Her only response was a breathy moan.

He had to get her help. He couldn't lose her when he'd just found her. With shaking hands, he brushed a strand of wayward hair away from her glistening face.

Her breathing shuddered before another one didn't come.

"No!" Pete grabbed her and pulled her onto his lap.

The movement must've dislodged something because she gave a gentle cough.

He inhaled a relieved breath before he noticed that her skin was now ice cold. "Jena!" Her body was limp as a rag doll's and just as unresponsive. The pain squeezing his chest deepened. A rumbling growl rolled from his throat. All higher reasoning fled. He was devolving into a shape he'd never been in before. His shoulders broadened, his jaw lengthened to make room for long incisors that slid slowly out. Lengthy claws pierced his fingertips. He had just enough sense not to scratch Jena with them.

The pulse in her neck mesmerized him. He took in a deep breath and inhaled the siren song of fresh blood. He shook his head. Blood? What the hell? That was his brother Zamush's gig, not his. He didn't crave blood. Well, at least not unless he was in animal form enjoying the freedom of the hunt.

Pete shook hard. The sounds, sights, and smells around him receded until his senses became muted in a thick sludge. An all-consuming urge to sample Jena's blood took over. Unable to stop, Pete pulled her lusciousness close to inhale the fragrant essence that layered this woman. He took a tentative lick on her soft neck, over her birthmark.

Ecstasy exploded.

A deep inhale filled him with the spicy core of her in his arms. The sensation of his incisors lengthening barely registered. Nothing mattered... nothing but sharing who he was with her. Strict instinct made Pete lean closer with his mouth wide. A thin line of drool dripped from his exposed fangs.

He struck and bit deep.

When Pete struck and his teeth pierced the delicate skin of Jena's neck, ambrosia exploded into his mouth. Her feminine moan became lighthearted background music. He suckled her essence in deeply. The metallic goodness consumed him and settled the burning unrest twisting his insides.

One draw, then two. Riding on instinct, Pete slowly withdrew. Twin pinpricks of dark-red blood beaded down her throat. The word now pounded over and over in his mind.

With a muted growl, he bit the thin skin of his wrist. He tore a wound big enough for his blood to flow free. He had to share a part of himself with Jena to finish the process. The process of what, he had no idea.

Pete shoved his weird behavior to the back of his mind. Instinct ruled, and one thing he was sure of, if he didn't do this, she'd die. The claws retreated in his fingertips as he watched the life-giving liquid pool in her mouth.

With a careful push, he closed her jaw. "Swallow, arammu." He petted her throat for encouragement. "That's it, take it all." He kept his voice a low whisper, holding his breath. He waited to see if she did as he demanded.

A painful eternity passed before her tender neck convulsed. His racing heartbeat thundered hard in his chest. "Come on, my fierce *I'Lati*. Show me your warrior spirit." With a forefinger, he opened her mouth for her to take more. She jerked, but he kept her steady.

"No, just one more." Pete squeezed her mouth open and placed his bleeding wrist over it for her to suckle. He crooned encouragement. Every draw she took sent a spiral of desire straight to his cock, and he groaned. With half-open eyes, he watched Jena's cheeks hollow as she suckled.

When her actions caused a tinge of pain to ride up his arm, he pinched her jaw to release her hold.

Her sexy cinnamon-colored eyes continued at half-mast, while her lips pursed to chase him.

"No, my *arammu*. That's enough."

He refused to examine why he'd done such a weird-ass thing. If he did, he'd have to admit it freaked him the hell out. Instead, he concentrated on the bow of Jena's scrumptious lips. With trembling hands, he captured the side of her face. Their gazes locked. His lids lowered as he covered her lips with his. He made sure his touch was light and tender.

Her response was immediate. She grasped the back of his neck and pulled him into a fiercely fervent kiss.

The mating drive gripped him hard and low. Everything faded except being held in this woman's arms. Sharing the faint flavor of their combined blood, the natural urge to join with her overwhelmed him as a piercing hunger squeezed Pete. He was starved for his woman. With another breath, he savored her uniqueness, reveling in who she was on every level. Her sharp wit. Her snarky humor. The sensual way she moved. She connected with him and offered him completion.

Which should have scared the shit out of him. Here he was, a man who had his heart ripped apart so many centuries ago. None of that meant anything now. The only thing that counted was Jena. She was everything.

He wrapped a hold under her waist and nudged her legs apart to give him room to nestle within the cradle of her thighs.

She jerked from their kiss with a hissing gasp.

With his weight on his arms, he searched her expression. Did he somehow hurt her? "Are you okay?" His breath caught as her face scrunched.

She held a hand to her forehead. With a groan through clenched teeth, she closed her eyes. "What the deuce?"

Her pretty eyes opened.

"It feels like a tank ran over me."

Her pain-filled stare hurt his heart.

Her glance moved over him until her attention stayed on the side of his face. With a gentle touch, she reached over and caressed his cheek. She came away with dry flecks of blood. "Why is blood coming out of your ear?" She rubbed her fingers together and the flakes floated away.

"What do you remember?" Pete scooted over when he realized he halfway covered her with his heavy body. What was wrong with him he seduced a woman who had just awakened from a traumatic injury? He slid off but kept her wrapped in his arms.

He examined her rosy face and even breaths, then moved closer and inhaled. Her aroma was that of a healthy, aroused female. But her underlying tinge of acidic pain made him grimace.

Jena flinched. "The last thing I remember was standing in your kitchen when you tackled me." She frowned as she glanced over his shoulder. "This doesn't look like your place. Where are we?"

Pete loosened his hold and scooted to help her sit up. Dust from the broken-down mattress puffed free when they moved to get more comfortable.

"Well, you didn't get run over by a tank." Pete tried hard as hell not to jostle her. "But you've got to admit the aliens weren't very nice when they came for a visit."

Her mouth dropped. "Aliens? Are you kidding?"

"Afraid not. Their stench hit me before that sonic blast slammed into my house."

"Didn't you tell me those aliens wouldn't get here for several months?"

Her adorable nose squished when she pounded the stained and dirty mattress.

"And how in the hell did they find us?"

Pete rubbed his scruffy jaw. "Well, now... that's a good question." He focused on her. "Let's back up to what happened earlier. Did you give that Claude guy your address?" The thought of her giving some asshole her address made his hackles rise.

Not that he had any hackles in human form.

She snorted and crossed her arms. "As if." Her head moved to the side as she studied him. "But what does that have to do with aliens attacking your house?" She huffed. "Are you trying to tell me Claude is an alien?"

Now there's a thought. Not that he believed that older man was an alien, but the faint aroma of an Akurn surrounded him. "No, not exactly." He rubbed his jaw as he focused inward. "But it wouldn't surprise me if he was working with them."

Jena's tanned face paled as she rubbed her stomach. A new fragrance spiraled from her. It made Pete's nostrils flare as he tried to identify what it was. It was almost... wild? No, wait. He took in a deeper breath. That smell had a weird mixture of natural scents combined with something familiar.

She smelled like... him.

He jerked and straightened. How... what did that mean?

Jena moaned and flopped an arm over her eyes. "I don't feel so good." Her words were mumbled and slurred. She rolled to her side and whimpered.

Alarmed, Pete brushed her hair back from her face. Her flushed skin burned.

Sweat beaded in rivulets down her temples.

"Jena, what's wrong?" Shit, she was fine a minute ago.

She paled and wrapped her arms around her waist. "I don't know!" The last word screeched. "I can't.... ahh!"

Her legs kicked straight, and she flopped to her back. Arms flung wide as her back bowed on the bed, like a scene from an old movie about a possessed child.

He didn't know what to do. He swept her up and stumbled when her icy body touched his naked chest. Jena's teeth chattered as violent shivers made it hard to hang on to her.

Snuggling her as close as possible, Pete walked back and forth and murmured reassuring words in his native, extinct tongue.

Jena thrashed.

He was positive if he hadn't kept her in a solid hold, the exaggerated twisting would have broken several bones.

Then she went rigid before she collapsed. Her breath came shallowly before stopping altogether.

"NO!" Eyes wide and frantic, he clutched her tightly.

A sharp lavender light filled the room.

Pete squeezed his eyes shut, cradling Jena. When the blaze dimmed, he looked around. A movement on the floor caught his attention.

Bright icy-blue eyes with slitted pupils narrowed in a glare from a Siamese cat.

What have you done to my pet? Why is she not breathing?

Pete was speechless. How in the hell did the cat find them?

Answer, Adamou. Time is precious, and you are running out of it.

The feline's arrogance snapped Pete out of his stupor. He glowered at the animal. *Get out of my way. I don't have time for your platitudes. I've got to help Jena.*

The chubby feline gave a derisive snort. *Obviously I'm going to have to take over before you let her die.*

Between one blink and the next, Bubbas changed. His body mass tripled and he stood on muscular human legs. His torso, from the neck down, was compatible to a human male's. From the sculpted muscles in his arms and forearms, to the bulging tree-trunk-sized thighs. His chest was a rumble of brawny thickness. Instead of a six-pack, this creature boasted an eight-pack. He was hairless, even around his semi-flaccid penis.

It was the head of the creature that gave Pete pause. A very, oh shit, what the hell is this pause. While the body may have resembled a human's, the head and neck did not. The beast looked like something straight out of an Egyptian Temple. The face was that of a Siamese cat's, but with long black hair tightly interwoven into two thick braids reaching his waist.

The sparkling blue eyes of the feline were the same, right down to the slit pupils. The smirk creasing the creature's snout told Pete Bubbas enjoyed making him uncomfortable.

"I told you we've been here a long time." The cat spoke English in a rumbling voice that sounded like it came from deep inside a well. Each syllable reverberated. The accent was hard to follow.

"Who, or what are you?"

"I am Maathes, a direct descendant of the Egyptian goddess Bastet and one of her temple priests. You will hand me my pet so I may save her." The creature held out his clawed hands for Pete to put Jena on them.

Pete didn't hesitate. Normality wasn't around and help was too far away. He hadn't gotten hold of his family. And he doubted there was a Transkip mirror around except at his house.

He stepped back as a lavender glow encircled Maathes and Jena.

The blinding light didn't last for long. The glow faded, and they were visible again.

The tight squeeze in his chest loosened as he watched her breathe.

Maathes placed her on the lumpy mattress and stepped back. "This will stabilize her for now. But the transition is going to be hard on her." The cat/man stood tall, his seven-foot frame taking up most of the room.

"Transition? What do you mean, transition?" The acid in his stomach rolled as he dreaded the answer. Pete had never exchanged blood with anyone before. Ever. Why he did so with Jena was beyond him.

"Do not be obtuse, Adamou. You have claimed this female as your mate. She must become you. It is your duty to ensure she successfully passes through the next phase without injury." The enormous cat/man stepped toward Pete. "I promise you, you will suffer dire consequences if further harm comes to my precious pet."

Pete wisely moved away. "Back up, buddy. You may be bigger than me, but I doubt you're ornerier. Even if I lose, I'll make you work for it."

The cat/man gave a creepy smile around very sharp, feline teeth. "Very good, Adamou. There is hope you are a fit mate for my pet." He patted Pete on the head.

Pete slapped the beefy hand away and stomped to sit next to Jena on the bed. "Okay." He tried not to glare at the creature that just saved his woman's life, but he didn't mind admitting the arrogant son-of-a-bitch rubbed him the wrong way. "Tell me, oh-not-so-wise-one, now what?"

"In order for me to answer that, I will give you a small history lesson." Maathes crossed arms over his expansive chest. "As a guardian of this planet, it has been up to me for thousands of millennia to continue keeping the peace between the several cultures that have an interest here. It is only our grace that allowed the Akurns to stay. I assure you, we are not happy they are coming back, intending to destroy all the hard work we've done here."

Maathes flicked a wrist, and a long staff appeared.

Pete hadn't seen a was scepter in thousands of years. It was an ancient emblem of divine power and authority in Egyptian culture. He thought a golf club was modeled after it years later.

Not that he was stupid enough to say that to Maathes.

The Egyptian demi-god waved his cudgel, causing a picture to materialize.

If Pete wasn't mistaken, it was an actual live feed of the Akurns swarming through his house. "How in the hell did they find my house?"

"Since they took a sample of your brother's DNA, they've traced all of you. You're just the lucky one they got to first." The slit of the feline's bright blue pupils expanded. "However, by my calculations, you only have a few hours before they detect you are here. As soon as she can travel, you must take my pet far away from here. And I feel it necessary to warn you of something else."

A sour taste filled Pete's mouth. How could things get any worse?

"The enemy that attacked our home has put an alert out on the human system." The cat's head cocked. "I believe the humans call it an APB. You are being hunted by every known agency that has access to that. There've also been many alerts discharged through the planetwide communication of social media. I suspect if any of them see you, they will forcibly detain you."

Pete rubbed the bridge of his nose. "So, what you're telling me is not only are the Akurns hot on our trail, but so is every human law enforcement between here and San Francisco?"

The tall creature straightened. "That is so. I urge you to practice extreme caution."

A loud moan from Jena caught their attention.

"Since you can pop in here uninvited, why don't you pop us all out?" Pete sat on the mattress and gathered Jena in his arms.

Maathes raised a whiskered eyebrow. "I do not have the capability of doing so, otherwise I would. As it is, I am violating several council mandates to confer with you as much as I have." The large creature bent at the waist and glared at Pete. "Any further interference on my part will not be tolerated. It would only cause severe consequences for all of us." He straightened and crossed his arms over his massive chest, the scepter held tight. "Be aware, Adamou, I will have you in my sight at all times. She is vital in keeping the Earth protected from the Akurn invasion. We must keep her safe at all costs." The smile the cat/man gave was wide with teeth. "Or I promise you, there is nowhere on this planet you can hide where I will not find you."

A lavender glow encompassed Maathes, converting his humanoid form into the huge, bulbous Siamese that stared at him.

I go now to your family in San Francisco. I will aid you by apprising them of your inability to contact them. The cat's deep brown tail wrapped around his sitting form. *The change in my pet has begun, so I will leave.* A regal nod. *In the words of my people, may Bastet's power defend you and set you free.*

The cat disappeared in a glow of lavender brilliance.

Before Pete could dwell on the strange conversation, Jena's moaning increased.

He spent the next few minutes rocking and holding her steady as she thrashed in his arms. At one point, she twisted and squirmed out of his grip. Before he grabbed her falling body, she landed on her hands and knees, head down.

Her chestnut hair was a curtain covering her face. Her breath rattled.

"Jena?" Pete crouched facing her, waiting to see if she reacted to his voice. "Honey, you..."

She jerked and stared at him. Blank, dilated orbs glared before something under her face rippled.

Pete gasped and fell on his ass. Damn, he'd only seen something like that in the movies. He reached out when her nose twitched and her mouth contorted in a hard grimace. When she bared her teeth, he swore her eyeteeth had lengthened.

He pulled his hand back into a fist to stop from taking her in his arms. He wasn't sure if holding her would support the change he feared she was going through.

"Jena? Arammu, tell me how to help." He kept his voice low and soft.

With wide eyes, her face stopped the flowing movement and morphed into something different.

Watching her cheekbones lengthen, her jaw broaden, and her forehead expand made him speechless. Her exquisite image transformed into...

... him.

Pete swallowed hard. His mouth dried as she changed yet again. This time into a version of one of her twin brothers. All too soon, it took on another shape. Not just her face. Now her body bowed, and she stretched with fingers splayed and head thrown back. A howl escaped when she turned into an average-sized wolf.

A pure, snow-white wolf. The wolf's ears swiveled as if searching for a specific sound while her espresso eyes widened. The confusion and pain contorting her animal expression made it easy to feel and understand what she was going through.

Holy shit! His eyes widened as he watched Jena sprawl on the floor back in the shape of a wolf.

She whimpered and flopped to her side, her pink tongue hanging out.

Not knowing how else to help, Pete morphed into his black-and-silver wolf. Crouching on four legs, he crawled until he was close enough to nuzzle her snout with his. After he gave her some licks, she rubbed him back with closed eyes.

What's going on? Why do I feel so funny? And is why Pete licking my face?

Pete stilled. The voice in his head was clear, as if spoken out loud... in Jena's tone. He held his breath to see if he imagined it or not.

The white wolf's eyes opened and stared back. *I wish you could talk and tell me what's going on.* The wolf shook her elegant head. *Nah, nothing's that easy. He said nothing about being able to read minds.* A rumbling growl echoed from her tummy. *Crap, how can I be hungry at a time like this?*

Jena? Pete scooted his snout closer and nudged her jaw. *Can you hear me?*

The female wolf jerked. *Oh great, now I'm going crazy. I'm hearing Pete's voice in my head.*

No, Jena. Pete placed a paw over hers. *It's me.* He gave her a joyous bark. *I can't believe it! We can talk mentally while we're in different forms.* He licked the side of her face. *And it seems like it won't hurt us to do so!*

His heart lightened when she licked him back.

When they parted, her brown gaze narrowed on him. *Okay, Mr. shape-shifting, alien man.* Her head lifted, and she sniffed. *I'm neither one of those things, so why am I sitting here as a...* Her eyes widened as she studied her white paws. *What the hell am I? Did I turn into a dog?*

No, my arammu. He sat on his haunches. *You've changed into a wolf. A beautiful, glorious alabaster one.* His heart thundered as animal lust coursed through his veins. Panting, he lay on his four legs and kept his distance.

His ears twitched as her heart picked up a faster rhythm.

She shook. *Am I stuck like this forever? Can I get back to who I was before? How did this happen?*

Jena. Pete made sure he kept his tone gentle. *I think you're like me in more ways than one. Just as I can transform into my natural self, I believe you can too.*

But what if I can't? I don't want to stay like this for the rest of my life! Jena jumped to her feet and growled. *Turn me back right now! I can't take care my brothers like this! They need me...* Her hackles rose. She bared her teeth and crouched on her front legs.

Damn woman was going to hurt herself. Pete leapt to her side and firmly took the scruff of her neck in his jaws.

Instead of the alpha move calming her, Jena attacked.

Chapter Seven

~Sub-Prince Murduk~

Sub-Prince Murduk studied the headshot of the commander of FarDeep base on a floating vid monitor. Sitting in his private office, Murduk leaned back in his massive formfitting chair behind the command desk and steepled his fingers under his chin. His ankle perched over his opposite thigh. He glowered at the man who droned on and on about the needs of the base.

Murduk snorted. If he believed everything Commander Kud spouted, he'd hyperventilate with boredom. When the military elder finally shut up, Murduk let the silence speak for itself.

"Sirc." Kud's pale, hairless face remained stoic. "May I go over the update on the search for Princess Inanna's offspring?"

Murduk flicked his forefinger with a slight nod. He resumed his relaxed demeanor in the chair. No need to give the observant Kud any further ammunition on how critical it was to find Inanna and her "children".

"I am pleased to inform you we have isolated the genetic footprint of the princess's offspring. With this information, we've accessed the humans' population database and come across a promising specimen."

Kud's thin lips creased in a sly grin. "Apparently, this child of Inanna's has had several interactions with their law enforcement division. While they've wiped his actions from their records, his blood sample has stayed in limbo in their system until we successfully retrieved it."

"Your people could analyze the humans' primitive scientific operations?" Murduk'd been concerned that the remaining personnel on FarDeep base wouldn't be able to continue the critical search without the lead scientist, Thoth.

Kud frowned. "Yes, Your Highness. Using the genetic information Thoth maintained in his systems, we have located this potential offspring. Rest assured, the abnormal creature will soon be within our grasp."

It was hard to identify the foreign emotion that jolted through Murduk's chest. He leaned forward and held the muscles in his face still. "Do you have a specific time frame for accomplishing this?"

The commander cocked his head as if listening to an internal conversation. "Yes, sire. His domicile has been located. As a bonus, we've also been able to locate one of Thoth's created female hybrids, which I am pleased to report is in the same vicinity. We are now approaching both premises. Once we've detained her, we'll immediately stimulate her genome to absorb and destroy the abomination's abilities. In the meantime, even if he's not at his residence, we've activated the Goraxag, the best-known tracker in the galaxy. Once it locks onto its target, nothing can stop it from reaching its prey." Kud thrust his chin out. "I assure you, Highness, on my next contact, I will announce we have one of Inanna's male offspring's in containment."

~Jena~

Jena lost control. She was stuck in the backseat of a runaway freight train, strapped in with no way to escape. With horror, she watched the midnight wolf lunge to clamp on to the scruff of her neck. The bite might not have been painful, but it was tight enough to cause her instincts to erupt. Hard and fast, she twisted out of his grip and bared her teeth. With a loud roar, she attacked.

His dual-colored orbs narrowed with menace.

A massive black paw swept against the side of her head. Not hard enough to hurt, but hard enough to make her land with a thud on her side. She shook her head and rolled to stand on four legs. With snout lowered, she snarled.

Jena, my love, please stop. I don't want to hurt you. But I'll take whatever measure I can to get you to calm the fuck down.

Pete's voice created a crack in the animalistic throes that bound her. She struggled until it occurred to her—the more she fought herself, the harder it was to take control. With a deep breath, she closed her eyes and willed herself to relax. With each calming inhalation, she loosened until she regained control. *Pete? Is that you?*

The black wolf tilted his head before sitting on his haunches. *Jena?*

Yes, I think it's me. Crap, what a stupid thing to say. *I had a little trouble, but I think I've got a handle on it now. Can you help me get back to who I am?* Her strength evaporated. She flopped on her side and rolled blurry eyes as the ebony wolf came closer.

He gave a happy chuff and rubbed the side of her neck. *Yes, I can help you. But you've got to do what you're told without question. Think you can do that?*

If Jena didn't know any better, she'd swear the other wolf laughed at her.

Well, that depends. How weird was it to banter with Pete while she panted and licked around her snout with her long tongue? *Are you going to tell me to do something stupid?*

The sharp puffing laugh from the wolf made her relax.

I'll refrain this time. Listen, I know you're exhausted, but can you stand? It'll be easier to shift when you aren't lying down.

Jena forced herself to blink, trying to clear her eyesight and un-fuzz her head. *I think so. Give me a minute.* She rolled on her belly before pushing up on wobbly four paws. After stumbling, she remained steady enough to gloat with her snout tilted. *Ha! Did it.*

He treated her with a regal nod. *Okay, now envision who you are. Grab the concept of who Jena King MacFarlane is. Close your eyes, keeping the image of yourself focused. Let's start by visualizing your feet. You got it?*

She nodded.

Yeah, examine your ankles, then move up your legs. Now imagine your pelvis and hips, past your waist, and then your glorious breasts. Now include your arms and shoulders and your neck. You still with me?

Jena murmured an "uh-huh" in her mind and smiled at his breast remark. She was getting into this whole visualizing exercise.

Now focus on your lovely neck, your jawline... His tone lowered into a sultry croon. *Your full, luscious lips and that cute mole just above them.*

Pete's masculine drawl made something tighten low inside. She had a hard time listening to his words when the texture of his voice caught her in a spell. Everything receded except the picture he painted in her mind. She had no trouble seeing herself through his eyes.

Your thick, chestnut hair as it brushes over your shoulders and falls in a silky curtain down your back. The bright-brown eyes that match the color of your hair perfectly. Don't forget the smattering of light freckles that cross your perfect, pert nose.

Normally Jena would have snickered at his poetic descriptions. But she was so caught up in what they were doing, she didn't acknowledge the slight pain that twisted through her. Her face scrunched and her fists clenched as she became immersed in who she was. The cool air against her naked skin confirmed she'd turned back into her human form.

A light touch on her shoulder made her jump. Eyes wide, Jena fixated on Pete. The world around her went away and all she could see was the dilated pupils of his brilliant dual-colored eyes.

Her breath caught as the intensity built between them. Heat sprawled up her neck as she opened her mouth to say something pithy. She never got a chance.

He grabbed her by her upper arms and pulled her into a scorching kiss.

It turned out to be a kiss of a lifetime.

His tongue swept through as something part growl, part purr left his throat.

A savage ache squeezed her nipples into hard points and lust flexed hard in her womb. All thoughts fled. She reveled in the sensation of his warm, slick skin and matted chest hair as they slid against her. Wrapping her arms around his neck, she pulled him tight and staked her claim. Arousal became a never-ending hunger. Everywhere they touched, pleasure tore through and stole her breath.

Pete's spicy heat made her head spin as he plundered and conquered. The man cupped her ass cheeks and pulled her up on her toes. Their groins aligned as her wet core stroked the velvety hardness of his cock. His fresh masculine scent of leather and licorice created icy-hot shivers in her.

When he broke free to suckle and nuzzle her neck, she groaned in protest. "Pete, no, I..." She couldn't get another word in.

He claimed her lips as he lifted her in his arms.

Eagerly, she wrapped her legs around his waist and locked her ankles together. Her heels rested above the curve of his solid steel ass. The action forced their sexes to rub in alignment.

He joined her in a responsive moan.

Inside. She wanted him inside her. Grabbing the shaggy carob strands at the base of his neck, she pulled him away. The intense blaze in his turquoise/gold eyes made her tremble.

Her eyes dropped to his swollen, glistening lips as his pink tongue came out to lick the bottom one. She tightened her grasp on his silky hair. Sensations blended as her lady bits swam with desire and bathed his hardness.

Her lids slid to half-mast. "You..."

Pete's slow, sensual smile allowed the two deep dimples to come out and play.

"Yes, you demanding woman. I'll be more than happy to do what you so elegantly dictate."

His grip on her butt rotated her pelvis over his rigid steel. His heavily veined shaft rubbed against her swollen sex, making her wild with the need for him to fill her.

With a swift spin, he carried her to the edge of the dilapidated mattress on the floor. "Yeah, baby. Tell me what you..."

He didn't finish. A soul-shattering caterwaul filled the air and made the ground shake.

Jena had heard nothing like that before.

Pete went ramrod still. His head cocked and his eyes widened. "Holy shit! We've got to make a run for it."

His tight grip under her arms lifted her to her feet.

He narrowed his eyes as he studied her. "Once we get out of this room, we've gotta shift."

His deep sigh fixated her attention to the firm muscles of his chest.

"I hate to ask this of you, but can you turn back into a wolf? When we make a break for it, it'll be easier for us to go in animal form." A snort. "If we're lucky, the difference in our scent will confuse it long enough to give us time to get away."

The fear widening his eyes was easy to see. A sudden coldness gripped her core. She'd just turned back into herself, and now he wanted her to reverse that? She shook her head. No, no, she couldn't possibly...

"Hurry, there isn't much time before it gets here."

The urgency in Pete's voice rattled her. "Before what gets here?"

Pete grabbed the side of her face and looked deep into her eyes. "It's called a Goraxag. A tracking creature the Akurns use to find prey. I, unfortunately, ran into that type of creature before. It's an ugly, barely intelligent beast. But once it gets your scent, it doesn't stop until it finds you. As far as I know, their success rate is one hundred percent."

He lifted his head and flared his nostrils. "It's close." Those colorful orbs zeroed in on her. "Hurry, we've got to change into our wolves and run." Pete's grip tightened as he peeked out the side of the raggedy curtains covering the single window. One of the few that wasn't boarded.

"I see nothing, so it's as clear as it's going to be." He released her and yanked the door open. The hinges creaked, but gave him enough room to poke his head out.

Jena stood on her toes and tried to peep around him.

He pushed her back before she saw anything. "Smells clear for now. Let's go."

She squealed when he grabbed her hand and pulled her outside. "Pete! We're naked! How..."

An earth-shattering screech shook the top of the pine trees.

She gasped and stumbled behind Pete's long strides. The sharp pine needles and cones on the thick forest floor cut her feet as dry dust rose in minuscule clouds.

They didn't go far before Pete stopped.

Jena missed plowing into him by pinwheeling. "Holy crap! Warn a girl next time."

Pete ignored her outburst and faced her. "Okay, here's a good a place as any." He looked her up and down. "You ready?"

"Ready? Now?" Her stomach twisted into a rock. "Can't we just..."

"No."

With eyes blazing, he let go and took a step back. Between one blink and the next, Pete changed from a man to a wolf. The midnight fur gleamed as the dual-colored eyes narrowed on her.

A snap from his massive jaws made her jump. "Okay, okay. Sheesh, give a girl a chance, will ya?" The last word lifted in a squeak. With an acid-rolling stomach, Jena closed her eyes and envisioned a white wolf. Damn good thing she was a veterinarian and understood the intricacies of several animal natures. If she was lucky, one of these days she'd peek in a mirror and see what she looked like as a wolf.

As soon as she closed her eyes, her body pulled apart and went from one form to another. It didn't take long, but it freaking hurt.

When she opened her eyes, the first thing she saw was the back end of a black wolf with his tail lifted. Acute sensations bombarded her. Layers of smells, sounds, and intense eyesight made it hard to sort things out.

Deer spoor to her right fought with the fresh scent of squirrel to her left. Bird calls resumed and battled for dominance over the orchestra of zinging bug noises. A quick movement under her paws highlighted an anthill, the inhabitants going about their business.

A blur of black rushed to her side and nudged her.

Jena! Quit staring at your feet... we gotta go!

She chuffed at Pete's wolf and bounded after him.

Running through the forest as a wolf was exhilarating as well as exhausting. It was easy to keep up with Pete, but it was hard to ignore the life-filled forest that tried to grab her attention. A nauseating stench hit her and made Jena stop and sneeze. The odor left a foul coating on her tongue. It smelled like the sweet decay of a dead animal rotting on a field of spoiled hard-boiled eggs. It reminded her of the time Nick entered a hot dog eating contest and got sick afterward. The bathroom reeked for days.

What's that smell? Jena's eyes watered as a blurry image of the black wolf came close.

It's the Goraxag I told you about. The damn thing is getting closer. He lifted his snout and turned back the way they came. *I think if we go this way...*

A dumping crash made them both leap backward.

A gigantic split-toed reptilian foot stepped on a downed hundred-foot pine tree. Then another foot stomped the tree log next to it.

Jena eyed the creature the feet belonged to. Her muzzle dropped.

It was an enormous beast with massive horns adorning its gnarled head. A foul breath escaped the creature's slanted nostrils set in a cavernous nose. Six beady black eyes randomly littered the forehead, much like a spider.

What she assumed was the mouth were three separate round holes. One on the chin and two on the jawline that came with a row of massive fangs.

The gnarled head sat atop a compact, powerful body that resembled the underbelly of an alligator, in a sickly green-and-yellow-khaki shade. The creature had two boulder sized arms that protruded from its hips and ended in pincers. Spiky bones and membranes in the four wings stretched outward before folding on its back.

In a holster wrapped around its waist, bizarre tools or weapons dangled at its side, clanking and swaying with each movement.

Cognizant thought fled. Jena switched to instinct and backed away. Her muscles tensed to sprint when the blur of Pete's black wolf sailed beside her in a giant leap.

In midair, he changed form. He went from wolf to a replica of the creature.

Right down to the oppressive stench.

Terror held her immobile. The only thing to do was stare at the ensuing battle and stay out of the way.

When Pete crashed into the Goraxag, it sent them rolling on the ground in an enormous ball of alien monster.

It was hard to tell the difference between them. Then she spied the one with the weapons strapped in a belt around its waist. That had to be the creature.

Jena searched around to see if she could find something to use as a weapon.

Screeches, grunts, and piercing wails from the battled thundered and echoed. Maybe it was time to get out of wolf form. If nothing else, as a human everything wouldn't be so loud and she'd be able to think.

She closed her eyes and changed with minimal pain. Nice. She might grow used to this weird shapeshifting stuff. Clipped grunts caught her attention as the fight took the two combative monsters close to the edge of a twelve-foot drop. Studying the rim lip, Jena noticed a huge rock that teetered at the end of a ledge above them. Hmm, all she had to do was go up there and push the boulder hard enough for it to roll down on the creature's head.

Rushing to her goal, she ignored the deep cuts and scratches on her bare feet from the forest floor and bushes. Hand over hand, she climbed up the steep side until she reached the large rock. Peering down, she watched the massive alien creatures separate enough to swipe at each other with their pincers. Her eyes widened when Pete raised a two-pronged foot and used the toes to slice a broad gouge in his opponent's upper thigh. Thick puke-orange ooze spurted and created a river down its boulder-sized leg.

As the Goraxag staggered backwards, it threw a bladed instrument at Pete. It embedded in the shapeshifter's side with a solid thunk.

"NO!" Jena shouted. She was about to scramble down to go to his aid when the monster tripped backward and fell over a huge boulder. It landed on its back with a thud and an ear-shattering screech. The stone next to her rocked back and forth. With a whoop of joy, she got behind it and pushed when it rocked close to the edge.

She had just enough leverage to force the stone over. A thundering rumble and the boulder hit her target. It didn't smash its head like she'd hoped, but it pinned one of its shoulders to the unyielding dusty forest floor.

The creature raised a bloodied pincer-hand to shove it off. It must have thought Pete was no longer a threat, otherwise it would have seen death coming.

Morphing back into his human form, Pete rushed and grabbed a flat steel blade from the creature's holster. He swung the shiny sword over his head, his thick chest and arm muscles bunching. With a triumphant roar, he brandished the sharp steel in a straight swoop and decapitated the Goraxag.

Jena jumped for joy with raised fists until she watched in horror as Pete's eyes rolled to the back of his head.

He dropped in a boneless heap, the embedded knife in his side creating a stream of red blood soaking the forest ground.

"Pete!" She screamed and ran down the incline, leaping over the sprawled legs of the dead Goraxag. The alien's head was the size of a medium boulder she swerved to avoid.

The bright light of the afternoon sun reflected off the unblinking, six black beady eyes.

Jena ignored the lingering pungent stench of the creature and rushed to Pete's side. "Oh my God!" She rolled him onto his back. The action caused the knife to slide out and gave her a chance to examine the wound better. She might not have been a human doctor, but being a vet gave her a fighting chance to staunch the deadly injury.

A huge gash split his waist just under the rib cage. Grabbing both ends of the damage, she pushed them together and frantically looked around for something to either hold the wound closed or stop the rapid flow of blood.

Nothing. There was nothing she could use. Dammit, she didn't even have any clothes to rip off that would help. Tears flooded and fell as she gasped for breath.

"Hang on, Pete. I swear I'll think of something..."

One minute Jena blinked through a river of tears, and the next she was in a dense tropical rain forest. Towering trees and vivid vegetation surrounded her.

Pete slumbered on a cloud of swirling mist, his face relaxed, with a slight smile.

The warmth of his skin was devoid of the fresh blood she'd been desperate to slow. She jerked and gasped at the unblemished area. It was as if there had never been a wound there at all.

Pretty lady... pretty lady for Adapa's son.

Jena squealed and turned around, searching for whoever was talking. A branch on the ceiba tree above her rattled and caught her attention. At first there wasn't anything to see, but upon looking closer she noticed a black bird scuttling to the edge of the limb.

Her eyes widened. That was no bird. That was something different. She squinted. Was that... was that a small dinosaur? The four-winged creature resembled a two-foot microraptor.

It tilted a triangular head and studied her with a single stern, unblinking black eye. Yes... yes, you are the one for Ara-Riyad. The sharp-looking beak parted and squawked. *You will be... You will be good for wild son.*

Jena put a hand over her pounding heart. *What the deuce! Are you speaking to me?*

The silky ebony head nodded and pushed off the tree limb. It glided down and stood next to Pete's prone body. *Wild son... wild son with broken heart has a powerful need for his female.*

Her stomach dropped. Female? He has a female, er, a woman in his life?

Look at her, going with the flow, talking to an extinct animal like it was a person. She'd suffered so many life-changing events in such a short time, it wouldn't surprise her if she turned into a certified crazy person by now. Her lips pressed. Was Pete involved with another woman? No, for now she'd ignore that horrendous possibility and help him. Later, when he was better, they'd have a serious conversation...

No... no. The microraptor fluttered its wings and shook its head. *Ara-Riyad has need of you. Only you. Now you must, you must decide.*

She scrunched her nose. *What is an aura rye ad?* She put her hands on her hips. *And decide what?*

Ara-Riyad is before you... before you, awaiting his fate. Come see. The dinosaur hopped closer to Pete and waved a feathered forearm toward him.

Jena gasped when it glanced at the sleeping Ara-Riyad, um, Pete.

That sexy, muscular chest rose and fell with each breath, and Pete's face was relaxed.

The soft glow over his heart was hard to look away from.

An old-fashioned lock that appeared to be ancient formed and embedded in his skin. The golden color was smudged and blackened with age. Around the keyhole were various etchings of swirls and curlicues.

What is that? Why does he have a lock stuck in his chest? She glared at the upturned triangular face of the dinosaur. *Who are you, and why are you here?* She looked around. *For that matter, where in the hell are we?*

The small dinosaur closed its dark brown eyes and swept a forearm across its feathered chest. *I am Ash... I am Ash. The spiritual guide for Adapa's sons.* The creature glanced at her with narrow eyes. *But I warn you... warn you. I can only advise you to a certain point. It is you... you who must decide the final outcome.*

That's the second time you talked about a decision. What kind of decision am I supposed to make? She glared at the creature.

The answer is with you... you only have to look. A small claw pointed to her clenched hand. *You have all you need in your possession. You must decide if all that is Ara-Riyad is destroyed, or if you are brave enough to listen to your heart and go against that which they have created you to perform. Brave enough... brave enough to endure the pain.*

With fists on her hips, she tapped her foot. *Could you be any more cryptic?*

Without warning, a sharp pain pierced the skin of her right palm. Jerking, she opened her hand and glanced down at a golden skeleton key. Jena studied the slight glow of the lock on Pete's chest before bringing the key closer to examine it. It had the same color and etchings as the lock in his chest. She brought it nearer. The more she stared, the more she had a wild urge to insert the key in the lock and turn it clockwise. That instinct drove her hands to shake.

Female... female that which belongs to Ara-Riyad must listen to her heart. What is best... what is best not only for him, but what is best for her. The small Ash waddled to her and placed a gentle clawed grip around her ankle. *Close eyes... close eyes and look inside. There you will find your answer.*

The animal disappeared in a smoky mist.

Jena clutched the key and searched around her. The microraptor was gone. A heightened glow caught the corner of her eye.

The lock on Pete's chest brightened.

She held the key in a tight fist and knelt by the prone man. Sweeping an errant lock of spice-brown hair from his forehead, Jena let her fingers trail down the side of his boyishly handsome face. Thick sable brows framed his closed eyes, thick enough to give her a spurt of envy. His snub nose had a bit of whimsy that matched his dangerously deep dimples. Full lips were luscious pillows she craved to explore. A scruffy five o'clock shadow coated his rugged jawline. It did little to hide the sharp cleft in his chin.

Her gaze wandered past his firm throat and settled on his brawny chest. A smattering of dark hair encircled the pebbles of his flat nipples, and a line down the middle pooled around his groin. His flaccid penis was a thing of beauty. Even softened, the uncircumcised member gave a hint of its majesty at full mast.

She bit her lip and stifled a moan. She loved being his lover. With determination, she clutched the key in her hand as it warmed. Jena uncurled her fingers and watched the metal glow at the same rate the lock in Pete's chest did.

What did that dinosaur say? Oh yeah, she had to search within herself for the answer. Whatever that meant.

She glanced at Pete. A sense of urgency tightened her shoulders. Time was running out. The glow from the lock and key got brighter, nudging her to insert the key. Instinct made her want... no, need to turn it clockwise.

Wait just a damn minute. Great, now she was arguing with herself. She sat back on her heels and clenched the key, taking it out of sight. She had to think this through.

Ash, that barely helpful animal, told her she had to go against what she'd been created to perform. Of course, he had to tack on something about pain after that enigmatic remark. It stood to reason, if she put the key in the lock and turned it counterclockwise, it would really hurt. But going against that inner compulsion would somehow save Pete.

Her arms shook. She bit her lip harder to stop from inserting the key. She shifted to look at Pete and her heart melted. Not only was he the best-looking man she'd ever seen, but he had the personality traits she'd always looked for in a partner. A lighthearted sense of humor coupled with an innate grasp of protective honor. He was solicitous and gentle with her when he needed to be, yet he could be stern without being disrespectful.

With all of that, how could she possibly consider doing anything to harm him? And she knew without a doubt, that if she inserted the key and clicked it to the right, it would destroy him. Oh, he may not die or anything that dramatic, but it would eliminate everything he was. Including the ability to shapeshift.

Jena licked her lips. This was it. This was what she was meant to do. Before she met him, she'd assumed her purpose was to take care of her brothers after their parents' death. But she'd been wrong. Her existence was interwoven with this man. That admission made something click inside. There was no doubt in her mind she and Pete had to be together. It was up to her to make that happen.

Sweat rolled down her temples and the middle of her back. As with anything worthwhile in life, it took effort. And sometimes that included a little pain. All she had to do was to be brave enough to do the right thing. She inserted the blade of the golden key into the glowing lock.

Time to fulfill her destiny and save the man.

Jena pinched the bow at the top of the key and turned it left. A torturing stab shot up her arm, making her fingers numb. The agony lingered, then spread throughout her body. Hot pokers squeezed every nerve ending until she was afraid her head would explode.

She refused to let her pain dictate the course of her life. Holding the key steady with sweaty fingers, she forced it farther to the left. It barely moved before another jolt of pain made her gasp. Wiping the sweat from her eyes with the back of her other hand, Jena leaned with white knuckles and turned it harder. Damn thing acted like it was fighting with her. It hardly budged.

With a low growl, she put both hands on the stubborn key top and yanked it hard with her entire body. A resounding boom exploded from the lock and flung her backward. Everything went black.

Chapter Eight

~Special Agent Claude Reese~

C laude Reese stood in the uninhabited Tahoe National Forest and watched a bizarre brawl he'd only seen in the movies. Agent Raven and a small contingent of special troopers were with him, observing as two combatants fought to the death. The man who'd interfered at Jena's house pulled a sword from the holster of a huge bizarre alien creature and used it to decapitate the beast.

After Jena screamed the name "Pete", she ran from a steep incline and rushed to the wounded man.

Agent Raven moved as if to intercept.

Claude put a restraining hand on her arm. "No." He nodded at the frantic Jena as she exclaimed, "oh my God" and rolled the unmoving man onto his back. "I want to see what she does." Claude made his tone low so only the agent next to him heard.

Agent Raven frowned. "Are you sure? We've got to grab her before the aliens get here. And you and I both know they're not far behind us."

Claude patted her arm reassuringly. "Yes." He glanced at her sideways. "Have the team surround this area. That way when the Akurns show up, we'll have the upper hand." He pointed to the carcass of the grisly alien with its head several feet away from the body. "Order a unit here to retrieve that creature. I'm sure Director Obsidian will be more than happy to have his scientists get their hands on it."

Agent Raven nodded as she spoke inaudible murmurs into the team radio attached to her shoulder.

Claude turned back to watch as a naked Jena knelt next to the wounded man who was also nude.

Tears streamed down her smooth cheeks as she pushed together the gaping wound in the man's side.

Not for the first time, he compared her to his former bank employee, Julienne. Jena was obviously the other woman's twin, but there were major differences. Julienne was a typical bank worker, with soft curves and a blinding intellect.

He'd never seen that woman without makeup and a business dress suit.

Jena went for the natural look and was more athletic and tanned.

He studied Jena when she stopped moving.

Her hands became slack on the gaping wound as she sat back on her heels with her mouth slightly open and her brown eyes wide.

"What's she doing?" Agent Raven whispered beside him. "And what in the hell is that?" She sucked in a gasp.

A golden light encircled Jena and the injured Pete until Claude couldn't see them. The operator next to him jerked as if to rise. He restrained her with a firm grip. "Stand down!" He gave a stern, low-voiced, no-nonsense command. "Tell the troops to do the same. Now!"

"Stand down!" Agent Raven didn't hesitate. "I repeat, stand down!"

Out of the corner of his eye, he verified they obeyed the orders.

Almost as soon as the golden shield around them appeared, it dissolved. When the image cleared, Jena and the injured Pete were lying on their backs on the forest floor.

Jena moaned and rubbed her temple.

"Move on my mark, and not before," Claude intoned firmly.

The troops moving in too quickly would screw this up. He wasn't about to let this opportunity slip through his fingers. The rush of the unknown made his blood pump faster and his breathing deepen.

~Jena~

Holy shit! That freaking hurt. Every muscle, nerve ending, and exposed skin rippled with decreasing pain. Jena put a hand to the side of her head and whimpered. Careful not to jostle too much, she sat up on a nest of pine needles littering the forest floor. She winced. Damn needles scratched her ass cheeks.

A male groan caught her attention. Ignoring the agony when she moved, she rushed to Pete. The image of the tropical forest became a distant memory as she studied the bloodstained area at his waist. A quick swipe to clear the excess dried blood away so she could grab and pinch the wound together again. At least that was her intention.

But there wasn't a wound to grip. In its place was a fresh swath of healthy skin.

Pete moaned louder and settled on his elbows. His brilliant, large, oval, dual-colored eyes fluttered before they opened and stared at her. "What happened?" He rolled to his hands and knees and twisted as if searching for something. "Where's the Goraxag?"

"Over there." She pointed to the disgusting head with burnt-orange blood coagulating under it.

Pete relaxed, and his smile created those sexy dimples on his scraggy face.

He sat with his arms wrapped around bent knees. With a sheepish grin, he gave a loud whoosh with a chuckle. "Well, thank the Goddess of Love that's over." The grin slid into a frown. "We'd better get the hell out of here while we can." He lifted his head and sniffed.

"Hang on a minute!" Jena touched the dried-blood soaked side that was now flaking. "You just suffered a life-threatening wound. Where did it go?"

In the blink of an eye, Pete leapt up and pulled her to her feet. Legs bent, he put his palms out. "Get behind me. Someone's here." He grabbed her and forced her against his back.

Jena squealed. Her cry ended when she mashed against the solid muscles of his back. Trusting him, she hugged his trim waist.

Various people in military tactical gear surrounded them. The weapons pointed at her and Pete were not something easily avoided—no matter what kind of animal he turned into.

Pete must have come to the same conclusion. He stood tall, shoulders back, with arms crossed over his exposed chest. He didn't even try to hide any part of his bare body. "Well, what can I do fer ya folks?"

His nonchalant attitude made her squeeze his waist. She hid her nude self behind him. No reason to give everyone a free peep show. She peeked around Pete's broad torso.

A man dressed in a black suit and tie sauntered between two of the combatants.

Her breath hitched. It was Claude Reese. But this Claude wasn't the same guy she'd gone to lunch with the other day. Nor was he the bully who forced himself into her home.

The suit and tie were a working outfit, complete with a gun in a holster at his side, and some law enforcement badge strapped to the belt.

She wasn't close enough to see what division it came from. She trembled.

"Jena."

Claude's hazel-eyed stare increased her shakes.

"You need to come with me." He gave a wave to encourage her to leave her haven behind Pete's back. "Hurry, before they get here. I promise I'll take you somewhere safe and into protective custody."

Jena snorted. Was this guy for real? She shook her head. "I did nothing wrong, and I'm not going anywhere with you. Just who do you think you are?"

"I'm with the federal government, and it's my job to protect you." Claude gestured to the military force surrounding them. "There are some enemy combatants determined to kidnap and harm you. I'm here to prevent that."

Her fingers clutched Pete's forearm. "I don't think—" She screamed the last word as Pete twirled her around and landed on the ground with her underneath him.

A ringing zing passed over where he'd been. If he hadn't moved, something would have hit him.

She squirmed to look through the arch of his arm and torso.

Embedded into the throat of the men standing next to Claude was a shaking spear. Instead of a gaping wound, a blinding blue/white light flashed before the man burst into a puff of gray ash.

The spear floated in midair before it made a 180° turn and flew back to the hand from which it came.

Jena gasp and scooted, trying to get a better look.

"Stay still." Pete whispered bare inches from her ear. "Where the fuck is Raiden or Michael when I need them?"

Doubtful he meant the last comment for her. Pete's bulk wasn't as heavy as it should be. She suspected he kept most of his weight on his knees and arms. But all the same he was a big man, and it was hard to breathe.

A blast of gunfire made her jerk. Bullets pinged and zapped over and around them. Pete clutched her tighter, as if to protect her from the combat. Where their bodies touched, his warm skin became icy. If she didn't know any better, she'd swear she was under a steel cage. She bit back a scream as her heart raced when he flinched. A bullet hit him? She had to find out if they hurt him. Twisting underneath him, she struggled to see what was going on.

"Stop squirming."

Pete's baritone made her shiver. He didn't sound hurt. "Are you okay? Your skin's cold and hard." She raised her voice against the loud gunfight above her.

"I'm fine. I just harden my skin so that if a bullet hits me, it'll bounce right off."

Well, wasn't that convenient? Jena would give anything to see that. But all she could see from her position under him was his Adam's apple bobbing.

Without warning, Pete vanished.

She shielded her eyes and squinted at the bright glare of the sun above. Hard hands grasped her and yanked to her feet.

Held fast, she tottered as a bare foot landed on a sharp rock. She twisted to get loose, but the two agents holding her didn't budge. She gave the jerks a glare before the chaotic scene around her made her mouth drop open.

Pete struggled in a similar predicament. But instead of humans in military gear, two strange looking, alabaster-white men restrained him in a tight grip and one slapped a round, iridescent disc over his mouth.

Her eyes widened as the disc expanded and buried the lower half of his face, leaving his nose free to breathe from.

Pete's oval, dual-colored irises blazed in his red face. He yanked and squirmed, but his captors held fast.

With quick efficiency, one of the men snapped silver metallic restraints on his wrists that they wrenched behind his back.

A small group of men who looked like the two holding Pete moved forward.

"I demand to speak to Commander Kud immediately!" Claude barked. He put himself between Pete's captors and hers. He faced the strange albino fellows with his palms out.

"You dare demand anything from us?" One of the men in the group stepped forward. A burly mountain of a weird-looking man stood in front of Pete and his captors. His words came out heavily accented, as if each syllable stumbled over one another.

With his arms crossed, he reminded her of something out of an Arabian Night's tale. Except this guy had blinding-white skin and hair, along with narrowed blue/green eyes, and a deep scowl that wrinkled his forehead. A thick alabaster rectangle beard several inches long adorned his sharp chin.

The man wore a golden helmet with a spearpoint poking out the top. A thick gold breastplate with a round lapis lazuli symbol containing a starburst of bright gold proudly displayed in the middle covered a tan cloth tunic. Billowing pants in the same color as the tunic were tucked into ankle-high brown boots that curled up at the toes.

His belt was double strapped around his trim waist with an eclectic variety of weapons attached to it—something shaped like a boomerang, a long broadsword, and a silver cylinder that had to be more than just harmless decoration.

"Tell Kud I was working in tandem with the Honorable Thoth. I assure you, Commander Kud will not take it kindly if you deny this opportunity for him to speak to me." Claude's demeanor was cool and collected.

Even with his back to her, she could tell he faced the scary-looking guy with crossed arms. Probably had a matching scowl. No telling who Thoth was, but she'd been watching Pete.

His eyes widened at that name.

Over Claude's shoulder, it was easy to see the annoyed expression crossing the albino's face.

With a pronounced lip curl, he put his arms out. A golden metallic band that encircled his wrist lit up.

Between him and Claude, a life-sized holographic vision of another white guy's profile appeared. This elderly man wore a one-piece gray suit. Instead of the shoulder-length hair and long rectangular beard hanging from his chin, he had a military buzz cut and a clean-shaven face.

The image turned and spoke in a strange lilting language to the man who called him up. After a brief, staccato conversation, the guy turned cold light-blue eyes to look at Claude.

"Apparently Bahadur deemed it necessary that I communicate with you, human."

This must be Kud, the man Claude demanded to talk to. He had the same rumbling accent as the other albino men.

"I only agreed to talk to you to assess if you have information about where Thoth is. Therefore, speak."

Claude gave a slight bow before straightening.

Jena would've given anything to look at his expression. It would be nice to see if any of these alien people made him nervous. She glanced at the guard holding her before checking out the other agents.

Each one had a gun drawn.

She bit her bottom lip and suppressed a shudder. Just her luck, to find herself in the middle of harsh negotiations with a gaggle of aliens. If everyone went for it, she and Pete wouldn't stand a chance.

"Commander Kud, thank you for agreeing to talk to me." Claude clasped his hands behind his back. He spun the gold ring around his wedding finger as he spoke. "While I don't know where Thoth is, I propose a compromise that will benefit us both."

Kud raised a pale, pencil-thin eyebrow. "Is that so? What could you possibly have that I would want?" He twirled an elegant finger to encompass the group. "We outnumber you and have greater firepower." His narrow lips curled into a mocking sneer. "I may be magnanimous enough to allow you and yours to leave unharmed. But only if you do so now without the male or female."

Claude reached for something under his jacket. Jena couldn't see what he held, but when he thrust it out to show Kud, the alien's eyebrows rose and his eyes widened.

"Excellent."

The mocking tone in Claude's speech made Jena catch her breath.

"You know what this is. I expect you will now be amenable to a compromise, yes?"

Kud's thin lips became a mere slit. "Very well, proceed." His tone came out brittle and sharp.

"This man is a unique specimen among humans, and I believe he might be who you're looking for." He turned and gestured to her with his free hand before turning around. "Because of that fact, my proposal is I'll take this worthless female off your hands and leave you with a much better prize." His back went ramrod straight. "When we part, I vow I'll continue to assist you in any way you deem appropriate. Also, if I find the Honorable Thoth, I'll contact you if you give me the means to do so."

Kud's expression smoothed out. He gave Claude a bland, blank stare. His head tilted before he answered. "I must examine this male before I render my decision."

The alabaster man, Bahadur, shouted a guttural order to the men holding a struggling Pete.

Two mammoth alien guards dragged him to the holographic image.

Kud studied Pete. "Lift an eyelid so I may look at his eyes closer."

One guard jerked Pete's head to the side and lifted a lid, exposing the overly large orb for the commander's inspection.

The bright yellow sunburst around Pete's pupil expanded, leaving the turquoise color in a thin line.

It didn't take long for a satisfied smirk to slide across Kud's pale lips. He straightened and glanced at Claude. "I agree to your proposal. You and yours may leave unimpeded. No need for you to contact me, I will be in touch." He turned to address Bahadur in clipped tones before the holograph vanished.

Bahadur glared at Claude with a guttural growl as he took a gold cylinder from his waistband. He kept his stare steady as he twisted the device.

A bright orange light illuminated like a flashlight before turning into a black hole. Inside the maw, a kaleidoscope of swirling stars and jet streams rolled in a myriad of colors.

Bahadur barked a short syllable and the guards holding Pete walked straight to the flicking image. Without breaking stride, they went through the hole and vanished.

Jena gasped. Pete! Her stomach dropped.

The rest of the aliens followed Bahadur and disappeared from the forest. On the heels of the last alien passing through, the hole folded and faded without a sound.

The forest floor was untouched, as if it had nothing to do with her world disappearing through a black hole.

Claude turned and signaled for a couple of his goons to hold her. "Quick, let's move before he changes his mind." He crimped a jagged, round object the size of a baseball and flattened it before sliding it into a slot in his holster beside his gun.

The agents holding her spun her away.

"Wait!" An African-American woman in combat gear rushed to stand in front of Jena. She shoved a large military jacket at Jena. "Here. Let her put this on."

"That won't be necessary." Claude waved at someone behind Jena. "We'll have her covered up soon enough."

They rolled a stretcher with a light blanket to her.

"I'm not hurt! I don't need..." She struggled and squealed as the two guards lifted her and laid her on the hard, thin mattress.

With quick efficiency, they strapped her in and pulled the blanket to cover her up to her chin.

"Hey, what do you think you're doing?" She couldn't move. Her fists clenched as her forehead beaded in sweat. "Let me go!"

Claude came over with a hypodermic needle. "This will relax you. It'll only sting for a moment."

With a gentle push, the needle pierced the side of her neck. A rush of something hot spread from the injection point. "Why are you doing this to me?" Her eyelids were heavy, and her vision blurred. She squinted, trying to focus on Claude.

"I assure you, my only intention is to keep you safe."

She didn't feel the pat to her shoulder, just watched the blurred image of his hand moving. Every part of her body numbed. Heavy lids were impossible to keep open, so she embraced the darkness.

~Pete~

Pete's easygoing nature was long gone. The last sight he had of Jena was her pale, trembling features. Those assholes restraining her wasn't something he'd easily forget. His roaring snarl was choked because those fuckers had put something over his mouth. Of course, if his mouth and hands were available, his snarling would be the least of everyone's worries.

The two guards holding him kept a tight grip. All he had to do was stiffen his muscles and he wouldn't suffer any bruises. Now that he dealt with the stinging pain, he looked around.

Fuck! He had to be on that moon base his brother Zamush told them about the other day. The one Ben and Julienne found themselves stuck on. The ceiling, walls, and floor were a sturdy, iridescent metal that might be a mixture of titanium and diamond. No windows, so he couldn't see outside to verify his suspicions.

Pete walked with his new best friends down a narrow corridor with minimal lighting. He squinted in the low light. Hadn't his mother told him the Akurns weren't used to bright light?

The guards stopped in the middle of the hallway as their leader, Bahadur, turned to him.

The sneer on the man's pale face made Pete smile. He just loved it when he irritated the shit out of the bad guys.

"Disgusting piece of *yetu*." The man spat at him in the Akurn language. "Release the *kartr* from him."

The thing covering Pete's mouth dissolved, as did the bindings on his wrists.

Once the restraints evaporated, Pete wiped his sweaty lips with the back of his hand. His smile widened. No way would he let this idiot know he understood everything he said. Well, except for whatever the hell a yetu was.

"Put him in there." Part of the wall dissolved, revealed a small, one-room holding cell.

They shoved Pete in.

He stumbled but righted himself before he landed in an undignified face-plant. He turned with arms crossed and spoke in English. "Okay, asslips. Now what?"

"Now you wait until the commander decides what to do with you," the brawny Bahadur replied in halting English before barking a command in Akurn to enclose the wall.

The last thing Pete saw before the door snapped in place was the alien guard sneering down his nose and glaring. Well, at least he didn't get injured this time. He rubbed his chest and looked around. He wasn't really taking in his surroundings; his thoughts were of Jena. No telling what agency that guy Claude worked for.

A new glance at the claustrophobic space wasn't helpful. A creature who craved the outdoors, he hated being stuck in a room the size of an average cell. He rubbed over the pain in his chest.

The walls, floor and ceiling had the same iridescent sheen as the corridor. A narrow bunk was on his right, while a toilet and sink were on the left.

Oh nice. The Akurns were kind enough to include a flat pillow on a hard-looking mattress. Give his captors five stars for their shining example of hospitality etiquette. He flopped onto the cot and cradled his head in his open palms. With an unseeing stare, he watched the bland ceiling.

Not for the first time did Pete lament how limited his telepathic abilities were. But he had one thing his brothers didn't. All he had to do was touch someone, and he'd get enough of their psychological imprint to mimic them. Then, at the earliest opportunity, he could walk around free as a bird. He had sufficient computer skills that, if he found one not in use, he'd be able to locate the nearest Transkip mirror and head home.

He couldn't do anything about his growling stomach, though. So he might as well get some sleep. Shutting his eyes in the dim light, he relived making love to his captivating Jena. He fell asleep wearing a small grin.

~Special Agent Claude Reese~

The helicopter ride back to Langley, Virginia was uneventful and smooth.

Claude took the time to set up a hospital bed for Jena and arrange to have some scientists study her. While he was sincere about keeping her safe from the aliens, he had to find out why they wanted her. Physical tests would be the first part of unraveling her mystery. After that, interrogation would be in order.

"Director Obsidian, we have the female you requested in custody." Claude spoke into his encrypted satellite phone.

The metallic, synthesized voice of the director replied, "Excellent, Special Agent Stygian. Has she been harmed in any way? Does she need medical attention?"

Claude glanced at the comatose woman. Absently, he noticed how young she appeared with her face relaxed in slumber. "The detainee is unharmed. To keep her calm, we've injected her with a sleep agent. I assure you, she's resting peacefully and will remain unconscious until we're ready for her to wake up."

"I don't have to stress that you're not to harm her in any way, do I, Special Agent Stygian?" The metallic voice came through hard as steel. "A preliminary assessment is acceptable, but under no circumstances is she to endure any physical or psychological harm."

Claude's jaw clenched. "In order for us to determine why the aliens want her, we may have to..." He cleared his throat.

"We might require a more invasive method of gathering information."

"If you cannot discern what you need by preliminary inspections, you are to report those findings to me immediately. You will not deviate from my orders without my express approval." The director cut off the communication.

Dammit. Claude hated this bureaucratic bullshit. He'd been in the Bureau long enough that he should be able to do the job as he saw fit. He put the satellite phone back into his jacket pocket.

Agent Raven sat across from him with her arms folded and a blank stare. She must've perfected that look while she worked for the NYPD. It was a flawless, nonthreatening expression that hid any emotion.

Didn't matter. He really didn't give a shit what her opinion was. She just needed to do her duty. "Once we land, you're to oversee her security until I set up the personnel to do the preliminary examination."

She gave a brief nod, her face blank. "Yes, sir."

Satisfied she'd do an exemplary job of putting Jena in a secure location, he pulled out his phone. Now he could concentrate on finding the personnel to carry out what he wanted done. He scrolled through several of his contacts before he came across one that made him smile.

Ah, perfect. This individual would go outside the director's mandate if he requested it. While causing physical harm to Jena wasn't something he looked forward to, he'd never hesitate if that's what had to be done to protect his country.

Chapter Nine

~Sub-Prince Murduk~

Sub-Prince Murduk rubbed his forehead and studied the current economic reports. Things were far more dire than he'd suspected. The shield around the planet was deteriorating at a faster pace than anticipated. The life-sustaining food crops were half of what they had harvested in years past. In another six months, food would become a scare commodity.

And that would be the least of their worries. If they somehow missed taking what they needed from Earth to upgrade their planetary navigational system, they'd end up being pulled into the sun. Akurn would explode in a fiery end long before all would starve to death.

Swiping the report away from the floating computer monitor, Murduk called up the latest news feed from his security force. A new illegal criminal fraction, with the ridiculous moniker of the Warriors of the Abandoned, WOTA, targeted royal households. Most notable of these were the families who'd proven their powerful alliance to him repeatedly.

In the silent darkness, late at night, the criminals would skulk into noble households and eliminate the patriarch as he slept in his own bed. Any coveted females or children were kidnapped, the male servants spared and left alive to tell the tale. Valuables were looted while the property remained intact and not defaced.

Escalating outcries for justice sounded loudly from the remaining nobility. The majority demanded Murduk find and crush the criminals without delay. Publicly, the underlying warning was clear. If he didn't produce the leader of the WOTA—Sychar—for a public execution within the coming month, the nobles would claim the right of Nabalkuta, the official process in which warlords could overturn the present monarchy by a combat to the death.

He quashed the cowardly urge to flee. He was no coward. He'd never let a handful of entitled pricks dictate what he did or didn't do. He snorted. When the first noble threatened him, Murduk made sure the man had an unfortunate accident. While the man's death would never be traced to him, he wasn't foolish enough to take a chance doing the same to the other treasonous morons.

Studying a list of those houses making the loudest demands, he jerked when interrupted by Uruk as the man scrambled into the room. Uruk's usual sour expression was missing. He skidded and halted with a small bow. His trim body quivered as if experiencing an unknown emotion.

Intrigued, Murduk didn't wait for the man to talk. "Report!" He leaned back with steepled fingers.

"Sire, good news!" The guard cracked his knuckles.

Murduk's eyebrows rose. Uruk was acting more like their pudgy friend, Nungal, rather than himself. He couldn't remember the last time he'd seen the man this agitated about anything.

"We believe we have one of the princess's sons in custody on FarDeep base." Uruk smacked his lips. "I have Commander Kud awaiting your attention."

Adrenaline rushed through Murduk's system. His hands fisted. He cleared his throat and sat straight. "Put him through."

The headshot of the FarDeep base commander replaced the list on his floating monitor. A self-satisfied smirk creased Kud's angular face.

The older man gave a slight bow, exposing the disturbing image of Kud's shorn head. Under normal circumstances, Murduk would've insisted the man wear his hair like any other decent Akurn. However, being billions of miles away, he felt it prudent not to stress the situation.

"Highness." Kud straightened. "We believe we've captured one of the princess's abominations." He stroked his pointed chin as he leveled a clear-eyed gaze at Murduk. "Unfortunately, without the scientist Thoth, we can only guess."

"Display," Murduk demanded and leaned forward. The floating monitor split into two, leaving the headshot of the commander in one while the other showed a dark-haired creature in a containment unit.

Murduk squinted. "Visualization increase twenty-five percent." The image widened until he had an unobstructed view of the alien. A sudden lightness created an unusually wide smile that creased his face. He might be mistaken, but he was positive he'd seen that creature with Inanna lurking in the background as he spoke to her. Even if the animal wasn't one of her sons, him being in the room with her meant he had to be someone she valued.

"What have you done with him to this point?"

Commander Kud shook his head. "We would never presume to do anything without your express direction, Highness."

Murduk sat back and rested his bearded chin on a forefinger. "Very good, Commander. You have my permission to experiment as you see fit." He pointed a finger at Kud's image. "However, you are not to terminate the subject even if he turns out not to be one of her sons. If you deem that is necessary, you are to contact me first immediately." He pounded a fist on the armrest. "You are to handle him with the utmost caution with stringent controls enforced."

Kud's chin jutted as he gave a stiff nod. "All will be as you command, Highness. We have several worthy scientists who worked with Thoth regularly. I assure you, uncovering the creature's origins will not be an issue."

Murduk waved a dismissive hand. "I would expect no less." He leaned forward and glared. "Remember what I've told you. You are not to end him without my express permission. Understood?"

Kud's rigid expression slid into a soft smile.

The uncharacteristic appearance gave Murduk an internal shiver. How he'd love to watch what Kud had planned for the unwary abomination.

"I assure you, Highness, that animal will yearn for death long before you mercifully grant it to him."

~Pete~

Cool forest air brought a refreshing scent on the soft breeze. Pete leaned his head back and flung out his arms to bathe in the warm glow of the summer sun. His toes curled on the forest floor as the downed pine needles crackled under his skin. With a groan of elation, he stretched before opening his eyes to enjoy the pristine scenery.

"You okay, Pete?"

A soft feminine voice sent a searing bolt of awareness straight to his groin. He spun around and faced Jena, grabbing her into his arms.

"Jena!" Gripping her tight, he nuzzled the side of her head and inhaled her intoxicating feminine scent. "Thank the Goddess of Love you're okay." He nestled closer, caressing her soft, naked skin flush against his.

Jena stepped back. Her dilated cognac-brown eyes searched him, and her face flushed. She closed her eyes, and with a tight grip at the back of his neck, she pulled him to her. She captured his lips with her eager ones.

His mind shut down. The music of her rich, feminine groan embedded deep inside of him. He grabbed the globes of her firm ass and pulled their groins together. The friction caused his dick to swell harder. As the kiss intensified, something nagged and vied for attention. The back of his neck tightened as the annoying sensation spread down his spine and up to the back of his head.

This wasn't right, this wasn't real. It couldn't be.

He framed her face and gently pulled away.

Her closed eyes blinked open and remained at half-mast, focused on his lips. She licked hers.

His racing heart drowned all sounds.

"What's wrong?" she whispered.

Pete couldn't resist. He hugged her and nuzzled the sweet spot between her neck and shoulder over her birthmark before pulling away. "We're not really here, you know." With a firm grip, he pushed away and stepped back. "I think were in some kind of shared dreamworld." He scanned the surrounding area.

Her smile was mischievous. "That another one of your weird alien things?"

With a disgruntled sigh, he let her go. Running his fingers through his hair, he gave a sheepish grin. "Probably. But I've gotta admit, it hasn't been something I could do. I've never entered the dreamworld before. At least I think we're sharing a dream." He snapped his fingers. "Quick, tell me something I'd never know about you. That way I'll know you're really here and I'm not just imagining you."

Her eyebrows rose. "Like what?"

"Like something you'd tell no one else." He stepped closer and took in a deep breath. "No lying now. I can smell it if you did."

She giggled.

How far gone was he that her giggle made his cock twitch?

She gathered her long chestnut hair and pulled it over her shoulder to pet.

The cutest little smile creased her lips. His breathing quickened as he imagined her stroking him instead.

"Well, okay. But you've got to promise not to laugh."

Pete cleared his throat. "I would never."

She let go of her hair, letting it float to her waist. A flush crossed her cheeks. "Well, um, I've secretly wanted to explore uncharted wilderness and discover unknown species professionally." Her eyes bored into his, daring him to make fun of her.

He pressed his lips together to keep them from widening into a smile. Not that what she said amused him, quite the contrary. Her confession made him lightheaded. He loved the outdoors and spent most of his life exploring the planet's wilderness in all his various forms. More than once he'd lamented that he couldn't traipse through uncharted wilderness safely anymore.

"Your turn."

Her demand made his smile run free. "Fair enough." His head tilted. "I've always wanted to pursue the art of abstract painting."

Jena whooped. "That's great! I never, in my wildest dreams, would imagine you'd like to do something creative like that."

She flung her arms up before she crossed them, partially blocking the view of her mouthwatering breasts.

"Does this mean were really in a dream and not lost in the forest somewhere?" She glanced around before her attention swung back to him. "Everything seems real to me."

"Yeah, to me too. But listen—" He stepped closer and looked her straight in the eyes. "—I'm not sure how much time we have here, so we'd better make the most of it. What's the last thing you remember?"

Her delectable little nose wrinkled.

"That jerk Claude put me on a gurney and strapped me in. He gave me some kind of narcotic that made me pass out." Her gaze slid away from him. "I must still be asleep because I have no idea where I am." She gripped his forearms. "What about you? You disappeared with those creepy aliens through some kind of black hole."

"Yeah, assholes took me to their moon base."

Her gasp was loud. "They have a base on the moon? Our moon? How...?"

The sensation of wrongness around his neck squeezed down his back. "Listen. We have little time." Grasping her soft hands in his, he stared at her beloved face. It was important for her to pay attention to what he said next. "I will come for you, no matter what. But if you can, call my brother Raiden at this number." Pete rattled off the digits. "You got that? Tell him who you are and that you're with me." Damn, he had so much to tell her, but now wasn't the time.

"Listen, there's one more thing." God, he hoped she believed what he said next. "You remember turning into a wolf?"

At her brief nod, he continued in a rush of words. "You can also turn into anyone you touch." Once she had more experience with shifting, she wouldn't need to rely so much on touching someone to change into them. It was just easier to do it that way.

No time to waste on her blank look and slack expression. "Anyone you come in contact with you can mimic, morph into them. It's not just a wolf you turn into. You remember how I turned into that Goraxag? You can do the same thing." He ignored her shaking head. "If you get a chance to touch their skin, all you gotta do is visualize them in your mind and your body will do the rest."

He hoped.

The squeezing sensation now engulfed the rest of him. Time was up. Gathering her in his arms, he held her close and breathed in her enthralling scent. "Stay strong. I'll come for you. I don't know how or when, but know this, you are my only concern." Before she dissolved, he whispered in her ear. "You're all I think about. I believe I'm in I love with you."

Damn. Wasn't he just the master of bad timing?

Pete startled awake from a sharp pain piercing his chest. He massaged a clenched fist over the ache in his heart. With a low moan, he rolled to a sitting position and wiped the sleep from his eyes. He took a blurry look around. Nothing to see, except for the toilet across from him. With a grunt, he got up and used the facility before flopping back onto the narrow cot.

With a yawn, he stretched his arms over his head until vertebrae popped between his shoulders. With nothing else to do, he might as well try to contact Raiden telepathically. He leaned back and closed his eyes. Resting the back of his head on his palms, he visualized his elder brother. With tentative mental fingers, he searched their well-worn mental path.

Nothing. Except a searing headache for his efforts.

He rubbed his eyes when a slight breeze on his naked skin made him jerk. He sat up as the side wall disappeared.

Four Akurn guards rushed in; two grabbed him a painful grip.

"Damn, chill out, fellas." He spoke in English, not letting on he was fluent in the alien language he grew up with. Since the guards held him with gloved hands, he wasn't able to get an imprint to mimic one of them later.

"Bring the abomination this way. Scientist Naram-Sin has everything ready." The guard who spoke led the way.

The fourth guard followed them.

The passageway was void of any other personnel. The corridor was round, shaped like the inside of a submarine and covered in the metallic iridescent material. Maybe they were underground like a bunch of moles. Nice, the floor was warm instead of icy.

He wiggled his toes in appreciation. Now would be the time to observe his surroundings before he shifted. That way he'd get the lay of the land, so to speak. Once he escaped these jerks, he'd hide or locate a Transkip mirror. If baby bro Ben could do it, so could he.

They didn't travel very far, just to the end of the corridor. With a tug on his arms, they turned right into an open doorway.

What he saw made him skid to a halt. He jerked, but they didn't budge. Oh, no fucking way. The only thing in the room was a cold metal table. He knew what that table was for. Alien autopsy was not a party he planned on attending.

They yanked Pete into the room and dragged him straight to the gleaming, sadistic slab. Without another word, the guards shoved him on the table. The cold metal burned his ass and shoulders as wide straps flipped over his forehead, shoulders, waist, thighs, and ankles and imprisoned him.

"Son of a bitch, let me go!" He snarled and twisted to no avail. The sound of his heartbeat thrashed in his ears. Beads of sweat dotted his forehead as he clenched his hands. Shit, he couldn't shift into anything tied up. It'd be great to turn into something like a Goraxag right about now. But with him trussed up like a freakin' steer at a rodeo, he'd end up with less than perfect results. The only thing to do was bide his time. That way, he'd morph into one of those idiots and then hightail it out of this sadistic clown show.

A white blur caught his attention. Moving his head wasn't an option, so he had to wait until it slid into his line of sight. The wait wasn't long. One of the whitest men he'd ever seen came into view. Nothing close to Caucasian white, but a pure alabaster, blazing, you're-blinding-me kind of white. Pete squinted.

"Ah, let's see if you're what they hope you are." The alien's Oxford English accent was flawless. Damn, even in real life the Brits couldn't get a break from villains using their accent.

The Akurn's deep-turquoise eyes would have been arresting on someone who didn't have the unblinking sadistic gaze of a fanatic. High cheekbones sharp enough to cut glass were the prominent features of his homely face. A mismatched full lower lip pouted under a thin upper one. A thick, almost translucent unibrow bisected his pockmarked forehead.

The man tucked an errant strand of platinum hair behind an overlarge ear. A one-piece silver suit straight out of the campy old Buck Rogers series from the seventies covered his lanky frame. Tacky would be the nicest thing to say about the guy's clothes.

"Whoever you're looking for, that ain't me. So why don't we just skip this whole alien probing thing and call it a day, eh?" Pete gave him his best fake smile.

The alien did an unexpectedly human thing and waved a forefinger with a tsk sound. "Now, now. No need to worry yourself, my boy. Oh, we're going to have so much fun!" Deep crinkles fanned his eyes while his crooked mouth slid into a smile that was creepy as hell.

With that announcement, the guy wiggled a thin cylinder with a sharp needle winking in the bright light. Neon green goo oozed from the end. "Let's get you relaxed, hmm?" The alien shoved the needle into the side of Pete's neck.

Pete squeezed his eyes shut and hissed at the pain. Mother fucker! The injection burned as it seared through his system. "Assss.... hoooll..." he slurred. Fuzz thickened in his brain as everything muted.

He wasn't lucky enough to lose consciousness. It didn't take long to wish he had. There wasn't a place on his body left untouched, inside or out. When the Akurn sliced him open to take tissue samples from his various organs, he wanted to howl in agony. Only his mouth and vocal cords refused to cooperate.

To make matters worse, the bastard didn't give him the satisfaction of touching his bare skin. Fucker wore gloves the whole time. Pete swore centuries passed before the blurred shape of the alien stepped back.

"I must say..."

The melodic tones of the unrealistic British accent made Pete shiver.

"I've never had the pleasure of examining such a perfect human before." The alien gave a deep, heartfelt sigh. "I'm just disappointed you're not one of the princess's offspring. How delicious would that have been?"

Good thing Pete couldn't smirk. The stupid son of a bitch didn't need to know Pete controlled his DNA and "turned" himself into a true human. He closed his eyes. Hopefully this little dickhead was done. He was tired, and if he lost control, he'd revert to his true self—a wonderful cocktail of Akurn and Adamou.

"Take this thing back to its cell."

The alabaster scientist left Pete's blurry line of sight as he spoke in the Akurn language.

"I'll inform Commander Kud of my findings. It will be up to him to decide what to do with it."

"Yes, Honorable Naram-Sin." One of the guards waved a hand by Pete's head, making the straps disappear.

Two pairs of rough, calloused grips grabbed him under the arms and yanked him off the table. The tips of his feet dragged as they pulled him out of the sterile examination room. Once they reached his cell, they dumped him on the floor. The wall closed, leaving him blissfully alone.

Laid spread-eagle on the floor, Pete groaned as excruciating pain radiated from every part of his body. It took some doing, but he let go of the hold he had on his DNA. Thank the Goddess of Love his natural healing abilities began repairing the damage.

Pete jerked awake, gulping a deep breath. Where the fuck was he? Was someone playing a practical joke on him? Damn it, the last time he was left naked was after a particularly rambunctious night he had with the daughter of a prominent chieftain in a Mongolian village. Who knew the father was serious when he told Pete to leave his daughter alone? Besides, she was the one who sneaked into his tent late at night where she schooled him on the various means of erotic pleasure.

But that was a couple thousand years ago, and he damn well hadn't done anything to get tortured and humiliated this time. He snorted and sat up with splayed legs and hung his head. Shit, his ass was freezing. The burning cold of the metallic floor made his teeth chatter.

Fucking aliens just had to throw his happy ass on the ground. Vision fuzzy, he spied a spigot next to the toilet. With any luck, there'd be water. With a grunt, he rolled off the icy floor went to put his hands under it. A trickle of brackish water came out. At least it was enough to splash his face and take a couple of swallows. While the metallic taste was nasty as hell, he doubted the Akurns would poison him this way.

The cot was his next destination. He flopped onto his back on the less-than-soft surface. One leg dangled off the side while the other rested with a bent knee. With an arm over his eyes, he took an internal inventory to see if he had any injuries not healed. While nothing overt screamed for his attention, something wasn't right.

Pete made his mind go blank and took a couple of deep breaths. He slid his arm off his eyes and looked at the iridescent ceiling. Okay, phase one complete. He'd fooled the Akurns into thinking he wasn't who they were looking for. Which meant one of two things. Either they'd kill him outright, or they'd have a jolly good time doing some more bizarre experiments on him. Neither option worked for him.

One good thing about the guards dragging him, the halfwits had touched his bare skin. So now he was the proud owner of the genetic material he needed to morph into one of those assholes. All he had to do...

The wall disappeared. The same two guards came in. Dumbasses didn't even have their weapons drawn. They must have thought him too weak to worry about. Especially after his wonderful experience with that fugly alien scientist.

No reason to hide his gigantic smile. "A-yo, how's it hangin' guys? I'm so glad you could join me. And here I was wondering what to do to pass the time." He sat up and polished the nails of one hand on his naked chest and admired the results. "I've gotta tell ya, boredom ain't my thing."

He never gave them a chance to respond. He laughed at their wide-eyed expressions as he leaped from the cot to grab their weapons. Yeah, nice of them to be careless enough to leave them loose in their holsters. With little effort, the jerks were soon down and out. It only took some well place kicks, jabs, and satisfying face-plants with his hardened knuckles. Being a master in several martial arts disciplines came in handy on more than one occasion.

Pete eyed the unconscious guards, trying to guess which one was closest to his size. After a quick decision, he stripped the guy of his uniform and put it on. The bland pantaloons were a tad long, but it billowed out like a puffy balloon and gathered at his ankles. An equally boring cream-colored cotton tunic draped over the pants, and a sleeveless red vest completed the outfit. The thick animal-hide boots were the last thing to put on. Once the material covered his foot, the boot adjusted to his size. Perfect fit.

Hey, when this was all over, he'd take one of these boots apart and figure out how they worked. Then sell the rights to a famous footwear company to add to the family's considerable wealth.

He picked up one of the laser spears from the floor and slipped it into the strap of a crisscrossed holster on his back. He put a silver cylinder into its holder around his hips. Given his long history as a weapons expert, he took time to examine the remaining weapons. With careful deliberation, he dismantled them without making it look like they were harmless and put them on the unconscious clothed guard. At least he hoped that's what he did.

Well, lookie here. It was that oval thing they'd put over his mouth. And Lady Luck hadn't left him just yet because next to the gag was a pair of hand restraints. With a sly smirk and chuckle, he placed both on the helpless guard he'd liberated his outer clothes from. The gag thinned and blended over the man's mouth. Pete jerked the guy's limp hands behind his back and restrained them with a satisfying click.

Yeah, how do you like that, Mutha Fucker?

He knelt next to the clothed guard and put two fingers on the man's pale temple and pushed a suggestion that the naked guy next to him was Pete. He also scrambled the memories of their fight. Not being a powerful telepath or one with empathic senses, Pete's suggestions wouldn't last very long. Hopefully, long enough for him to make a quick escape.

Okay, everything was ready. He morphed into the exact image of the near-naked guard. Not for the first time was he grateful his internal senses remained sharp no matter what form he took.

He shook the clothed man to wake him up. The alien winced and blinked before his eyes stayed open.

"Excellent execution, my friend." Pete patted the other's shoulder as he spoke in flawless Akurn. For the first time in a long time, he was grateful to speak the language his parents raised him with. "I can't believe how quickly you subdued that abomination." He nodded at the still-unconscious guy with the gag over his mouth.

The guard followed his gaze as his eyes narrowed at the bound, so-called prisoner. "What am I doing on the floor?" The bigger man scrambled to his feet.

"After you punched him, you accidentally fell over his feet." Pete leaned forward to show his concern. "You hit your head pretty hard. You feeling okay?"

The guy snorted as if he didn't believe Pete. "I'm fine. Let's finish this. Grab him under that arm and I'll take this one."

Together, they lifted the unconscious man, whose dead weight was heavier than he looked. Following the other guard's lead, Pete held tight on his end. "Where are we taking him again?"

"Commander Kud wants him terminated, but that crazy scientist Naram-Sim wanted to play with him some more." The guard's pale-turquoise eyes slid to look at Pete with a leer. "I promise you, Mattaki, I'll share the credits he'll give us to keep quiet about it. Trust me."

Pete bit the inside of his cheek to stop from making a comment. He doubted this guy meant what he said. Trust wasn't something he'd give him. "Of course I trust you. Where does Naram-Sin want him?"

"You know damn well he wants us to take him to that un-used portion of the base where he has his private laboratory set up." The bigger man stopped and narrowed his eyes. He lifted his side of the prone man and shook him. "Did this guy hit you too? That why you're acting so strange?"

Pete shrugged with a sheepish grin. "Yeah, that must be it." He rubbed a temple. "Sorry. I'm sure I'll be fine soon enough."

The pale Akurn pursed his fat lips. "Fine. Let's go."

Dragging the unconscious Akurn between them down the iridescent metallic hallway, the other guard stopped and waved a hand over a slight indentation in the surface over a lighted blue dot.

A portion of the wall disappeared, revealing a small rounded space just big enough for the three of them to enter. A series of dots appeared when the wall solidified, and the guard waved over the yellow one.

Pete had to brace his legs when the room jerked to the right in a continuous motion.

Ah, that's what he had to look for. A slight indentation with an unblinking blue dot to open a door to an elevator. He examined the unblinking colored dots as the elevator yanked downward. The dots were a veritable cornucopia of rainbow colors. Each one had to take them to a different section. Too bad he didn't know where they went. Except for the one in yellow, the button his cheery companion had touched.

"Do you think Naram-Sin will let us play with this first?" The taller guard shook his side of the prisoner. "I would love to taste me some alien flesh."

Pete raised his eyebrows. Well, wasn't this guy just a paragon of virtue? "I doubt it." He forced a regretful sigh. "Besides, I find its appearance disgusting." Over the centuries he had a lot of ways to describe himself, but disgusting was never one of them.

"Who cares what it looks like?" The guard leered at the prone prisoner between them as he massaged his crotch. "I'm not gonna look at its face while I fuck its ass hard."

The skin around Pete's mouth tightened as his throat burned. He hung his tightly clenched fist behind his back. Just two seconds. That's all the time he needed to knock that smirk off the asshole's mug. Instead, he kept his expression relaxed. "You can ask. But I doubt he'd let you mess up his experiment."

The elevator car stopped, and the wall disappeared.

"Probably right." The guy mumbled as he yanked the prisoner and stepped out. "But it won't hurt to ask."

The only answer Pete had was a grunt as he followed. Hauling the dead weight of the unconscious guard was secondary to examining his surroundings. The air here was thick and musty, like it hadn't been used for quite a while. The light was dim and made the iridescent metal appear dull.

Instead of a smooth corridor, intermittent openings in the walls revealed various enclosures. Most were empty, but some had broken machinery and various indescribable discarded items strewn about. All but one room had piles of bare bones. He stared as he passed an open doorway with a tibia bone lying across the threshold. A faded shoe still covered the foot.

Looking left and right as they walked, he could only conclude this must be where people mysteriously disappeared. Perfect, he was in the right place.

Up ahead, a white light blazed from an open doorway.

Ah, that must be their ultimate destination. Taking a deep breath, he gave himself a few precious nanoseconds to examine who was in the room as they entered.

Yeah, his luck held.

The only person in the room was that sadistic scientist Naram-Sin. His homely face flushed an ugly color as he pointed at the unconscious prisoner between Pete and the other guard. "Tizqar, what is the meaning of this?" He stomped toward them with his thin arms flying. "Why is Mattaki striped of his uniform and tied up?" He narrowed his light-turquoise eyes as he stared in Pete's direction. "And why is this abomination in his clothes?"

"Oh, that's a mean thing to say! I thought I looked good in his clothes." Pete smirked and burst into action. He jerked the unconscious guard out of Tizqar's grip and flung the heavy body at him. That would keep the other guy busy. He rushed to the scientist.

"Stop! I'll use this on you." Naram-Sin had one palm out while his other hand brandished a slim black cylinder with a protruding needle.

No telling what was in it this time.

Pete didn't hesitate. "No, thanks." Behind him, the other guard grunted as a thump sounded. He must've pushed his buddy's body off him. With a leap, Pete got behind the scientist, wrapped an arm around the man's neck and tilted his head. Using his free hand, he grabbed the cylinder and punched it on the scientist's exposed flushed neck. A quick press on the protruding button at the end injected whatever was in it.

Naram-Sim squealed like a scared piglet.

Pete shoved the scientist away from him.

The man turned around and trembled. He opened his mouth before his eyes rolled to expose the white sclera. With an undignified flop, he crashed hard to the floor.

A brawny arm grabbed Pete around the neck. A flash of silver caught his eye. Freakin' idiot didn't know who he was dealing with. He bashed his head backward, and the satisfying sound of a broken nose echoed in the small room. The arm holding him let go. Pete twirled and knocked the guy out with a few quick punches.

Huffing, he scrutinized his surroundings.

The first unconscious guard was still out for the count. Yay for that. The muthafucking sadistic scientist wasn't moving. Well, at least he wasn't awake. He was twitching and moaning as if in the throes of some bad dream. And his little bud Tizqar was going to be in a world of hurt when he woke up.

Yeah, Pete old boy, you've still got it. He let loose a whoop and smashed all the weapons except one. Grabbing the blaster, he looked for a high setting. Flicking what he hoped was the right toggle, he took another look around. Satisfied with the damage he'd done, he left through the open doorway. After he made a happy push on the tiny orange light in the wall indentation, the door shut with a creaking whoosh.

A quick adjustment for maximum power, and he shot the control where the orange dot was. As sparks and smoke flew, he tucked his head in the crook of his arm. The acidic scent of burnt metal stung his nose. When the flashing died down, he dropped his arm.

The entire side of the wall had melted, along with the door.

Pete grinned. Yeah, those guys weren't getting out soon. Just like the gunslinger he used to be in the old west, he expertly twirled the weapon at the trigger guard before flopping it back into the holster at his hip.

He spun around to find the elevator. A sharp pain twisted his abdomen. Grabbing his lower gut, he gasped and put a hand against the wall to steady himself. Another searing pain squeezed until it was hard to breathe.

When it faded, he stood and wiped the sweat from his brow. What in the hell was that? Not wasting time, he found the blue dot of the elevator shaft. He waved the door open and stepped inside. He quickly studied the columns that held the various dark colors. Maybe this thing worked like an elevator back on Earth and the lower button would take him to the last floor.

He waved over the last one in gray. Another jolt of agony hit. It was getting worse. The pain now escalated to his stomach and started up his throat. He paid no attention to the movement of the elevator until the door dissolved open.

Blindly, he stumbled out. The door dissipating behind him barely registered. He doubled over. Another shot of agony put him on his knees. A cloud of silty dust rose, making him choke. Coughing, he placed a palm to his mouth and drew it away, covered in blood. What in the fuck did that scientist inject him with earlier?

That was his last clear thought. The pain of hitting the ground made him pass out.

Chapter Ten

~Jena~

Jena jolted awake. The echoes of Pete's last words made her head rush. Had that been a dream, or was it somehow real? She swung into a sitting position and covered her eyes as she struggled to calm her racing mind. It had to be real. She swore she'd been with Pete. Taking deep breaths, she concentrated on calming her racing heart. The faint scent of his signature aroma lingered. She licked her lips, searching for a taste.

His flavor faded. She dropped her hands and glanced around. At first, the bland scenery confused her. Then it all became too horrifyingly clear. The taupe walls, vaulted ceiling, and thickly padded floor. She sat on a twin mattress covered by a thin, white sheet. The only other item in the place was a small toilet in the corner.

A bubbled black object stared from the ceiling's corner. A camera. Great, she was in a padded room under constant surveillance. Well, at least she wasn't wearing a strait jacket.

Ignoring the camera, she rubbed her temple. What was the last thing she remembered besides that vivid dream? Oh yeah, that asshole Claude had her put on a stretcher and injected her with something. Before she passed out, he spouted an asinine fairytale that he was trying to protect her. What a crock. He wanted something from her. The only question was, what could that be?

A sharp click and the steel door to her prison swung open. Looked like the bad guys were here to tell her what that something was. She raised her brows when the two people who walked in the door were anything but psychiatric orderlies.

Both wore black suits and ties with a white shirt. The one on the left was a man in his thirties, straight out of the military. His Latino features were hard, his dark brown eyes narrow and focused on her.

The second person was the same woman who had offered her a coat. The African-American was around the same age as her companion, with an equally alert expression. Her dark-eyed glance darted around the room as if she expected somebody to show up and attack. She crouched as her hand covered a bulge on her hip. No doubt that was where she kept her gun.

"I am Agent Coal, and this is Agent Raven." The Latino stepped aside and waved a hand to the open doorway.

As he moved his arm, Jena glimpsed his holstered weapon.

"You have to come with us."

She bit her lip. Her first inclination was to say something snarky, but that probably wouldn't be the smartest thing to do. She stood and for the first time noticed she wore light-blue hospital scrubs. Warm booties covered her feet. At least she wasn't walking around naked anymore. She crossed her arms and tapped a foot. "Agents of what? Where are you taking me?"

The man's dark features tightened. "That's for the Special Agent in charge to answer. Come on, he's waiting for you."

She pursed her lips. "Fine. Lead the way." With a forced, dignified huff, she dropped her arms and followed them into the brightly lit corridor.

The hallway wasn't long. They reached a set of elevators at the end.

He pushed the only call button and the doors slid silently open.

Tamping the urge to run, she stepped into the small elevator lined with imitation wood. Her companions crowded in with her.

Agent Raven entered last. She put her back to Jena as if she was expecting somebody to jump them before the doors closed.

The upward ride was short and sweet. When the car stopped, the doors slid open.

The woman stepped out, with Jena close behind. Now was her chance. The echo of Pete telling her she had to touch someone before she could turn into them gave her the courage to do it. Pretending to trip, she stumbled and fell.

Agent Raven turned and grabbed her by the arm.

Contact. Skin contact. A hot zap stung her arm. She was numb for a brief second where they touched. Damn, she hoped that didn't happen every time she touched someone new. But if what Pete told her was true, she could change into the woman whenever she wanted to. "Oh, so sorry about that. Hard to believe how clumsy I am. You know, getting kidnapped and all."

She skipped away and nearly collided with the solid man behind her. The heat from him warned her they were too close. She'd be lucky to morph into one person. No need to confuse herself by touching him as well.

"This way."

The two guards switched places. Agent Coal took the lead as Agent Raven took the rear, walking backward.

Why was the woman acting like she expected somebody to attack from behind? Jeez, they had to be on their home turf, right? What, like someone was going to pop out of thin air and rescue Jena? She swallowed a snort. Doubtful.

This corridor had the same boring, beige industrial vinyl that matched the paint on the solid concrete block walls. Steel door frames highlighted obvious offices.

She craned to look into the small windows of the doors but wasn't tall enough to see inside the closed-off rooms. What surprised her was no one was around. The place was empty of other people. Which, come to think of it, might not be a good thing. Shit, no witnesses.

The ramrod backside of the tromping man stopped in front of an open door. "In here." He pointed to the entrance.

Keeping her expression blank, Jena strode into the room and braced herself. Good thing, since it was Claude who was apparently the Agent in Charge. Her face heated, and she clenched her hands to stop from slapping him.

The attractive older man sat behind an oak desk and used two index fingers to peck on a keyboard attached to a laptop. When she entered the room, he looked up with a smile and stood.

The door clicked closed behind her.

"Ah, Jena. So good of you to join me."

Her left eyebrow rose. "What, like I had a choice?"

He gestured to a chair in front of the desk. "Come, sit. We have a lot to discuss."

She glanced over her shoulder. The two bodyguards were nowhere in sight, but she doubted they went far. With a jutted chin, she sat down. She folded her hands over her flat stomach and crossed her legs with a narrow-eyed glare. "Okay, you've got me. Now what?"

"Would you like some coffee?" He gestured to a one-pod coffee maker and a tree of little pods of various flavors.

Oh look, we're going to play nicey-nicey like civilized people. Kidnapping aside. But the mere suggestion of coffee made her mouth water. With an internal sigh, she nodded. "Yes, dark roast please."

Her lips tightened at his warm smile. The more she was around the man, the more she didn't like him. Right now, she'd bide her time and get as much information as possible.

After that, she'd figure a way to sneak out.

"Here you go."

Claude handed her a steaming mug of coffee. The mug was white with a recognizable blue logo, proudly displaying the profile of a bald eagle. The cup he carried back to his desk held a different colored logo—black with gold lettering and the words "Special Agent" across the bottom.

With fresh eyes Jena examined the room they were in, inhaling the heady aroma of the coffee before taking a sip. The neutral tan nylon carpet matched the darker color on the drywalls. Several diplomas, awards, and accolades adorned one wall while a sizable picture window graced another. The view had to be from a second or third story since the only thing to see were green, swaying treetops.

Claude's executive desk matched the towering credenza behind him. A slim, silver laptop sat on one side of his desk while a manila folder rested in the middle.

"So, what could the CIA possibly want with me?" She tapped her mug with the famous logo.

Claude settled into his overly large dark leather chair. He took a sip from his cup, then placed it on a CIA coaster. He reached for the folder and opened it. Taking out an 8 x 10 photograph, he slid it over to her. It was a matted picture of an elderly man dressed in some kind of ancient Middle Eastern costume. Except for dark swarthy skin, this man was so pale it was almost translucent. His alabaster hair was in tight waves that brushed his shoulders. A solid, two-inch wide white beard covered his chin and hung to the middle of his throat, leaving his jaws bare.

The baby-blue eyes might have been attractive except for that chilly fanatical gleam.

"Do you know this man?" Claude leaned forward with his fingers entwined.

She shook her head. "Never seen him before. Who is he?"

"How about this one?" He pulled out another picture and placed it over the first one.

She gasped at the hard set of a rigid jawline prominently displayed. While this person was younger than the man in the first picture, this one caused her to shiver, and not because she took any pleasure in the image.

Cold ice-blue eyes, set deeper than normal, made his Roman nose prominent. Thin lips creased in a cruel smile. His platinum ringlets flowed under a gold circlet.

While the man's overall appearance wasn't unattractive, the frozen expression would make her give him a wide berth. "No, thank God."

Another picture.

"How about her? Seen anyone like this?" He pushed it to her. "Ignore the color of her eyes, she's wearing contacts."

Wow, beautiful. woman. Jena raised her eyebrows. While the other two looked like the personification of a bad guy, this young woman was anything but. The picture was a professional head shot. Her silky hair framed an oval face; the strands hung in thick blonde, auburn, and platinum highlights. Even in the matted picture, her pale, unblemished skin was translucent and glistened with health. Her almond-shaped, emerald-green eyes were framed by deep-brown eyelashes. The image stared with an ideal blend of intelligence and humor.

Jena had to admit she'd never seen a more perfect-looking woman in her life. She pushed the picture back. "Nope. Don't know her either, eye-color aside." She crossed her arms and legs and sat back. "You going to spend the entire day showing me pictures? Why not tell me why I'm here so we can quit wasting each other's time?"

His derisive smile made her face heat.

"Just one more picture. Do you recognize her?"

At first it was hard to figure out what he showed her. It looked like a picture of her. Except, in the picture, she had a professional haircut and makeup on that she'd never worn in her life. She gasped and grabbed it for a closer look.

The structure of the face might the same, but as she stared, subtle differences became obvious. While she had a small mole on the corner of her upper lip, it was missing from this picture. Also, her own face was a little thinner and her cheekbones slightly higher.

The woman wore a professional business suit, something Jena wouldn't get caught dead in. She frowned at Claude. "Who is this? And why does she look like me?"

Claude sat back, gripped his wedding ring, and twirled. "You don't know? Are you sure?"

Her fingers twitched, crinkling the photograph. She hissed when she saw what she'd done and slapped it on the desktop. "Quit playing games. Tell me who she is." A slow burn crept up her throat. She bit her tongue to keep from making a smart-ass comment.

Silver eyebrows lifted over Claude's hazel eyes. "All right. Her name is Julienne King, and I believe she's your sister."

The air in room became heavy and thick. This must be the woman Pete told her about. Not that she'd admit anything like that to the ass in front of her. "I don't know what you're talking about. I don't have any sisters."

Claude shook his head. His professionally styled silver hair didn't move. "Oh, my dear, you are so wrong." He put the tips of his fingers under his chin and narrowed his eyes. "However, since you were unaware you even had a sister, I doubt you can help us find her. No matter."

He stood and faced the picture window with his hands clasped behind his back. "Our primary purpose for bringing you here was to protect you."

"Protect me?" She couldn't help the mulish expression. "You sure have a funny way of going around protecting me. And just what is it you're supposed to protect me from?"

Claude glanced over his shoulder. "Our aim is to secure you from those men I showed you. What I'm about to tell you is highly classified and cannot not leave this room." He turned to face her. "Before I go any further, you must give me your oath you won't repeat what we discuss. Agreed?"

She eyed him with a sharp nod. She wasn't stupid enough to disagree with him. Not for a minute did she think his only motive was to protect her. He wanted her for something else that had to be more important than identifying a person in a picture. Claude knew more about those people than he admitted.

"Let me ask you a quick question." Claude sat in his chair. "Do you believe we're alone in the universe?"

She loosened her folded hands. "I've never given it much thought. But I'd like to think I'm open-minded about the whole thing."

He mimicked her stance. Except he twirled that ring. "Good. That'll make this much easier." He gestured to the pictures fanned out on the desk. "These good folks are from a planet called Akurn, which is actually a part of our solar system. The planet has an elliptical orbit around the sun every 3,600 years. As a matter of fact, Akurn will arrive in transportation range of Earth within the next couple of months." He shot her a quick glance.

She relaxed her face, hoping it would encourage him to continue. When she said nothing, he did.

"I assure you, these aliens are not friendly. They plan to ravage our planet for various minerals and resources for themselves. As far as we can determine, they intend to put Earth in chaos before they arrive. Their goal is to get humans to fight amongst ourselves, creating a global war." He snorted. "As if that would prevent us from noticing them coming in and taking over."

"That's kinda far-fetched, isn't it?"

His smile wasn't comforting. "I'll let you decide that for yourself."

He lifted a remote control and turned on the TV behind her. The first video was about a small bank in Las Vegas that was under federal oversight for a huge, blatant money-laundering scheme. The president of that bank was missing, along with several key employees. Among the pictures of the missing managers was her sister, Julienne.

The segment stopped with the newscaster linking that bank failure to a cascade of financial institutions experiencing the same thing. The anchorwoman warned that if the feds didn't step in and halt the progression, the financial crises of 2008 were going to look like child's play.

The next video showed a burgeoning fuel shortage escalating. The elderly woman reading the news cautioned that the oil-producing countries had enough raw oil, but with the threat of the financial industries in America collapsing, they were holding back their reserves. They demanded an unprecedented amount of money, goods, and services up front.

Claude clicked off the TV.

Ice squeezed Jena's stomach. Living in a small rural community in Tahoe, she didn't pay attention to world events like she should have. Her brothers. She gasped and splayed her fingers over her throat. "My brothers. I've got to get out of here and find my brothers." She fought the sense of dizziness that threatened to overcome her.

Claude moved from his desk and sat in the chair next to her. He took her hand in his and patted it.

She almost missed what he said because of the numbing tingle that shot through her.

"My dear, I'm sorry to tell you this, but we can't locate your brothers."

Her heart dropped. Nick and Nate were camping with their friend Chris and his family somewhere around North shore of Tahoe. Cell reception there was spotty at best. She saw no reason to tell Claude that. She'd rather her brothers stayed out of all this craziness. Especially with the CIA involved. "You've been searching for my brothers? Why?"

He tightened his hold on her hand.

She pulled back, but he didn't release her.

"The Akurns are searching for you and your sisters. Because of that, they may use your brothers as leverage to coerce your compliance. What I want to know is why."

His hard hazel-eyed stare made her throat close. When he said nothing else, she gasped and successfully pulled her hand from him. "You think I know?" Heat crept up her neck. This guy was pissing her off. "Look, what you're telling me makes little sense. If those, um, aliens want me so bad, why did they let me go with you?"

The older man leaned back with a satisfied smirk. "Because the weapon I had with me convinced them they were better off taking that guy you were with instead of tangling with us." He shrugged. "I suspect they took him for pride's sake." His hands rested on his lap as he twirled the wedding ring.

"You told them you'd let them know if you found some guy named Thoth. So, why do you need me?"

"Because they're desperate to find this woman, and I want to know why!" He lifted the photograph of the young blonde woman from the desk and shook it. "And they believe they need you to locate her. While I have no idea why she's so important, their actions have convinced me we'd better find her before they do." He tossed the photo back onto the desk. "From the minuscule intelligence we've been able to gather, she's a catalyst that will help us save Earth. They won't continue with their plan to invade without her."

Jena tried to think if Pete had mentioned a woman the Akurns wanted. He said how the aliens were going to use her to lure Pete into a trap and somehow take his abilities away. Once they had him, they'd use the threat of killing him if his mother didn't surrender to them.

She glanced at the twenty-something woman in the photograph. That woman couldn't possibly be Pete's mother. The only explanation was Claude and Pete were talking about two different people.

Jena rubbed her temple. "I'm afraid I can't help you. I don't know those people, er, aliens, nor have I seen anyone like them." She let her hand flop on her lap. "Listen, I'd help you if I could, but I have a hard time understanding why they even want me." She narrowed a glare at him. "So, are we done here?

I've got to find my brothers and make sure there aren't any crazy aliens out to get them." She stood and spread her hands. "To show there are no hard feelings, I promise not to hold it against you that you forced your way into my house." She waved a hand. "Much less how you brought me here against my will."

Not an ounce of remorse crossed Claude's handsome features as he sat behind his desk. He didn't hide the fact he reached under the lip before he leaned back. "I'm afraid things aren't that simple, Jena. I want to know why the Akurns are determined to locate you and your sisters. And I'm convinced you know more than you're admitting." He made a shooing gesture.

She jerked when hard hands gripped under her arms. Gasping, she struggled. Damn, she didn't hear anyone come in. "Hey, let me go, you assholes!"

Claude flicked a gaze to the goons holding her. "Take her to the kitchen. Time to cook up some answers." His attention turned from her struggling to the computer screen on the end of the desk.

Without a word, the agents dragged her out.

The journey out of Claude's office wasn't as nice as the first time. Once they cleared the doorway, the African-American woman slapped some zip ties around Jena's wrists. Thank God the woman didn't put her hands behind her back. That would be all kinds of uncomfortable.

"You sure you got them on tight enough, Raven?" The Latino man gave Jena a savage tug and forced her to walk beside him.

"Why? You afraid she'll get away from you, Coal?" The woman replied with toneless inflection. She took up her position in the rear, walking backward with her gun drawn.

Maybe her two new friends didn't get along. That would be something she could work with. All she had to do was get them separated. After that, she'd somehow make her little lady friend unconscious, turn into her, and escape the CIA building undetected. Yeah, no problemo. Then the fun would begin. She'd rescue Pete, who was evidently a prisoner on some alien base on the moon. Huh, she'd get right on that. Too bad veterinary school hadn't prepared her for this weird crap.

A sharp pain shot up her arm where Coal held her in his punishing grip. Jena tugged.

He squeezed harder.

Damn, she was going to end up with a deep bruise that'd last for days. "Ow, you're hurting me."

"Don't worry about it, sweetheart. We're almost there." Without breaking stride, the man approached a metal door and banged it open with a splayed palm.

He dragged her down an internal steel staircase. The agent's clanking boots echoed.

The farther they traveled, the dimmer the lights were. After a couple of stories, they reached the bottom.

With his free hand, Coal pushed the bar across a metal door and hauled her through. They entered a large bay filled with unmarked black, white, and tan vans. Some had side and back windows, some didn't.

Just her luck, her companions took her to a windowless white van.

Agent Raven swung the back door open, revealing side benches minus a backrest. The rear of the van was an enclosed box, with no view of the driver's seat.

"In ya go." Coal halfway lifted her up and pushed her inside.

With both wrists bound, Jena was afraid she'd fall on her face. Instead, she stumbled and landed with an undignified thump on the hard bench. The door slammed, plunging her into darkness.

The vehicle dipped as the agents got in. The engine started and backed up before lurching into drive.

As the van moved and picked up speed, she whipped back and forth.

A couple of bumps and sharp turns before the vehicle resumed a steady pace.

Jena concentrated on her breathing, hoping it would help keep the shakes to a minimum. She clenched her fingers and closed her eyes. She'd rather dream of Pete and the last time they were together than worry about where she was being taken to. A tender, smooth sensation calmed her shuddering nerves as she recalled his smiling, dimpled face in glorious detail. The tan of his skin highlighting his muscled torso. The laugh lines fanning from his unique colored eyes, the larger oval of bright aquamarine with the starburst of yellow around the black pupil dilated when he gazed at her. Others might find the habitual smirk that creased his full lips insulting. But she loved how he put everything in a humorous vein.

Not to mention how when he smiled those killer dimples came out. Damn, they were all kinds of sexy, especially when he had a scruffy beard. Every time she saw those deep pits, all she wanted to do was lick and nibble her way around them until she zeroed in on his plump, tempting lips.

The heat of his mouth was a prelude to the fire in his body when they joined. The sensation of his ridged cock sliding inside her made her wet just thinking about it. His arms wound around her; one under the globes of her ass while he held her steady. The intense yearning caused an ache that took her breath away.

Enough. She'd better worry about escaping instead of indulging in her growing feelings for Pete. Even though he was fast becoming her everything. She racked her brain, trying to recall what Pete told her the last time she'd seen him. God, it all happened so fast. How was she supposed to remember it all?

Okay, Jena. Stop whining and concentrate on one thing at a time. Pete gave her a contact number to call his brother, some guy named Raymond? No, wait. That wasn't it. Raiden? Yeah, that sounded better. But where was she going to get a phone? She glanced around the dark van. Not here, that's for sure. A sliver of sunlight framed the back door, but that didn't give enough light to see anything else clearly. Not that she expected to see much.

And if she got hold of this Raiden, what was she supposed to tell him? That Pete somehow landed on the moon? She'd then have to confess he told her so in a dream. He said something about them being in some dreamworld. Jeez, how crazy was that? Who's to say she didn't hallucinate that conversation? Maybe it was all a bad dream. She really wasn't here in the back of a windowless van heading to a place called the "kitchen", which she was sure had nothing to do with food.

All at once the futility of her situation hit her. With a silent sob, her face dropped in her bound hands as she let the tears fall freely.

"Please do not despair so, Jena."

She squealed with a jerk. Holy shit! What was that?

There, in the darkness, was a strange, oddly handsome man who glowed, on one knee in front of her.

Her eyes widened. She'd seen no one quite like him before, except in the movies. Straight, silky white hair parted in the middle. Hard to tell how long it was since it flowed behind him. High cheekbones, full lips, and a sharp cleft in his chin deep enough to make superman proud. He tilted his head. His larger-than-normal oval irises were the same dual turquoise and gold color of Pete's eyes.

Covering his lean figure was a linen tunic and pants that could be beige or white. Hard to tell since the freaking guy glowed. One hand rested on the top of his knee while the other fisted on the floor.

"I am Raiden." He spoke in a softly accented voice.

"You're Pete's brother?" Damn, the guy looked nothing like her Pete. Not only in his appearance, but his stern, no-nonsense face was a polar opposite of her man. "How did you find me?" Please let him be real. Please let him be real. She was so screwed if she'd lost her mind and started dreaming about a hero witch from one of her favorite TV series.

A sardonic grin made a corner of his lips curl. "I was looking for my brother when I found you." His head cocked to the other side. "Do you know where he is?"

Ugh. It pained her to admit her craziness, even to a hallucination she just met. She swallowed hard. "He came to me in a dream and said he thought he was on an alien moon base."

One of Raiden's platinum eyebrows rose. "Indeed?" He held his chin as his eyes unfocused. "That would explain it."

He didn't elaborate.

Jena was about to ask him what he meant when his exotic gaze focused on her.

"While that may pose a bit of an inconvenience, I believe with your help we will retrieve him with little difficulty."

She snorted. "Hey, I'd love nothing better than to join you, but I'm afraid my dance card is a bit full at the moment. I have a date with some sadistic CIA tormentors in their kitchen where they plan to cook up all sorts of experiments on me."

Raiden's other pale eyebrow rose in unison with the other. "Is that so?" His eyes dilated as he examined her from head to foot. "It appears you have bonded with Pete. Therefore, it should be little trouble for you to access his considerable abilities and escape your current confinement."

Wow, he talked like an old college professor she once had. "Yeah, um, maybe. But it's a little hard with my hands tied." She lifted her wrists bound in the white zip tie.

"I do not see any complication." He stood.

Dang, she had to crick her neck to look up at him. He had to be taller than Pete.

"Just harden your skin and break free. Keep your body in that hardened state when the vehicle stops. That way you can incapacitate your captors and thus assume the visage of one them." Raiden put his hands behind his back. "I, of course, will stay with you to guide and offer you my assistance as you go through the process."

She giggled. Okay, without a doubt her sanity had gone bye-bye. Instead of being terrified like a normal person, she found herself light as a feather. Hope might not be her best friend, but *dayum*, she'd rather take her delusion's advice rather than wallowing in a pity party all by herself.

Chapter Eleven

~Jena~

The van jerked to a stop.

Thank God Raiden taught her how to harden her skin. And when it was hard enough, Jena yanked her wrists apart and the zip ties popped free. When Raiden asked her if she'd touched a guard, she admitted she had.

He gave several suggestions on how to visualize morphing into the woman.

While what he recommended helped, it was the image of Pete and the warm way he suggested she shift that enabled her to turn into Agent Raven.

When the van doors swung open, two pairs of eyebrows rose as mouths dropped.

No time to laugh at their comical expressions or think what to do next. With a high leap worthy of her college track team days, she flew out of the back of the van and smacked their heads together.

In unison, their eyes rolled before they fell unconscious on the ground.

Yeah, she may not know any self-defense moves, but years of keeping her rambunctious teenage brothers and their friends in line came in handy. Guess being hard as a rock was super helpful when knocking bad guys out as well.

She brushed her palms together with a nod of self-satisfaction and glanced around. It looked like she was in a secluded hanger big enough to hold the two private jets parked side-by-side. She tilted her head to listen, hoping no one else was around. Good, nothing moved. Her snoring friends had invited no one else to the party. Yay for small favors.

"Jena, exchange clothing with the female officer. When done, grab her cell phone and call me at this number." The ghostly image of Raiden disappeared.

Yeah, yeah, yeah, change into the woman's clothes. Thanks for the advice, Captain Obvious. Releasing a whoosh of tense breath, she made quick work of his suggestion. She didn't bother dressing Agent Raven with the scrubs, just left them on the floor beside her. The toned woman was decent enough, but no way was Jena going to wear that cute boy-short set, even though it was a stunning shade of red.

A nice thing about assuming the shape of someone else, she had no trouble fitting into their stolen clothes. After lacing up the rugged combat boots, Jena put the various weapons and communication devices on the holster wrapped around her hips. She checked the Glock before putting it away. Her adoptive dad took her target practicing throughout her childhood, making her comfortable with most guns. Not that she'd ever shot anyone or any animal.

Finding the woman's cell phone wasn't a problem, so Jena slid it into her back pocket. She grabbed the zip ties from a pouch and bound the unconscious folks' hands and feet. Nice, there was a tool chest against a wall. She trotted over to look for some duct tape. Eureka, right on top.

She bit off strips long enough to put over their mouths, securing their silence. With her fists on her hips, she briefly snorted at a job well done. Pulling out the phone, Jena dialed the number Raiden gave her.

"Jena?" His modulated voice made her relax. "Did you accomplish that which needed to be done?"

Jena smiled at the way Raiden talked. His careful, unhurried way of speaking must drive Pete crazy.

"Yeah, got the guards snoozing away and wrapped up like a Christmas present." She glanced around the empty airport hangar. "Now what?"

"Keep this line open while Michael runs a trace."

The murmuring in the background let her know Raiden was with someone.

"In the meantime, tell me what you see."

After a brief description of the place, she laughingly admitted she had no idea how to fly a personal jet.

"Are there any vehicles you can appropriate?"

"Just the van we came in with."

"That will have to do. I believe that vehicle has an embedded tracking device we could not dismantle." A man's voice mumbled in the background. "Ah, apparently you're just outside Langley, Virginia."

She snorted. "That makes sense. The CIA kidnapped me, after all."

"Yes, you said that previously."

Raiden's tight tone put her on alert.

"Are you sure it was the CIA that held you?"

Jena got in in the van. "Yep, a douche-wad named Claude snatched me. He seemed to know all about your little alien friends and that they're coming here to take over." Woo-hoo, that arrogant asshole Agent Coal left the key fob on the dashboard. She placed her foot on the brake and pushed the button to start it. "Okay, I'm in the van. Where am I going?"

"Michael is sending directions to the phone's GPS. We have a satellite office near there. Once you get there, go to office 1b. Call me when you arrive." He disconnected.

Okay, short and sweet. She could work with that. Hopefully, whoever she met at their satellite office would help her. A quick glance at the phone let her know the directions were ready. Hmm, the phone was synced with the GPS in the van.

A tap here, a tap there, and voila! The GPS screen was good to go.

She swung the wheel to turn around to leave the way they entered, passing through the open door, and she shot out into the paved driveway. She squinted at the sun that was high in the sky. A quick glance at the center console revealed a pair of mirrored aviator glasses. She slipped them on and relaxed with a hum.

Following the directions, she headed south and merged into the minimal traffic. She rolled down the window and put an elbow on the open ledge, enjoying the warm summer day.

Jena arrived at a typical u-shaped industrial park. The bland buildings were no taller than three stories. And bare of any landscaping that would give it a pleasant appearance. At least there was plenty of parking up front.

With a casual toss, Jena left the fob on the dashboard. She pushed the sunglasses up her nose with a forefinger and headed to the building entrance. It wasn't too hard to find suite 1b.

What next? The place didn't have any windows to peek in, just a solid door. Should she knock or walk in?

The gray door swung open.

Jena jerked when the last person she thought she'd see stood there. Raiden towered over her with an overlying aura of barely suppressed power.

His dominant allure had her shivering. "You're Raiden?" Stupid question, but it was the only thing her scrambled brain came up with. How in the hell did he get there so fast?

His slight smile was warm. He stepped back with a welcoming gesture for her to come in. "Yes, and you must be Jena."

She nodded but didn't go far as he shut the door behind her. With wide eyes, she glanced over his shoulder. "This is it?"

It was a bare room. A blackout curtain covered the lone window, and an industrial fluorescent strip light glowed from the ceiling. No furniture, no carpet, and nothing adorning the naked drywall except for a massive mirror. The gigantic thing took up most of the opposing wall.

She blinked at her reflection, confused at first. Oh right, she looked like the CIA agent and not herself. Mesmerized, she approached the image with a hand out. Touching her fingertips to the cool surface, she took in her wide-eyed expression with an open mouth. Which she shut since it made her look like a brainless codfish.

"Do you need assistance to change back into your normal self?" Raiden's voice lowered to a whisper.

Jena glanced at his image behind her. He stood close enough for her to feel his body heat, but not so close he caused her to be uncomfortable. Eyes closed, she concentrated on her natural appearance. A twinge and a couple of aches settled before she opened her eyes. Her normal reflection stared back.

She gave Raiden a sheepish grin and pulled the tight top out of the pants. Agent Raven may have been around the same height and size, but Jena's breasts were larger. She had to hold the panels of the industrial white shirt closed to keep the buttons from popping off. No way would she flash Pete's serious brother. "Nope, got it." Turning away from the mirror, she faced him. "Okay, let's get going." She marched to the door. "Let's go find Pete."

"If you are amenable, I want to take you to our headquarters in San Francisco. That way we can pull our considerable resources together to locate him faster. Would that be all right?"

She glanced at him over her shoulder. "Sure, whatever you say. Anything to find Pete." She started for the door, but Raiden stopped her with a gentle hold.

"I'm afraid you're going in the wrong direction. We need to leave through there." He waved to the mirror. "This is not a mirror, but a transportation device called a Transkip. Let me demonstrate."

He flourished a graceful hand at the mirror. The reflection rippled before it changed into a scene of a long, brightly lit hallway. Ceiling lamps and various wall tables adorned with floral and sculpture motifs completed the opulent sight. A classic Aubusson red-and-gold carpet runner covered the maple flooring.

She gasped. "How? What?"

Raiden took her hand in a light grip. "Come. Don't be afraid. Let me introduce you to the rest of Pete's family. They're excited to meet you."

Jena swallowed. Normally, walking headfirst into a mirror would be a last thing she'd want to do. But dealing with so much weird stuff lately, what was one more wacko thing? Squeezing his fingers, she had to ask. "Think you can keep the CIA from finding me there?

His laugh was infectious. "I assure you, where we're going, they have no way of following."

The man never gave Jena a chance to think about it. Raiden pulled her through the mirror. Between one step and the next, she left the empty room and walked down the luxurious hallway. A quick glance over her shoulder caught the image of the bare office vanishing. Now her retreating reflection came into focus. She looked ahead, confused. Did she just go from Virginia to California in one step? At the very least, shouldn't it feel different than walking through a regular door? Shouldn't there be a feeling of her stomach dropping? Where was the change in air pressure?

"Come, sit and relax. I'll have some refreshments brought in."

He led her into a stylish sitting room. Huge bay windows dominated the place, allowing bright ribbons of sunshine to flow and spotlight the expensive neutral carpet. A gray circular sectional couch with a colorful variety of throw pillows dotting the cushions took up most of the area, surrounding a spherical coffee table with a sturdy maple frame. Two cinnamon-brown leather recliners faced the couch. A miniature modern-art sculpture made of brass adorned the middle of the table.

Raiden held her elbow as she sat on the plush couch.

The three-tiered bay windows highlighted the famous Golden Gate Bridge. The iconic Transamerica building dominated the view from a side window.

A low droning sound came from behind.

Jena swiveled.

A floating robot hovered at the end of the couch next to her. It was humanoid in appearance, the upper body encased in gray double plastic with a round head that sported two orange lights in the middle. It had shoulders, but at the elbow, two forearms branched out with straight, pincer fingers. The bottom half of the drone tapered to a flat pedestal.

Jena had seen prototypes like this in various online vids, especially from Japan. She didn't know they were available to the public yet.

"What may I serve you?" The metallic sound was without inflection.

Even her AI voice recognition system at home had more personality.

"Do you want something to drink or eat?" Raiden remained standing as he gestured to the drone.

She nodded. "Yes, please. I'd love some water." Even though she was starving, she doubted the empty pit in her stomach was from the lack of food.

"DD-72, two bottles of water, please." Raiden folded his hands in front of him as he looked around the room. "Anyone from the family here?"

"Affirmative. Master Ben and Mistress Julienne are awaiting your instructions."

Raiden studied her intently.

His unblinking stare gave her the chills. Not that she imagined he posed a danger to her. Instead, the tingle from his alien stare told her she wasn't hiding anything from him. Not even the secrets she kept from herself.

"If you are amenable, I would like to introduce you to someone you may already know."

Jena's heart thumped. With wide eyes, she covered her mouth with her fingers and faced the hallway. At first it was hard to see who came toward her since her vision blurred with tears. She blinked and watched a woman who looked just like her head straight for her with open arms.

Without a second thought, Jena jumped off the couch and rushed to her. Hugging and crying into the woman's neck, she didn't care she'd never met her before. She knew who she was down to her very core.

"Oh, my God. Oh, my God."

The woman whispered in a voice eerily similar to Jena's own.

"I can't believe you're real."

The hug was tight. Jena stepped backward and hung on to the woman's shoulders, who returned the grip. Through bleary eyes, she examined her sister in person for the first time. While they may look identical from a distance, this close, Jena could distinguish their differences. As someone who loved the rugged outdoor lifestyle, she could tell the woman she held in her arms didn't. Jena had a deep tan and maintained a toned body. The creamy pale skin of the other woman matched her fleshier physique.

Jena's dark chestnut brown hair was waist length; the other woman's hair was professionally styled and reached her shoulders. Her cognac eyes were a mirror image, expanded and filled with tears.

Her bottom lip trembled as her face flushed a deeper red. "You're my sister, aren't you?"

The more-than-obvious question made Jena laugh. "God, I hope so. Otherwise we're both part of a huge cosmic joke."

The woman's eyes twinkled. "Hi. I'm Julienne."

"I'm Jena."

"Come on, let's sit so we can get to know one another better." Julienne tugged Jena to the couch. "We've got so much to catch up on." She gave a nervous giggle. "I have no idea where to begin."

A familiar whirring noise came into the room. The drone Raiden called DD-72 held a tray holding two bottles of water.

"Would you like anything, Miss Julienne?" The metallic drone hovered over the coffee table and set the plate down.

Jena grasped the chilled bottle and took a couple of swallows of the refreshing liquid. Damn, she couldn't remember the last time she'd been this thirsty. With a happy sigh, she put the half-empty container on the table.

Julienne waved with one hand while keeping a firm grip on Jena. "No, thanks. I'm good." She eyed the water bottle before glancing back at her. "Do you need anything else? Are you hungry?"

Jena smiled so hard her cheeks hurt. "I'm good, thanks." She squeezed her sister's hand. "I want to hear all about you." She glanced at Raiden and his stoic expression. "But first, tell me how we're getting Pete back."

Julienne's lips pursed. "Pete's missing?" She focused above Jena's head. "You didn't tell me Pete was missing."

Jena turned to see who Julienne was talking to since Raiden stood next to her.

A tall, brawny man entered the room with silent steps. His defined build was visible through his casual clothing. The wavy, blond hair was stylishly short, its color resembling a Macadamia nut. His aquiline nose topped full lush lips, and he had a slight overbite. High chiseled cheekbones went well with the deep cleft in his chin. He had to be, without a doubt, one of the most gorgeous men she'd ever seen up close.

Except for Pete, of course.

"This is my husband, Ben." Julienne let go of her and held the tips of his hands he put on her shoulders.

He leaned down and nuzzled her neck before glancing in Jena's direction.

His eyes had the same large, oval-shaped irises with the dual colors of bright turquoise and sunburst yellow that Pete's and Raiden's did. He had to be one of Pete's other brothers. Wait... husband?

When Julienne glanced at Ben, her goofy smile told Jena everything she needed to know about the couple. "Have you been married long? Do you have any kids?"

Julienne splayed a hand over her stomach with a dreamy smile. "We got married in Vegas last weekend. As for kids, that's about eight months away."

Jena sucked in a breath. "You're pregnant? That's awesome!"

Ben beamed. "We were so excited when we found out she was pregnant." He aimed a slow, secretive grin her way. "So, how did Pete react when you told him? What did he say?"

"Say?" She frowned at him. "What could I have said to him for you to look at me like that?"

Ben threw his head back with a deep belly laugh. "Holy shit! I hope I'm there to see the expression on his mug when he finds out."

His cryptic answer made her face heat. "Finds out what?" She crossed her arms.

The crazy man stopped laughing and cleared his throat. But the smile remained. "Why, when you tell him he's going to be a father, of course."

~Special Agent Claude Reese~

"Please tell me I misunderstood what you just told me, Special Agent Stygian." The computer voice of his superior officer accompanied the blurred image on the monitor. "You had one of Julienne King's sisters in your custody and she somehow escaped? A woman with no combat skills or training escaped the top echelon of your team?"

Claude couldn't remember the last time his face heated under a superior's reprimand. Sitting in the comfort of his private office, he leaned back in his chair as he twirled the wedding band around and around. No matter how many times he tried to stop the nervous habit, it always got away from him. At least no one was around to witness his unease.

He cleared his throat. "That is correct, Director Obsidian. We discovered Agents Raven and Coal bound and gagged in the airport hangar where they were to escort the prisoner to our offshore accommodations."

"Offshore? You were taking an American citizen to our offshore facilities?"

Claude stilled at the monotone steel of the director's voice. Even through the computerized scrambling, the sheer rage coming through was loud and clear.

"The only reason to do that is to inflict emotional and physical pain in order to gather information. Did I not specify that you were not to harm those assets? By what authority did you subvert a direct order?"

"I was only following your dictate, Director. You wanted Julienne's sisters secured at an undisclosed location. The only way to ensure this was to take them to a maximum-security facility out of the country. We had no intention of interrogating the detainee while she was housed there."

"I also specified that I wish to speak to her myself. Which I cannot do at the offshore facility." The computerized voice remained flat.

Claude ignored that last reprimand. "While we search for Jena MacFarlane, I have it on good authority we have the location of one of the other missing sisters." On a second monitor, he pulled up a copy of the recent file sent to him. "A woman matching the general description of both Jena and Julienne has come up on the Nevada gaming commission database. This asset appears to be working in a small casino at the state capital in Carson City. A plan to retrieve her is being assembled as we speak."

The blurred image of the director moved as if leaning back in a chair. "Fine, Special Agent. As for now, your only concern is to get this new asset as well as Ms. MacFarlane and Ms. King. And when your team has them, you are to contact me immediately. And, I cannot stress this enough. You have no authority to decide where to locate them. That decision is mine. Do I make myself clear?"

Claude's lips thinned. He wasn't a child and didn't appreciate being talked to like one. "Yes, Director. Understood."

~Jena~

All of a sudden Jena was cold and sweaty, and all sound in the room receded. Her fingers shook as she tossed a panel of her hair over a shoulder. "What? No, I must have heard you wrong. I'm not pregnant!" Her laugh was hollow. "I mean, really. Pete and I have only gotten, um, together once."

The knowing smile from her sister caused her to frown even harder.

"As I'm sure you're aware—" Julienne smirked. "—it only takes once. That's what happened to me and Ben." She leaned back and gazed at the man standing behind her.

He wore a sappy grin as he gave his wife a quick kiss on the top of her head. Moving to the couch, he sat next to Julienne with an arm around her shoulders.

Well, Julienne had a point. It did only take one time to get knocked up. Jena's breath caught. She hardly thought about having children. She'd been so busy raising her teenage brothers, the idea hadn't crossed her mind. At least not lately. She squinted. "Wait a minute. If I'm pregnant, how in the world could you know? Especially since I don't?"

Ben's patient smile made her straighten.

"Pete has certain skills that normal humans don't have. Am I correct?"

Jena gave him a curt nod.

"Well, to make a long story short, my brothers and I have our own particular psychic abilities. I, for one, am an empath. Do you know that is?"

She cocked her head. "No, I've never heard that word before. Does that mean you're empathetic?"

Julienne snuggled under Ben's arm and wrapped a hold around his waist.

Her stare made Jena squirm.

Ben patted his wife's arm as he replied. "Yes, to a certain degree, but on a more profound level. I don't have to guess what another person is feeling, I experience everything they go through as much as they do." He gave a self-deprecating chuckle. "People may lie to themselves all the time, but emotionally it's harder to lie to oneself."

Jena's eyes widened. "Wow, that must be a pain in the ass." She grabbed her hair and twirled a slim string around her finger. "But what does that have to do with you saying I'm pregnant?"

"I can sense your daughter's emotions." He gazed at Julienne. "Do you feel her too?"

Julienne's gaze unfocused.

A comforting, warm sensation spread from Jena's core outward. She put a hand over her stomach as if to protect what was inside.

"Yes! I do!" Julienne laughed and grasped her husband's arm. "Oh my God, how did I miss that?"

"Be patient with yourself. Remember, you're still learning, my khoshgel." His indulgent tone was soft. He covered Juliann's stomach with a large palm. "Search inside yourself and feel the joy our daughter experiences with her cousin. Even now they are communicating and getting to know one another."

Jena's head spun. What in the hell were they talking about?

"If it's all right with everyone present, I believe it would be prudent to discuss the best way to retrieve Pete from the Akurns."

Raiden had taken a seat on one of the leather recliners. He steepled his fingers and stared at Jena. "In order for us to understand where he may be, please share what happened to you since the two of you met."

Wow, that was a tall order. After a deep breath, she gave as much detail as she could, from when she met Pete as an injured wolf, then at Heavenly Village and ended when he passed through the black hole as a prisoner of the aliens.

"You keep calling this guy from the CIA Claude." Julienne's brown eyes were wide as she leaned forward, hands clasped. "You wouldn't know his last name, would you?"

Jena scrunched her nose. "I think it was something like Reese. Why?"

Instead of answering, Julienne turned to Ben and grasped one of his hands. "That couldn't be the Claude I worked for at the bank, could it?"

Ben scowled. "That doesn't make any sense. I never got a feeling he was anything but what he appeared to be. How could your old boss be working for the CIA?"

"Jena, have you touched this individual since you acquired the same abilities as Pete?" Raiden's matter-of-fact tone sounded like he was discussing the weather.

The memory of Claude's skin touching hers in his office rushed back. "Yeah, when the asshole questioned me in his office, he touched my hands. Why?"

"I believe you can change into anyone you touch. Correct?" When she nodded, he continued and leaned forward. "This may be a crucial piece of information we have been missing. Would you mind changing into him so Julienne can identify this individual?"

She bit her lip. "Um, okay. But do you have any sweats I could wear? When I change into a bigger form, the clothes I'm wearing will rip." She gave a sheepish laugh. "No offense, but I refuse to prance around naked without you guys buying me a drink first."

"Oh Lord, you're smart-ass just like Pete." Julienne laughed. "Come on, I'll take you to the room where Pete stays while he's here. I'm sure we'll be able to find something you can put on for now."

Following her sister down the same elegant corridor that she'd come through earlier, Jena took the time to admire the various classic works of art and sculptures that lined the wide hallway. "This place is gorgeous."

"Come on, you can change in here." Julienne opened the first door they came to. It was a master suite worthy of any GQ magazine spread. Deep rich browns, tans, and a smattering of midnight black highlighted the decor. A California King bed dominated one side of the room while the other half was a gamer's dream. Embedded in the wall were five 28-inch monitors with various gaming consoles on the long table between a pair of high-end gamer's chairs.

While she looked at the player's paradise, the oil painting on an opposite wall caught her attention. "Oh my God, is that a Rembrandt?" She moved closer to peer at the masterful brush strokes. She took a step back to examine it from a distance.

When she realized what, or rather who the painting depicted, she sucked in a gasp.

"Is that... is that Pete?"

The image was proud and distinct. The man in the portrait wore the typical garb of 1600s nobility. His dark-sable hair was under a tall hat, complete with a conical crown rounded at the top and a narrow brim, with a single long strand of hair resting over his shoulder. A blistering-white linen shirt was topped with a matching wired collar with lace trim. Over the shirt he had a deep green slashed doublet that covered the sleeves.

The subject's pointed beard matched a wide mustache tipped up at the ends. His two deep dimples were a prominent feature of the canvas. The mischievous expression was all Pete, captured in exquisite detail by a master's hand.

She couldn't imagine how much this undiscovered portrait was worth.

With fresh eyes, she glanced around the room. Looked like she and Pete had a lot of things to talk about. His age being right there at the top of her list.

"Here, put this on. You can change in there." Julienne held a pair of gray sweats and matching top in one hand while she gestured with the other at an open doorway to an obvious bathroom.

Jena murmured her thanks and went in, shutting the door behind her. Glad to get out of the tight-fitting shirt and uncomfortable pants, she slipped on the sweats. It would be nice to have a bra, but at least the pants had an elasticized waist.

When they rejoined Ben and Raiden in the living room, another man sat in the other recliner. When they entered, the auburn-haired man stood as they approached.

"Oh good, Michael. I'm so glad you could join us." Julienne rushed over and grasped the man's hands and gave him a kiss on the cheek.

"Hi, Julienne. You're looking good. How do you feel?" His voice was soft as he glanced at her stomach before he squeezed her hands and stepped back.

"I'm great! Come on, I want you to meet my sister, Jena." She took him by the elbow and brought him to where Jena stood at the end of the hallway.

Jena swallowed the groan threatening to erupt. Holy cow, she'd never seen so many gorgeous men in one place in her entire life.

His deep reddish-brown hair was thick and wavy and held back in a tail. A full trimmed beard and mustache hugged his rugged jawline. His oval irises were the same turquoise and gold, with double-rowed dark eyelashes to highlight the exotic orbs. His wide stature gave him the typical look of a strong-featured outdoorsman—from the bulging chest muscles under the untucked T-shirt/flannel shirt combo to the trim waist and relaxed jeans. A motto splashed over his navy-blue T-shirt with the saying, "If a short psychic broke out of jail, you'd have a small medium at large".

She chuckled. But no matter how he dressed, she doubted this man spent a lot of time outside. His skin was too pale to have indulged in being outdoors much. In the room with the sun beaming through the large bay windows, he squinted as if the light bothered him.

"Michael is our resident expert on uncovering information on a variety of things we need to know about. If it involves the CIA, identifying this Claude person is imperative. He'll investigate and hopefully determine what the man's motives might be." Raiden spoke as Julienne led Jena to stand beside the couch.

"Okay. Give me a minute to get a hold on his image." Jena flexed her shoulders and shook her hands. She squeezed her fingers, clutching them on and off as her circulation pumped. With eyes closed, she envisioned Claude's attractive older features—his thick silver hair, hazel eyes, and trim physique.

Deep inside, she let go, keeping how he looked forefront in her mind.

Between one breath and the next, a warm sensation shot through her from her core outward. When she opened her eyes, her perception changed to that of a taller person.

A gasp from Julienne.

Ha, maybe she could do this. A medium-size mirror hanging on an opposite wall confirmed her assumption. The image of Claude dressed in the gray sweats stared back at her.

"Oh my God, that's Claude!" Julienne put fingers over her lips as she came over to stand in front of Jena. Her sister examined her with wide eyes traveling up and down her body. Walking around her, Julienne turned to Ben. "What does this mean? How is it my boss from the bank turns out to be part of a CIA operation?"

When Jena crinkled her nose at Julienne's statement, the heavier, unfamiliar masculine skin on her face made her stop.

"That's what I've got to find out." Michael crossed his arms over his wide chest with a guarded expression. "It never occurred to me the CIA was aware of the threat the Akurns posed to Earth." His hands fisted on his trim hips. "It wouldn't be a stretch that they have information on us as well."

"Julienne, I hate to tell you this, but that man was more than just a CIA operative. He was in charge of the people who took me. They referred to him as Special Agent Stygian, and trust me, he was calling all the shots. Oh, I almost forgot. He showed me some pictures and asked me if I knew the people in them."

"If you can describe what those people looked like, it would give me a great place to start." Michael scratched the side of his beard.

"Good." Julienne sat and crossed her legs. Her foot twitched back and forth. "While all this doesn't explain why Claude did it, at least it tells me why he didn't have any trouble shooting Bob Manning right between the eyes."

Chapter Twelve

~Sub-Prince Murduk~

Murduk gripped the balustrade of the railing that overlooked the palace garden in the ever-present twilight of the capital city, Eengurra, on Akurn. His trusted companions, Uruk and Nungal, remained silent behind him. His mind became blank as he strained to control his facial expression.

Control. Must maintain discipline at all times. No matter how glorious it would be to act on his instincts, screaming a demand to eliminate all those who opposed him. He envisioned that elimination happening in a slow, methodical manner, to every one of his enemies. Spilled traitorous blood would bathe the holy grounds of the palace in a rapturous, colorful display.

If he gave in and did that, it would drive home a warning to the citizens of Akurn to never oppose him. Everyone would fall in line. The populace would trip over themselves just to please him. He'd savor watching the noble warlords scramble as they fell over themselves to worship him, as was his due. The ignorant fools were oblivious of how bad things could end up if they interfered with his plans. The reckless actions those clueless imbeciles practiced were getting out of hand. It was time he made a bold move and put them in their place. Fear was the only weapon he needed to control the empire.

He fisted his hands and turned to his companions. "Any further word from Commander Kud?" The last he'd heard from the leader of FarDeep Base, he was examining a potential son of his missing sister, Inanna.

"No, sire." Uruk's gravelly voice had no inflection. "However, he stipulated he would contact you when he had a preliminary summary." The man shrugged his strong defined shoulders. "I expect things are running smoothly. Rest assured, Highness, he will gift you with a substantial report when ready."

Murduk stared at Uruk. It was possible the man was right. "Very well." He strode into his private suite. For once the place was void of the various naked men and women he insisted on having around him at all times. The urge to indulge in hedonistic pleasures was the last thing on his mind. "Are the warlords gathered?"

Both Uruk and Nungal nodded as they gripped their charged laser spears.

"Any resistance?"

"Old Warlord Ennugi is on his deathbed, but he sent his firstborn to take his place."

Murduk's face hardened. Ennugi had been one of his devoted supporters. No telling if the man's young son had the same inclination.

"Sire." Nungal tilted his gigantic head with unfocused, watery blue eyes. "I'm told there is a caller in the vestibule who insists they speak to you."

Murduk clenched his hands. "I don't have time for interruptions. Send whoever it is away." He'd kept the warlords waiting long enough. He had to ensure they didn't question his authority...

"Lord," Nungal interrupted. "This visitor is adamant to meet with you before you go to the warlords. They insist they have information concerning WOTA that will benefit you."

Murduk raised an eyebrow. "Is that so? Send him in." He'd remain standing so whoever dared interrupt him would have a minimal amount of his attention. Best not test the warlords' patience more than necessary.

"I am more than grateful you agreed to see me, sire." The musical female tone caught him off guard. Given their much-deserved status of sub-class citizens, females had no business meeting with the leader of Akurn unless he arranged it.

With his arms crossed and his legs splayed in a wide stance, he narrowed a glare at the noblewoman approaching him.

She glided with the self-assurance of a member of a royal house.

He supposed she was attractive in the run-of-the-mill beauty the nobles produced.

Butterscotch-blonde hair curled to the tip of her rounded ass that was just shy of being too lush.

His gaze drifted to an impressive set of opulent breasts. He grimaced at the unnatural surgically enhanced full lips.

Her mouth creased in a self-assured smile.

He stilled and glared with narrowed eyes. The laser focus of her pale-blue eyes jogged a memory. She was a tiresome debutante he'd dismissed a long time ago. While her father, Warlord Puzur-Assur, was a formidable noble, Murduk deemed this female not worth the aggravation of being involved with in any capacity. "What do you want?" He growled.

"Oh, my Lord. It's not what I want. But what you do." She bowed with a hand covering her heart and sauntered closer.

Her cloying perfume made his nose itch. He resisted the urge to step back. Holding firm, he stared down at her.

"I am Damkina from the House of Puzur-Assur. I would like to offer you my unwavering services." She straightened with a coy smile.

Oh, for the love of the Goddess. He didn't have time for this *wapiti* shit. He pushed past her. "Uruk, get rid of her." Before he reached the exit, an unknown male voice echoed in the chamber.

"Do you have information on our next target?" It was a recorded voice.

Murduk spun around and watched the vid she played from a recording device in her palm.

The image stilled as a cloaked figure stood in a room surrounded by indistinguishable forms as if in a private meeting.

"I'm afraid you misunderstood my offer, my Lord." She moved her head with a tsk. The thick curtain of her hair swayed across her hips. Her coy smile matched the fanaticism in her pale-blue eyes. "I'm not here to offer you sexual favors. I'm here to offer you a certain set of unique skills that only I can provide." She nudged the video display. "This is a brief sample of my ability to, shall we say, be discreet eyes and ears for you. While this is an unusable piece of evidence, it shows you my sincerity in uncovering these worthless traitors."

"Who is that speaking and how did you get this?"

"That, my Lord, is the traitor leader known as Sychar. How it came about—" She shrugged her delicate shoulders. "—I don't know, since I found it among some discarded household possessions. I believe I have a spy working in my home that we can use to our advantage."

For the first time since entering his chamber, the female showed some interesting qualities. Not that he believed her ridiculous explanation. He stepped into her personal space. "Are you offering to become my spy with the nobles?"

Damkina didn't move. "Yes, Lord. I can be an invaluable asset to you. As a daughter of a high-ranking warlord, I have unfettered access in and out of the nobles' households. I will observe and report all traitorous activities I uncover." Her sly grin matched the half-lidded gaze. She wet her lips. "As we all know, females are far beneath a male's notice. Hmm?"

"Is anyone else aware of your offer to me?" he whispered and crowded closer.

Her clothed breasts brushed against the leather breastplate he wore. Her breath deepened as her nipples hardened, making their sharp points obvious under her soft linen gown. "No."

Her throaty answer caused his dick to thicken. If this female thought to work for him, she'd better be aware of everything that entailed. He grasped, then tweaked one of those protruding nipples.

She sucked in a breath at the pain he created. Her eyes widened as a moan escaped. She leaned into his hold, grasping the top of his hand, and squeezed. Her gaze lowered as her mouth dropped open with a pant. "I assure you, I'm here to serve you in whatever ways you desire, sire."

Murduk allowed a restrained smile. It was easy to recognize the ambition oozing from this female. It was something he could work with. But first things first. She needed to be aware he was in control, not her. Ah, the multiple pleasures he could use to train this new spy. In more ways than one.

Those damn warlords could wait.

~Pete~

The last time Pete suffered this much pain was when he stupidly got caught by a band of cannibals when he helped discover Fiji in the 1600s. They sliced bits and pieces off of him before he hardened his skin. They tried to kill him, claiming he was a demon. He didn't bother to let them know how to do that. Short of cutting his head off, he couldn't be killed.

Instead of the pain being on the outside, this was an internal agony that reached every part of his body. He swore his blood was on fire.

What type of trouble have you gotten yourself into this time, Ara?

Holy shit, it was official. He done lost his ever-loving mind. Pete clenched his teeth as he breathed through the agony. His father was the only one who had shortened his name with that lilting accent. But that was impossible. Adapa had been in stasis for hundreds of years. No way was his father here. Wherever here was.

Pay attention, son.

Adapa's familiar rumble brought tears to Pete's eyes. His father's continued absence left an enormous hole in his soul. Now wasn't the time to indulge in that debilitating emotion. In normal circumstances, he'd figure out how to eliminate the poison that burned through him. But he couldn't gain control of the blazing narcotic to get rid of it and the pain.

Ara, open your eyes.

When his father used that commanding tone, Pete obeyed. His vision was blurry at first, but after a couple of blinks he focused on a see-through image of his father. A squeeze of pain made him clutch his stomach and moan.

I know you're hurting son, but we are here to help you hold on until your woman and brothers come to get you.

"Great, now I'm hallucinating." He grimaced. His fucking fingernails hurt. A stretch of agony consumed him, all the way to his goddamn fingernails. What kind of sick fuck made something that burned fingernails? He breathed through the pain and searched for the culprit internally. There wasn't any part of him that wasn't in torment.

His father's infectious chuckle made his heart ache. His parent had a dry wit that Pete identified with.

No, you're not lucky enough that I'm your imagination. I'm here to keep you focused and not let you wallow like a youngling until help comes for you.

The transparent image of his father moved into Pete's direct line of sight.

His father's image sat with his legs crossed and his fingers laced. He looked relaxed, as if he didn't have a care in the world.

I have a surprise for you. Adapa lifted an open palm and a golden glow gradually brightened.

If Pete didn't know any better, he'd swear a small sun floated above his father's hand. The indulgent smile and the loving glance he gave the bright light made Pete's eyes widen. The only time he'd seen that look was when his father watched Pete's mother, Inanna.

Is she not lovely?

Adapa's sappy grin made Pete smile through his pain.

Of course, you would think she is. Adapa answered before Pete had a chance to. *After all, she's your daughter.*

Yep, his mind had gone bye-bye. For the life of him, he couldn't imagine why he'd dream about his father and some bright light instead of indulging in the memory of making love to Jena. Closing his eyes, he rolled to his side and curled into a fetal position. Maybe if he ignored his made-up ghost, it'd go away.

Grandfather, my father might be in too much pain to think clearly. Should I begin?

The feminine singsong voice bathed Pete with a calm that coated his battered soul.

Of course, my dear. That would be best. His father's tone was gruff. *But I warn you, I will monitor you to make sure you don't get so weak that we cannot go back. When I tell you to cease, you must do so immediately. Agreed?*

Yes, Grandfather.

With Pete's back to the apparition, it was hard to focus on the gibberish blabbing on around him. Not that he cared. A shot of agony came from deep inside and stole his breath. Torture ripped through him and it took a while before the warmth on his forehead registered.

It was like a door opened, letting him see what caused his pain. Deep in his DNA, a foreign body grabbed and stretched his healthy cells and forced some mutation.

Oh, Father.

The tinkling feminine voice spoke inside his head.

I'm afraid we're too late to stop all of this on our own. We'll need Mother and Uncle Ben to help us.

A soothing warmth settled under Pete's temples and down the back of his neck.

I'll give you what energy I can to stall the bad thing from hurting you more until they arrive. Don't worry, Mother will fix you. I have to go, but you'll be okay until they get here.

The comforting warmth on his forehead disappeared.

Son, look at me.

With a groan, Pete obeyed. He rolled onto his back with arms and legs splayed. He opened his eyes to watch the see-through image of his father. The bright star now rested on his father's shoulder and twinkled.

I know this is hard for you to understand, but my essence is here with you. Through the energies of your brother's child and yours, they've given me enough strength to communicate with you like this. But be aware, the forces on this moon base are looking for you. You will be safe here in this unknown cave if you don't take it upon yourself to leave this chamber.

Was the man kidding? He couldn't move two inches from where he lay, much less get up and snoop around. Staying put sounded like a fine idea to him. Besides, he had to be hallucinating, anyway. No way was his comatose father here helping him with a bright-light companion.

Pete groaned and sucked in a breath. Hey, what do ya know? He felt a little better. For some reason he now could pinpoint where the pain started. He found he had the strength to manipulate internally to turn off some foreign molecules. If he finished that, then he'd go in and reverse the damage done to him.

You hear me, son?

He'd better answer. Even if he was delusional. "Yes, Father," he croaked. Damn, his vocal cords were thin and hard to use.

Good boy.

Pete opened his eyes and watched the transparent apparition float close. He bit his lower lip to stop the whimper at the love shining from his father's dark gaze. While he may be a grown man, he missed his father's wisdom and dry sense of humor. Not to mention the unconditional love Adapa had for all his sons.

"Will I see you again?"

Why not take this all the way and ask his imagination the most important question? Over the centuries they'd tried everything to stop the continued deterioration his parent suffered. It had been a final, desperate solution to put his father in stasis on the spaceship. Pete and his family clung to the hope they'd somehow find a cure for him.

With each new spark my sons create comes the added possibility I will be with you soon. The ghost image stood; the bright golden light remained steady on the perch of his shoulder. *I love you, Ara. Remain strong. I know your woman and brothers will be here in time for you.* His father's expression softened, longing sharp in his dark eyes. *Tell your mother I love and miss her desperately.* Adapa crossed a fist over his heart. *May the Good Goddess of Love keep and protect you all.*

The transparent image of his father slowly dissipated.

Unbidden tears filled Pete's eyes. Even though that had to be some feverish apparition, the vision of his father made him light.

And maybe, just maybe, the ghost of his father was right. Help was on the way. All he had to do was not die before then.

~Jena~

Jena shivered at Julienne's announcement about Claude murdering someone in front of her. That wasn't much of a surprise. Look at the way he forced himself in her house. Then he had her knocked out and taken her against her will to the CIA headquarters, planning to keep her hostage. He was a cold spy with little empathy for anyone or anything that stood in the way of his demented mission.

With eyes closed, she let go of Claude's shape and reverted to her natural form. Shrugging her shoulders and twisting her neck to get the kinks out, she opened her eyes and glanced around the room.

"Okay, but what about Pete? We've got to get him back." She stood with arms crossed and directed a stern glare at Raiden. "I've got a bad feeling he's hurt, and needs us as soon as possible."

Raiden's eyes twitched to the side as if he focused internally.

She tapped a foot. "Well, Raiden? What about it? Are we getting your brother or not?" When she didn't get an answer, she stopped tapping her foot and put her hands on her hips. "Raiden..."

"Hang on a minute," Ben interjected. "When he gets like that, he's operating on a different, shall we say level, than you and I do."

Jena dropped her fists and straightened. "What does that mean?"

"It means he's either talking to somebody or he's trying to find Pete on an astrophysical plane. Give him a minute and he'll tell us what he knows."

"Fine." She threw her hands up and flopped on the couch, her eyes glued to the platinum-haired man. For the first time she noticed the slightly pointed tips of his ears, like the guy was an elf or something.

Raiden's lids closed with agonizing slowness before lifting. His oval-shaped pupils expanded as he blinked again. He regarded her with lowered eyebrows. "I believe you are correct, we need to get to Pete as soon as possible." His gaze settled on Ben. "I assume you have the accurate coordinates to return to the moon base?"

Ben nodded with a slight frown. "Yes, I made sure I saved it in our Transkip database."

"Very good. You and I will travel there immediately and retrieve our brother." He stood and slipped on the casual loafers he had toed off earlier.

Julienne gasped and her grip tightened on Ben's forearm around her waist. "You're not going back there, are you?"

Ben patted the top of her hand. "My love, it's important I go since I'm the family's healer. If Pete is injured, I'm the only one who can help him."

"But what if one of those aliens capture you?" The color drained from Julienne's face.

"Well, we just won't let them grab us, now will we?" Jena glanced at Raiden for support.

"Wait, you're going too?" Julienne narrowed her eyes. "Why? Shouldn't you stay here and take care of business?" She glanced at Jena's stomach.

"I'm afraid she's an integral part of Pete's overall ability to heal." Raiden gestured toward Ben. "Just as you were in bringing Ben back from his catastrophic injury."

Julienne crossed her arms with a mulish frown. "Okay, I understand why the three of you have to go to bring Pete home safely. It doesn't mean I have to like the danger you're putting yourselves in."

"*Khoshgel*, I assure you, we'll be fine." Ben gave his wife a gentle kiss before standing next to his brother. "Do we need to get anything before we leave?"

"No, I believe expediency is necessary. Let us depart."

And with that, Jena followed Ben and Raiden down the elegant hallway to the large mirror. Look at her, going to the moon with a couple of hybrid-aliens to rescue her hybrid-alien lover.

Yeah, life didn't get any weirder than that.

Chapter Thirteen

~Jena~

"**S**hit, I never thought I'd be back here again." Ben muttered.

Jena was so busy gaping at the impressive display around her she didn't pay much attention to what he said. She'd followed him and Raiden through that large mirror and passed through to an area unlike anything she'd ever seen before. She wasn't even sure she could call it a room. She swore she was in a terrarium with the universe outside the thick transparent walls. A sea of stars surrounded her while an image of the white, blue, and green Earth hung in magnificent splendor.

The vision occupied one side of the room and the blackness of space dominated the other.

Her mouth dropped. Almost in a trance, she shuffled to the invisible barrier with her fingers out, as if she could touch her home planet.

"Here's the door."

Ben's voice sounded far away, even though he'd only moved a few feet from her.

"This will take us out to the maze of abandoned caves under the base."

A firm grip jerked her out of the fog she was in. Raiden nudged her to go after Ben.

"If we're fortunate, one day we'll come back and examine this place to our heart's content." His deep baritone held no censure as he motioned to an open door.

Her hand dropped as she gave him a sheepish smile. "Okay, I'll hold you to that." She followed the taller man into a darkened hallway. At first, she couldn't see anything.

Ben clicked a pocket light on.

Raiden did the same.

The door to the room behind them solidified closed.

"Here's your light." Raiden handed her a portable light. "You follow Ben, and I'll stay close behind." He swung the beam to shine on the middle of Ben's chest. "Ben, do you remember the way to that control room?"

"Yeah, this way." Ben turned and led them away with sure strides.

Jena flashed her light at the ground to get a better idea of what she walked on. Just dirt along with a smattering of small and large rocks dotted around. She peered closer.

The dirt itself looked odd. It was fine, like powdered sugar. Clouds of silty dust rose with each footstep.

She flicked the beam at the rock walls that reflected tiny sparkles. A movement out of the corner of her eye had her swinging her light higher.

A small reptilian creature skittered away.

She gasped.

Instead of having normal earthy colors, the body was fire-engine red, ending in a long, barbed tail, and was propelled by six double jointed legs. Before it disappeared into a hole in the wall, four fuchsia-pink eyes set in low sockets on the sides of its head glared at her.

She got a brief impression of the creature's narrow, flat nose along with pointed ears topped with whisker tufts that feathered the tips.

With a hard swallow, Jena followed Ben. Definitely not in Kansas anymore.

She hadn't gone far before her eyes watered in the dusty air. While she expected it to smell dry, she didn't expect the metallic tang that came with it. "Why does it smell so weird in here?"

"We're on the dark side of the moon, called the South Pole-Aitken basin. Scientists discovered underground here a pile of metal five times larger than the big island of Hawaii. We, of course, know this is where the Akurns built a base. Thus the metallic scent." Raiden's small chuckle echoed. "And the base provides the air we're breathing and the gravity we need to move about."

"Here it is." Ben stopped at a side wall and shone his light up and down.

That part of the surface didn't look any different from the rest of the rock enclosure.

He ran his fingers across the craggy landscape before poking a finger into a slight indentation.

A sharp click echoed as the wall separated and swung open.

Ben pulled it wide enough for him to slip through.

Not waiting for encouragement from Raiden, Jena stepped through the threshold into the softly blue-lit room.

It was like something out of a science fiction movie. In the rectangular room were floating transparent monitors above cushy command chairs.

The place gave her the shivers. Shouldn't there be people working here? "Where is everyone? Why is this place so empty?"

Ben headed for the large station in the middle of the room. It had its own console and monitor. "My best guess is they've lost personnel since the last time Akurn was here. I bet they don't have enough people to man the facility." He swept a hand over the blank screen to activate it. Strange hieroglyphics popped up. He acted like he had no problem reading them.

Raiden stepped away from Ben and the computers.

She raised her eyebrows and glowered. "Aren't you going to search for Pete?" She gestured to a computer set nearest him.

The slight grin matched the flush flooding his cheekbones. "I'm afraid technology and I aren't compatible."

"Yeah." Ben grunted as he waved at the monitor in front of him and rushed through several files. "Raiden has to stay far away from any computer system or he shorts them out."

"Really? I've never heard of anything like that." Jena stood behind Ben and watched his dizzyingly search through the aliens' information.

Ben gave her a sideways glance with a mischievous smile. "He's our secret weapon whenever we want to crash an enemy's network. He doesn't have to do anything but stand next to its mainframe and everything goes wonky."

"Does that mean you can't use a computer?"

Raiden scratched the side of his reddened cheek. "Only on a limited basis. I do my best to avoid things of electronic make-up, such as television or cars with computer controls." He clasped his hands behind his back, still holding his lit flashlight. "I can, however, utilize a cell phone for brief moments."

"Hey, Raiden. Look at this." Ben pointed to the monitor. "I think I found him."

Raiden pushed off the wall and stood a respectable distance behind his brother. He leaned as if it would help him read the information better. "Yes, that could be an excellent possibility. That individual is not entirely of Akurn physiology."

Ben waved a finger to change the image. A stylistic 3D picture popped up of a figure lying in one of the lower corridors. It didn't move, but then, was it supposed to?

While the picture was something Jena expected to see out of virtual glasses, it was hard to tell if it was realistic or not.

The floating screen split into two different monitors. On one, the prone image lay. On the other, various undecipherable letterings popped up. It appeared to be a readout of medical values.

"Well?" She gripped the back of Ben's chair. "What does it say? Do you think it's Pete?"

The monitor flickered with a distracting zigzag.

With a quick step, Raiden bounced back. "I'll retreat so you may continue." He went to the corner he'd been in before. As he passed several floating monitors, they quivered on and off.

"Damn, man. You are one disaster area," Ben grumbled as his focus never wavered from the screen he was reading. "Stay back, or better yet, wait in the hallway. I'm almost done." He looked over his shoulder and gave Jena a quick grin. "This has got to be Pete." He turned to the monitor and his smile changed to a thoughtful frown. "I don't like his vitals. They're all over the place. We'd better get to him as fast as we can."

Jena grabbed his arm. "What aren't you telling me?"

He patted her hand as his gaze unfocused. "I don't know. I'm worried because I can't feel his emotions. Come on, let's go find him. I'm sure he's waiting around for me to save his sorry butt." He gave a final swipe to the floating monitor to clear the file he'd been reading. He headed to the door with her right behind him.

"Raiden, let's get Pete out of the trouble he's found himself in. Again."

Ben's teasing eased the pressing weight holding her down.

They left the comfortably lit room and walked back into the dark, dusty tunnel.

Jena blinked. She shone her light around the nondescript passageway. Once again, she was between Ben and Raiden, with Ben's long strides never faltering.

At least he seemed to know where he was going.

The soft whoosh of the command center's door dissolving closed was an afterthought.

While not a serious spelunker, she'd explored her share of shallow caves in the Sierras. She might not be claustrophobic, but this darkened underground tunnel made her break out in a nervous sweat. At least it was wide enough to walk through without stooping. The three of them remained silent, which is why she heard the strange shuffling sound behind them. While the noise didn't echo, it caught her attention.

"Do you hear that?" she whispered, and swung the light around, bypassing Raiden's tall form. "I think there's something behind us."

Raiden and Ben both stopped and aimed their lights with hers.

Ben tilted his head. "I don't hear or feel anything." He looked at his brother. "What about you? You get anything?"

Raiden's eyes unfocused as his grip tightened on the handle of his light. After he took a deep breath, he shook his head. "No, I sense nothing." He waved his hand in the direction where they'd been headed. "Let us proceed."

Good thing her companions couldn't see the heat in her cheeks. Last thing she wanted was for them to think she was a burden finding Pete. After one last glance behind her, she followed them. She hadn't gone far when the same rumbling noise happened again. She bit her lip to stop from saying anything and took a deep breath.

Ever since she learned how to shapeshift like Pete, it had heightened her other senses. There. An almost elusive but pungent scent of something "other". She ignored the fading steps of the men and concentrated on her listening skills. There were definite steps scuttling behind them. Now that she paid attention to the sound, it came through loud and clear.

The image of the strange reptilian lizard thing popped in her head. What if it was something bigger? Something with sharp teeth and claws? Before she freaked out, Ben suddenly stopped. She raised her light to see what he looked at.

It was a fork in the tunnel. Equal in size, the corridor broke off into two different directions.

Ben glanced at Raiden. "I didn't see this in the schematics I read. Which way do you think we should go? I still can't get a feel on Pete's emotions, so I'm not sure which direction would be the best."

Raiden stepped next to him and flashed his light in the corridor on the right. "I suggest we analyze..."

Jena tuned them out. She suspected they were going to have a long, boring conversation. Now was the perfect chance to see if she was imagining things or not. One more quick peek at Ben and Raiden.

Their heads were together as they talked in low tones.

She clicked her light off. Being in the dark helped her rely on her other senses. Her nose twitched at a distinctive, unfamiliar scent. The shuffling ceased. Was an Akurn stalking them? Or something worse?

The droning male voices of Pete's brothers faded behind her. She shrugged to release the tension between her shoulders and crept forward. She stopped and focused before resuming. Her nose twitched as the aroma became stronger. The scent didn't seem to be from an animal. A memory floated by of a familiar smell from her childhood at the fair. A fun mixture that was part salty, part sweet, and reminded her of corn dogs. Added to the mixture was the mouthwatering sweetness of caramelized sugar and strawberry. Cotton candy?

She didn't move a muscle and waited for the sounds to come closer.

Now the shuffling was accompanied by a smattering of giggles along with stern shushes.

Jena's shoulders relaxed. She'd helped raise her twin brothers from infancy and was quite familiar with the sound children made whenever they tried to be sneaky.

The darkness hid her as she waited for them to get close. Then she clicked the light on. Frozen in front of her was something she never dreamed she'd ever see on a moon base.

Twin boys stared at her with wide, dark eyes and open mouths. They couldn't be over eight years old, their boyish bodies wiry as only a child's could be.

From the top of the mop of brown hair parted on opposite sides, to the light tan of their skins. Jena would have sworn the children were human, except for their eyes.

The boys' oval irises were large, their unusual shape a dual tone color much like Pete's. Instead of the deep turquoise-and-gold color, these boys sported dark brown with a bright-orange starburst surrounding oval black pupils.

Each wore a one-piece overall in dark brown. One boy wore a tan shirt while the other's was navy blue.

They stood gaping at her, holding hands as their exotic eyes examined her with up and down quick motions.

Their little bodies shook, but she doubted it was from fear.

The excitement was clear in their smiling, open expressions.

"Hello there, boys." She held the light to the side and leaned to look them in the eye. "Who might you be?"

It was if her voice broke the hold they were in. They let go of each other and hopped up and down with hands flying. Gibberish spouted between them. They looked at each other as one would start talking, then other would finish. They pointed at her as many times as they pointed at each other.

A warm palm on her shoulder made her jump. She swung around to see who touched her.

Ben focused on the children and not her. He gave a reassuring squeeze before he went to the youngsters.

They stopped talking and gazed at him with mirrored frowns.

He spoke, spouting the same nonsense that sounded like what the children used. In response, the boys answered with bodies bobbing. They scrambled closer as one grabbed Ben's light and peered into it. The other boy kept yapping with Ben.

Raiden joined the group and stood next to her. "Looks like Ben has made some new friends." He clasped his hands behind his back. "I apologize for not taking your suspicions more seriously. In my defense, I had forgotten how heightened your senses are. Quite similar to Pete's."

"Can you understand what they're saying?"

"Yes. They're speaking in the original Akurn language that our parents raised my brothers and me on." Raiden cocked his head as he watched the interplay between Ben and the children. "I suspect these two have wandered far from where they should be. I'm concerned that even now someone is searching for them."

He stepped forward with his hands behind his back, the light shining behind him. He spouted in the same gibberish with a musical lilt.

The twins faced him as one with mirrored frowns. Crossing their arms over thin chests, they sent him a mutinous glare.

She was quite familiar with that expression. Her twin brothers had given her the same look more times than she could count.

The boys frowned and shook their heads.

She peeked at Raiden, looked away, and hid a smile.

His grip tightened on the light as his eyes narrowed. It sounded like he repeated the same question and got the same results. Nothing.

"Oh, for God's sake." Jena tsked at Raiden. Obviously the man never spent much time around children. "Ben, offer them your light so they'll tell Raiden what he wants to know."

Raiden turned his frown on her. "Bribing children is not the appropriate way to elicit compliance from the young."

"Yeah, I get that. But if you want a quick answer, the best thing to do is bribe them with something they seem interested in."

Ben's slight overbite creased into a smile, and his eyes twinkled at his brother. "She's got a point, Raiden. We have to find out where these kids come from before their parents surprise us." He held out his light and twitched it back and forth in front of the boys, muttering some gibberish.

They squealed in delight and clapped their hands.

It didn't take long for the boys to spew, at least that's what Jena assumed they did. Hard to tell when she couldn't understand a word they said. But, by the expression on everyone's face, it sounded like they agreed.

"Hey." She nudged Ben. "Think they can help us find Pete?"

Ben's dark-blond eyebrows squished together. "Not sure. Right now we're only asking them where their parents are."

Jena resisted the urge to stomp her foot. Why was it men had a hard time multitasking? "It's more than obvious these two are explorers. If anyone knows where Pete might be, it's them."

The boys stopped playing with the flashlight and watched her with intense interest.

She narrowed her eyes and gave Ben a sideways glance. "I bet if you bribe them with another one of these lights, they'll agreed to help us find Pete before we take them to their parents."

"What's a Pete?" The question came from the twin in the navy-blue shirt.

Jena widened her eyes. "Did you just speak in English to me?"

The small child shrugged his thin shoulders as if speaking her language was no big deal.

"I only have to hear some of it first." His little nose wrinkled. "This English is like baby talk. So simple."

Great, an alien child telling her that her native tongue was baby gibberish. She nodded to the other twin. "Can he speak as well?"

The boy shook his head. "No. He's much better in the language of mathematics." He patted his brother on the shoulder, which the other pushed off with an angry bark. A quick exchange of garbled words passed between them.

Time to interrupt before this turned into an all-out brawl. "My name is Jena. What's yours?" She leaned with her hands on her thighs and gave the boys an inviting smile.

The boy in the navy shirt puffed his chest and pointed a thumb at it. "I am Dylan." He pointed at his twin. "My brother's name is Nalyd."

A soft chuckle from Raiden made her glance his way.

"They have mirror names. Nalyd is Dylan spelled backwards." He sent the boys an indulgent smile.

It almost hurt to stop her eyes from rolling. Trust a brainiac like Raiden to point something like that out. "Listen, Dylan, you think you can help us find my, um, boyfriend? He's somewhere in these caves and we're afraid he's really sick." She nodded to Ben. "He has a basic idea where he might be, but we're not sure how to get there." She gestured to the two separating tunnels ahead of them.

"Be that as it may," Raiden interjected. "It is imperative we make sure they are not being searched for first. That would impede our rescue attempts longer than necessary."

Dylan's nose wrinkled. "You talk funny." He looked at Jena. "What did he say?"

"He just wants to know if your parents are looking for you. Are they?" She gave them her stern mother voice and put her hands on her hips.

Nalyd muttered something in Dylan's ear while Dylan kept his eyes narrowed at Raiden. Nalyd's tone grew urgent and a rapid-fire argument ensued.

They were speaking in gibberish, so Jena missed what they talked about. She glanced at Ben, hoping he'd have an answer.

He shrugged with palms up. "Beats the hell out of me. Now they're talking in their own secret language." He gave her a sheepish grin. "Pete and I used to do that when we were younger."

Raiden rolled his eyes.

It was one of the few humanistic gestures she'd seen him do.

"No one had the heart to tell the two of you we understood every word you said."

Ben's smile grew wider. "Yeah, we knew that. That was part of the fun."

Dylan's sharp bark brought her attention back to the twins.

"Nalyd and I agree to take you to the elders. They can find your friend faster. But you've got to promise not to tell them where you found us." Dylan's small fist clasped on his narrow hips. "Okay?"

"Agreed." Raiden answered before either Ben or she could.

She wanted to protest, but he gave her a narrowed-eyed warning with a slight shake of his head. With a humph, she crossed her arms. Keeping the twins' whereabouts secret from their parents didn't sit right with her. But she'd go along with it for now if it would help find Pete faster.

"Come on, this way."

Jena smiled at Dylan's peevish tone as he darted suspicious glares at Raiden.

"We'll take the nearest skipper to get there faster." They turned around and headed back the way they'd come.

"What's a skipper?" She power-walked to keep up with the young boys.

"You know, a..."

Dylan's rumbling gibberish made her eyebrows raise. She glanced at Ben. His thoughtful frown put her on alert.

"I'm not sure. Let's wait and see what they show us."

Peachy. She hoped this wasn't some stupid delay. She swallowed past her dry throat and sped up so she wouldn't lose the racing boys.

"Do not despair."

Raiden's soft baritone jerked her out of her musings.

"While I cannot pinpoint exactly where he is, I can feel his essence is currently at rest. I believe we will get to him before that changes."

Well, that was good and all, but she wouldn't feel better until she saw him for herself.

Before she replied, the boys stopped by an indentation on the side of the rock wall. Nalyd pulled a small metal pebble from his pocket and threw it at the craggy surface. The metal hit with a high ping before it disappeared. The reflection waved until it became smooth, like a lake of water.

Jena watched the reflection of her eyes widening. She gaped at the image of her next to the tall, cool Raiden and the rugged good looks of Ben.

"Ah, it's a Transkip mirror." Ben crossed his arms. He glanced at his brother. "Think we can trust this?" He clasped his arms behind him as he leaned toward the reflective surface. Without breaking his examination, he spoke to Dylan standing next to him. "And where will this lead us?"

Dylan tilted his head. "You said you had to see my parents." He gestured to the vibrant surface, which changed from a reflection to a swirling kaleidoscope of colors.

"And you have no problem accessing this information?"

Dylan snickered something at Nalyd, who snickered back.

Ben dropped his arms with a disgusted huff. "Boys, we need your parents' help to find my brother who's hurt. Wouldn't you want to get to your brother as fast as you could if one of you were in pain somewhere dark and scary?"

Dylan rolled his eyes. "Are you serious? Come on, let's go."

The random flashes of color in the mirror morphed into a scenic picture unlike anything Jena had ever seen before.

It was like an elfin city out of a fantasy novel mixed with something out of ancient Babylon. An immense cavern, complete with majestic icicle-shaped stalactites with pointed tips from the craggy ceiling, appeared.

She'd love to know what liquid created them.

In the middle was a dark-turquoise pool with enough illumination that it gave the chamber a warm glow.

No time to examine the rest of the place before Raiden put a palm on her shoulder. Startled, she glanced at him. His calm smile helped to steady her.

"Let's get some help for Pete."

With an uneasy roll in her stomach, Jena went through the transportation device.

The silty atmosphere of the dark corridor changed to fresh air on the other side. Instead of dryness, the air smelled of moist, growing things.

She stopped and took in the magnificent scene.

The cool color of the rippling pool matched the golden glow from the cave's ceiling, along with the illumination twinkling from several lit fires. Wait, no. That wasn't fire flickering in the street lamps. It was a stationary light that looked like flames.

An arched bridge over the water connected the two sides of a city where figures of people moved back and forth. Two- and three-story square buildings littered throughout and could either be houses or places of business. Dominating the view was a huge majestic building against the farthest wall, supported by tall wide columns.

It reminded her of the ancient temple in drawings she'd seen of the hanging Gardens of Babylon. Large fern-like plants fought for dominance and surrounded the outside, while towering trees with sparse leaves and thick trunks were in strategic places. A wraparound balcony on the second story had plants draping like a living curtain over the railing.

While the image was astounding, the myriad colors of the plant leaves made her mouth drop. Some were green, but the majority were Aegean blue or eggplant purple. To give the area a bit of depth, there were a smattering of sunny-yellow and bright-red leaves scattered about. She was so busy gaping at the surrounding scenery, she didn't notice they weren't alone until something bright caught her eye.

Chapter Fourteen

~Jena~

A moving blue blur out of the corner of Jena's eye caught her attention. Her jaw dropped as she stared at n immense muscular man who had to be at least six and a half feet tall.

He crossed his powerful arms and stood with his legs splayed. His short-sleeved tunic left one massive shoulder bare. The clothing had embroidered gold piping around the left sleeve and across the edge that exposed his brawny chest. The man's thick wrists sported large leather bands etched with gold. The red sash tied in a knot at his trim waist ended in a tassel.

A pair of formfitting pants were tucked into knee-high, black boots. The golden headdress that adorned his head covered his ears, with an oval ruby emblem was prominently displayed over his forehead.

Deep-set eyes, either black or brown, were staring from below slashes of fixed set eyebrows. A bulbous nose sat above a full mustache that tapered into a lengthy chin beard in black. He was handsome in a barbaric, scary way.

Jena shivered. She sure wouldn't want to meet this guy in a dingy alley somewhere.

A woman next to him spoke in a singsong language that came out harsh and clipped. She might not be as tall or as muscular as the behemoth next to her, but she was no less formidable. Around the same height as Jena, her long blonde hair reached the back of her knees in a spiral of curls and braided tails. Parted in the middle, the flaxen tresses draped over a golden circle that fit around her temples and sported the same ruby symbol matching the male's.

Bluebell-colored eyes narrowed as the woman's full lips pursed. Rounded high cheekbones framed a pert, ski-slope nose. A floor-length, sleeveless, cerulean-blue gown covered her lithe figure. The gown's V-neck was an excellent frame for a wide golden necklace made of golden links. A cream robe draped over one shoulder and flowed to mid-thigh, held in place by a wide, dark navy-blue cloth belt. Her ethereal beauty was an ideal foil to the man next to her.

Raiden took a step forward with his left arm crossed over his chest and gave a slight bow. Never taking his eyes off the couple, he talked in what sounded like the same language spoken by the newcomers. He straightened and gestured with an open palm to her and Ben.

The only words Jena recognized were her and Ben's names.

Raiden dropped his arms, clasping his hands in front. When he spoke again, the names of Dylan and Nalyd came out loud and clear.

The woman's pale complexion flushed. Her bright-blue eyes glanced from Raiden to zero in on the young boys who were doing their best to hide between Ben and Jena. With a snap of her fingers, the woman gestured for the twins to stand before her.

Heads hanging, the boys shuffled to stop in front of her.

With her hand on a hip, she pointed to a cluster of buildings behind her and spoke in clipped, brief sentences.

Dylan twirled a toe on the ground with folded arms and shook his head.

Nalyd elbowed his brother and stood between him and the woman.

The way they were all acting, Jean guessed she was their mother.

Dylan replied quietly and grabbed his brother's arm.

With an impatient slash of a hand, the woman waved to someone behind Jena.

With a start, Jena bumped into Ben as she took in the group of well-armed men surrounding them.

Each one was as formidable and massive as the man she assumed was the twins' father. All the guards had an assortment of weapons strapped to their sides and hips and were holding... spears? How odd was it that an advanced civilization used spears?

Two guards flanked the twins and gave the woman a quick answer.

The children left with the men following close behind. The boys' quiet argument faded as they walked away.

Jena's smile grew wide. Boys, especially twin boys, were the same throughout the galaxy. She couldn't count how many times Nate had to stop Nick from doing something stupid. She rubbed her temple, thinking of her brothers. Thank God they were with Chris's family, camping. But time was running out. She had to talk to them before they headed back home. First chance she got, she'd borrow somebody's cell phone and call them to make sure they were okay. The last thing she needed was for them to go home and have either the CIA or a group of aliens trying to capture them.

Come to think of it, the twins could take care of themselves. The aliens and spies wouldn't know what hit them.

The woman watched the retreating children, but when they were out of sight, she returned her gaze on them.

Jena clenched her hands to hide the shaking.

With narrowed eyes, the blonde rested her fists on slim hips. Focusing on Raiden, she fired a stucco of rapid words in his direction.

He stood relaxed with his chin tilted, hands clasped behind him. His expression remained bland and nonthreatening. When the woman stopped speaking, he gave her a soft answer.

Raiden turned to Jena and Ben. "We've been 'invited' to join them to discuss why we're here. Just follow my lead. I'm sure we can convince them to help us find Pete."

Jena glanced at the guards surrounding them.

Each one wore a fierce scowl, as if they were ready to attack.

Wow, if this was a nice invitation, she'd sure hate to see what those guys looked like if they weren't so nice.

Jena was as silent as the others during their journey to the softly lit city.

The giant and his lady led the way, with Raiden behind them and Jena in front of Ben. There were guards on each side of her and her companions, along with a troop of guards following close behind.

While she didn't like the uncertainty of what they were going into, she had to admit the trip was awe-inspiring. Since there wasn't any sunlight, the soft glow from the electric fires complemented the ceiling and walls of the cavern. She took a deep breath of clean air. An underground cave should be at least dusty. But here the dominant scent was of growing things that had to add to the slight humidity. As they approached the arched bridge that overlooked the gentle, flowing river, the fresh smell of the rolling water tickled her nose.

The rock land bridge was wide enough to accommodate their little group while leaving enough room for other folks to come and go.

As they passed the citizens of the internal city, each made a slight bow with arms crossed over the chest as the alien man and woman greeted them with a brief nod, a smile, or even a word or two.

Once they crossed the bridge, the ground turned spongy.

Instead of dirt, she now stepped on what looked like grass. Not green grass, but multicolored blades that ranged from bright yellow to deep purplish black. The rainbow of colors surrounding them was breathtaking.

Jena was so busy looking around, it took her a moment to realize a group of city citizens had gathered.

They either pointed or clasped hands over their mouths while muttering.

Her face heated. She hated crowds and being the object of alien scrutiny didn't help. A broad palm on her shoulder squeezed gently. Jena met Ben's warm gaze.

"Don't worry. Raiden and I won't let anything happen to you."

His sincerity was touching, and she gave him a slight smile. Too bad she didn't believe he'd be able to keep his promise. The crowd noises let her know more had arrived.

Men, women, and several children were all gaping and talking in loud voices.

Thank God she couldn't understand what they said. She more than appreciated the armed guards stomping next to her.

"We'll be okay. So far, everyone around us is curious and not threatening." He gave her a last squeeze before letting go. "Just stay close to me and Raiden."

To keep her mind off of her looming panic, she studied the diverse crowd.

Some people had alabaster-white skin and hair with bright-turquoise eyes, while others had dark hair, skin, and eyes.

She looked closer. Wow, several pairs of eyes were like Pete's and his brothers'. Large oval irises with dual colors. Everything from turquoise and yellow to the brown and orange like the twins. Every once in a while a pair of eyes were emerald green with a red starburst around the oval pupil.

The flash of a familiar face made her heart race. Wait... no. Between one blink and the next, the image was gone. She tried to scan the crowd to see if she could find that person again, but nothing. She could have sworn she saw herself in that brief flash. How crazy was that?

As she watched the crowd intently, it dawned on her Ben was right. No one acted threatening. They really did seem as curious about her as she was of them. Once that idea kicked in, the tension between her shoulders loosened. She just needed to concentrate on finding Pete. It was hard to shake the growing feeling he'd suffered a mortal wound.

The large temple-like building loomed close.

Their little procession approached a set of marble steps that led to immense, arched double doors.

The building was smooth as if it was constructed from a single piece of white marble with minuscule slivers of color running through it. It was gorgeous and terrifying all at the same time.

As the giant and the woman came to the entryway, a door guard waved at an indentation on the side.

The doors dissolved, leaving the way open.

The elegance of the building took her breath away. When she entered with the others through the monumental doorways, all thoughts of antiquity went out the window.

The vast chamber actually had a futuristic vibe. Wide pillars attached to the floor and walls arched into a circle.

She tilted her head back. Damn, that ceiling had to be at least a hundred feet above her.

Iridescent lighting resembling flames held in scones sat on scattered pedestals. Adding to the ambience was a broad laser light directed at the ceiling that helped to illuminate the wider area.

The room was a spectrum of warm browns. The shiny floor was a rich brandy with golden ribbons in a paisley design. The arching taupe pillars were lighter than the sandalwood walls.

She doubted the material was wood. Yeah, like there was a forest somewhere around. With a deep breath, she inhaled the slight scent of cedarwood along with a hint of citrus. It made her smile. She cupped her arms against the chilly air and kept pace with the long strides of the people leading her.

They came to a set of double doors in the same design as the massive entryway.

One guard opened it to reveal a circular conference room.

Thick, wooden beams in an interlaced pattern adorned the walls from floor to ceiling. A wide light from the roof highlighted the equally enormous round table. Nothing was on the table except for a reflective, clear top.

Around the table were round globs of dark brown that made Jena think of yoga ball chairs on a base without wheels.

With an open palm gesture, the giant spoke to Raiden.

Raiden answered and turned to her. "He's invited us to sit with them so we can explain why we're here."

She shrugged with open palms and a slight smile. Like she had a choice?

The behemoth and his lady settled on the brown blobs.

Jena gasped when the contraptions morphed into high-backed chairs. Following Ben's lead, she sat on one next to him. As soon as her tush hit the thing, it changed to fit her dimensions exactly. Without a doubt, it was one of the most comfortable chairs she'd ever sat on. She settled back. Even better, her feet rested comfortably on the floor.

Ben opened the conversation in the same singsong language.

The beautiful blonde answered and nodded in Jena's direction.

Obviously, the woman was saying something about her. "What did she say?" She bit the inside of her cheek. It was hard to sit there while people carried on an incomprehensible conversation around her.

"She's concerned you have no idea what we're saying."

Whoa, how did that woman know what was bugging her?

Ben continued. "She's offering to install a translator nano in you so you can join the conversation. Would that be okay with you?"

Translator nano? "What in the hell is that? Will it hurt?"

"Nanotechnology is the manipulation of matter on an atomic, molecular, and super-molecular scale that can be injected or placed with a biomimetic device to activate." Raiden unhelpfully explained.

She turned to Ben with wide, beseeching eyes. "Please translate what he just said."

Ben's reassuring smile made her boiling stomach calm down.

"Just think of them as little tiny computers that will make whatever language you hear understandable. And no, it won't hurt."

It didn't take long to decide. No time for folks to translate things for her, and nothing was worse than being kept in the dark. "Tell her I'd appreciate that." She gave Ben a sidelong glance. "This better not take long. We've got to find Pete."

Before Ben could answer, a guard stood behind Jena's chair. With a quick move, he placed a gloved finger at the tender skin behind her earlobe. He did it so fast that Jena didn't react at first. While his initial touch didn't hurt, it created a burning pinch that dissolved. A wave of dizziness made her clasp the chair's armrests. She sucked in a breath as nausea threatened to make her pass out. Good thing it faded until the disorienting sensation stopped.

"Can you understand me?"

A woman's lilting tone grabbed Jena's attention. She glanced at the woman across the table. "Yes?"

The woman nodded. "Good, then we shall proceed. Who are you and why you have invaded the city of Azadi?"

"Hey, that's kind of harsh. We didn't invade you, Dylan and Nalyd were nice enough to bring us here so we can ask for your help." Jena folded her arms and glared. "Pete's life is in danger and we're asking you to help us find him before it's too late."

"Jena is correct in conveying the urgency of our request." Raiden jutted his cleft chin with a head tilt. "However, I believe we should start with the basics. If that will be acceptable to you?"

The giant's rumble took over the conversation. "Yes, I believe that would be best. You are in the city of Azadi, founded in secret from the Akurns. My wife and co-ruler is Edinni, and I am Damuzi." He stared at Jena.

She gave a quick nod for him to continue.

"We've never had unexpected guests here before, so you can understand our suspicions. How did you get to FarDeep Base? How did your missing friend get here? Are the Akurns aware you're here? Are they looking for you?" The man thumped a fist on the table and leaned forward. "I demand to know if you've put us in danger by being here."

"Those are all very reasonable questions. I will endeavor to allay any concerns you may have." Raiden sat back and regarded the couple with a relaxed expression. "We have come to FarDeep Base through a Transkip mirror from our home on Earth. We do not believe the Akurns are aware of our presence. And, as I previously stated, we're here to find my brother Pete, who the Akurns kidnapped. We believe they intend to threaten his life and use him as blackmail to force our mother to surrender to Sub-Prince Murduk."

"Why would Sub-Prince Murdoch want your mother? He can have any female he wants on Akurn without forcing a woman from Earth." Edinni's pale eyebrows furrowed.

Raiden glanced at Ben, who gave a curt nod, before he answered.

Jena had the wild idea Raiden was asking Ben's permission mentally before he said anything out loud.

"Our mother is an intrinsic key to Murduk's claim to the throne. Without her, he cannot hope to ascend legally to the monarchy."

The scowl on Edinni's face melted. She blinked several times and her chin trembled. "Your mother? What's her name?" The question came out softly.

Ben's grin was wide. "I just realized what your name is. Edinni. You were our mom's only friend on Akurn, weren't you?"

"Princess Inanna? Your mother is Inanna?" Edinni covered her mouth with splayed fingers. "Are you hybrids like our sons? Was your father an Adamou?"

Raiden gave a curt nod. "Yes, our father was one of the first." The corners of his lips drew down.

Edinni gasped and stood abruptly, leaning on the table. "I must talk to Inanna! Take me to her."

Jena slapped a palm on the counter to catch everyone's attention. "Yo, alien people! Focus. We're not going anywhere until we get Pete." A throaty growl erupted out of her. She glared around the table. They'd better get a clue real fast like. She meant business.

"Do not worry, little human." The giant Damuzi's grin was infectious. "Our security forces are currently scouring the unused tunnels around Azadi. I expect we will find your companion..."

The man stopped in mid-sentence and his eyes unfocused, as if listening to something internally. "Oh, yes. I am correct. We have located another hybrid alone in one of the lower canyons." He stood. "Come, our sentries have located him. Follow me and I'll take you to him."

~Pete~

Ouch! What the fuck are you doing?

Pete's weak attempt to slap his brother was pathetic. Especially since Ben wasn't physically touching him. He sensed Ben's body next to him, but it was his brother's essence traveling internally through him that was annoying as hell. While his brother did his healing mojo, the ass left twinges of pain as he chased the piercing poison out.

Oh, grow up, Ben's mental voice replied. *I'm almost done. I'll let you know when I'm ready to leave, so you can shift to complete your healing.*

Pete grunted. He'd never admit to his brother that whatever Ben was doing gave needed relief. He swore instead of having a normal nervous system, he'd turned into one giant glob of torment. It had gotten so bad he'd passed out because of it.

As the agony lessened, it gave him a chance to think clearer. *Shit! Jena? I've got to find her...*

Calm down! You freaking out will make this harder than it has to be.

Pete hissed when Ben yanked on something that stung his left arm. He swallowed the urge to snap back. He opened his eyes and blinked to clear his blurry vision. He was still in the damn cave he'd passed out in. Only now he wasn't alone. In fact, the place was crowded as hell.

His brother Ben sat cross-legged next to him with his hands over Pete's arm.

Sitting beside him in an identical position was their brother Raiden. His eyes were closed with hands clasped on his lap. No doubt Raiden lent his psychic strength to Ben.

On the other side of Ben was the most beautiful woman in the universe.

Jena knelt with her fists clenched on her thighs.

She gnawed on her bottom lip so hard he was afraid she'd break the skin.

Movement over her shoulder caught his attention. Behind the trio was a bunch of odd-looking, ah, people? Some of them looked like typical Akurns while the others could be a mixture of humans and hybrids, eerily similar in appearance to Pete and his brothers.

That small group had to be sentries, complete with weapons in firm grips with more harnessed on their bodies.

In front of that fun bunch was a giant of a man, with a woman right behind Ben. The enormous male wore the typical garb of the Akurn/Sumerian nobility. And in a flowing dress next to the giant was a pure-blooded Akurn woman. Complete with alabaster skin and dark blue/green eyes that reminded him of the bluebell flowers on his family's English estate.

Ben, he whispered mentally. *Don't move. There are some Akurns behind you.*

Yeah, I know. They're the ones who brought us here to save your happy ass.

Ben jerked something around Pete's heart that made it tingle. Until then, he hadn't realized it was thundering out of control. With each twinge from Ben, the hard whop lessened as did the rush of blood that filled his ears. To test his strength, Pete clenched his fingers. Dammit, he was still as weak as a newborn kitten.

The sensation of Ben leaving his body was like the forceful receding of an ocean tide. Thank the Goddess of Love, as his brother left, he took the remaining agony with him. Pete inhaled an appreciative, pain-free breath.

Ben's smile widened. He patted Pete's shoulder as he got off his knees and stood. He gestured to the man and woman behind him. "This is Damuzi and his co-ruler Edinni, of the secret city of Azadi on FarDeep Base."

"Pete!" Jena scooted over to grasp the arm Ben had released. "Are you okay? How are you feeling?"

Her beautiful cinnamon eyes filled with tears.

He gave her a lopsided grin. "Well, I'm sure I won't win any WAKO competitions anytime soon, but I think I'll live." He gripped her hand and glanced at Raiden, whose piercing gaze rarely missed anything. Not trusting the surrounding dynamics, Pete talked to his brother internally. *Friends or foes?*

Debatable. Raiden answered on their secret psychic path. *But I believe they mean us no harm at this time.*

Humph, helpful as ever. Thanks.

"Co-Regent." One guard stepped forward and made a respectful bow behind the massive Damuzi, who stood with arms crossed.

The ruler glanced over his shoulder at the Akurn who spoke.

The guard's alabaster skin and blinding-white hair with his deep blue eyes gave away his ancestry. "There are reports the lukurra are approaching this area. We need to leave immediately."

The word lukurra was an ancient name the Akurns used for enemy. Shit! He could barely breathe, much less walk out on his own. He sent Raiden a beseeching glare. His brother had better get him out of here and do it without making him look stupid. He swore to the Goddess of Love, if Raiden hefted him over a shoulder, Pete was gonna... do something. What, he had no idea.

The slight smirk creasing Raiden's face made Pete narrow his eyes.

The only thing his brother did was raise his palms. Show-off. Raiden didn't have to make any physical gesture for him to move something through psychokinesis.

He suspected his brother was putting on a show for their strange audience. Maybe if they had a taste of his ability, they'd think twice before turning on them.

Jena gasped, still holding Pete's hand as he rose several feet in the air.

He squeezed back to reassure her he was safe and snug in his brother's psychic talent. "It's okay, I promise."

She nodded and let go.

He floated past her as if resting on a cloud.

The group left the abandoned caverns without a word.

Pete closed his eyes during the journey to wherever Raiden and Ben let the strange group take them. The scenery didn't change and the jiggling between light and dark made his eyes photosensitive. Besides, the only things to see were rock walls and ceiling.

The semi darkness gave him a chance to think. One thing was crystal clear, he didn't like Jena putting herself in unnecessary jeopardy. Oh, she might have gotten his abilities to shape-shift, but that didn't mean she knew how to use them.

And how did she get away from Claude and his goons? Raiden and his other brothers must have found and rescued her. He gritted his teeth. And then those idiots put her in danger by bringing her here. What were they thinking? She was a civilian, for God's sake. She didn't have the training to deal with all this hostile alien bullshit.

He squirmed and clenched his fists. Look at him, he was no better than his brothers. He cavalierly dragged Jena into this mess without considering how it would affect her. Or her family. While Bubbas claimed he was going to protect her brothers, who knew if that happened or not? With the dual threat of the Claude's agency along with Akurns searching for her and her family, they were all in danger.

He turned cold. For once in his life, he'd do the unselfish thing and think of her welfare first. He had to force her to leave, to make sure she stayed as far away from this mess as possible. No, away from him as far as possible. But she'd never leave on her own. She had a nurturing personality deep in her core. It was up to him to make it impossible for her to stay.

A heaviness squeezed his chest. Only for her sake would he do this. He'd send her away by making her so mad she'd never want to see him again. If he treated her bad enough, she'd take her brothers and happily go to one of the family's remote safe houses and stay there. Only then would she be safe.

He sucked in a deep breath and unclenched his fists. Yep, that's what he had to do. And when this was all over, he'd go crawling back to her. If he was lucky, she'd be grateful he kept her and her brothers safe as he helped save humanity. Saving the planet would be a bonus in his favor. Wouldn't it?

His throat tightened.

Dammit. Looked like heartache, his old friend, was back. And she was meaner than ever.

Chapter Fifteen

~Jena~

If Jena's fingertips tapped any harder on the dining table, she'd either break the thing or her fingers. Her neck burned while she stared at nothing.

The previous day's scenario played over and over in her mind. Pete lying so still on that dirty cave floor, the normal tan of his skin a pasty white. Dry, cracked lips, half-opened eyes coated with a jaundiced milky yellow. Then Ben did... whatever he did. At least Pete woke up and breathed better, and his color came back.

When they returned to the city of Azadi, their little troop headed to the infirmary. The doctors there gave Pete a cursory inspection and declared him healthy.

Ben did another woo-woo examination while the other brother, Raiden, stood unmoving by his side.

The whole time, she sat beside Pete, holding his hand in a tight grip.

As Ben sat back, the beads of sweat at his temples shone in the dim light.

When Pete opened his eyes, the whites were clear of the sickly yellow.

She smiled when his gaze settled on her and then she squeezed his hand.

He pulled away and sat up. The strange one-piece suit he wore stretched and appeared to be several sizes too small.

With his back to her, he addressed Raiden. "Get her out of here. I don't want her anywhere near me. So, where can I go to shift and finish my healing?" He patted her hand like she was a distant aunt and leapt off the hospital cot.

His cool dismissal made Jena's eyes widen. She stiffened. "Excuse me?"

Pete swiveled to her. "What?"

"You want me out of here? You don't want me to be anywhere near you? If that's so, why are you telling your brother this and not me? What, you don't have balls enough to say that to my face?" Heat crept up her neck and flooded her cheeks.

Pete's full lips slid into a frown. He looked everywhere but at her. "You can understand what I'm saying?"

"Course I can. I'm not an imbecile, you know."

"They gave her a nano translator. She understands the Akurn language as well as we do." Ben's baritone was dry.

"Fuck." Pete's shoulders straightened as he faced her. "Look, I'm glad you and I escaped our captors, but to be honest, the only reason I was with you in the first place was because of the danger we were in. Now that we're both safe and sound, it's time for us to go our separate ways."

The formfitting suit he wore stretched, defining his chest muscles when he shrugged. He waved at his brothers. "They'll take you somewhere where you can meet with your brothers and be safe." He patted her shoulder and turned away with an absent smile. No dimples.

Jena stopped him with a hard grip and forced him to pay attention to her. "Wait just a damn minute. Explain to me what's going on."

He stepped back, making her drop the hold. He glanced around the room. "Can we have a little privacy here? I need to explain how things are to Jena."

Her stomach dropped. Was he dumping her? Hot tears threatened. She gritted her teeth and blinked them away.

No, she couldn't have misunderstood their relationship. She watched with crossed arms and gritted teeth.

The small group of eclectic folks left without a word, including his brothers.

Raiden stopped and put a hand on Pete's shoulder before he gave a quick nod and left.

As the double doors closed, the air became still and thick.

She stared hard at the man she'd given her heart to.

Pete got right to the point. "I'm sorry if you misunderstood what was going on between us. We were in a tough situation and, you know, things happen. Now that it's over, it's time for us to get on with our lives. You have your responsibilities and I have mine. The most important thing for you to do is get your brothers somewhere safe."

"Okay, let me make sure there's no misunderstanding between us now. Are you telling me you don't want to see me anymore?" She bit the inside of her cheek to keep from blurting something she'd regret later. "And everything we said to each other was just because of the stress of the moment?"

God, she hated sounding like a whiny little Victorian maiden out of some historical romance novel. But come on. She didn't imagine what they'd experienced together. Not to mention those murmured words of "I believe I'm in love with you" while they were in that dream state. Why wouldn't she trust what he said there? Everything else he'd talked about had been real.

Those killer dimples were nowhere in sight of his stony expression.

"What can I say? I got caught up in the moment. I'm sure we can appreciate how we enjoyed each other. You have other responsibilities besides putting yourself in the middle of a threat you're not prepared for. To be honest, I can't afford for some lovely woman to distract me when billions of lives are at stake. Right now, I'd rather concentrate on stopping an alien invasion." He cocked his head, crossing his arms to mirror her stance. "That's a bit more important than our little fling. Wouldn't you agree?"

Little fling? Even with the stressful dangers they'd been in together, she refused to think it was just a random hookup. "No, I don't agree." She squeezed her hands into fists under her arms. The fear of abandonment slithered through her, making it hard to breathe. "But I guess it doesn't matter what I think, does it? Sounds like you've made your mind up. Right?"

The hard glint in his eyes softened somewhat, but his lips pursed. "Yes, I believe this is for the best." He stepped away. "Maybe when this is all over, we'll meet again. Who knows what might happen then?"

After that dramatic piece of crap, he gave a small bow and left without a backward glance.

"Need help to bury the body?"

Jena jerked at the sound of her sister's voice. She'd been so absorbed in what had happened the day before, she never heard the woman come into the communal dining room. Julienne had joined their little group in Azadi after a tentative truce was established with the ruling body of the hidden city.

Sitting in a corner booth, she studied her sister. While it still unnerved her to see her face looking back at her, she found herself overlooking that detail the longer they were together. In fact, she was becoming accustomed to the minor differences she'd noticed before. Besides, she loved how Julienne looked at things, especially the woman's wicked sense of humor.

She smirked at her sister's comment as Julienne settled across from her. "Nah, I'm still contemplating the best way to do the deed." She didn't mind teasing a little with her sister about Pete leaving, but she wasn't about to share how the cavalier way he left hurt and made it hard to concentrate. For now, she'd hide the pain until she worked it out for herself.

Julienne shook her head. "I may not know Pete very well, but from what Ben has told me and my ability to read emotions, I don't think he's as casual about you as he's trying to convince you he is."

Jena scrutinized the expression on Julienne's face and resumed tapping a forefinger on the metal table. "I think I agree with you. That's what makes this whole thing so hard. I've never had such a strong connection with anyone so fast in my life."

She stopped tapping. With sudden clarity, she gripped the mug filled with a steamy beverage that tasted suspiciously like coffee. "And I'm pretty sure he felt the same way. But him talking to me like an insensitive asshole makes me rethink everything."

"Did you tell him about the baby?"

Her derisive snort echoed in the small room. "Hell no. First, I only have you and Ben telling me I'm pregnant, which I don't feel like I am. And second, if he acted like that without being told, imagine how fast he'd run then." She glanced to her sister's side. "Speaking of being alone, where's your hubby? He's usually glued to your side."

"He and Raiden are chatting with Edinni and Damuzi and the rest of the family on Earth. I think they're trying to form some kind of alliance to work together against the Akurns." Grinning, Julienne leaned back with her hands folded on her lap. "Sounds like a match made in heaven to me."

"Yeah, when they started talking about leaving me here 'to keep me safe'—" Jena made air quotes. "—I got disgusted and left. I told them to let me know when they finished planning my life for me. Not that I care what they dream up. I'll make my own decisions on what to do next. One thing for sure, I won't agree to anything that doesn't involve getting my brothers somewhere safe." She shrugged. "So, we'll see. But I guarantee you this, I'll do what I think is best."

Julienne mirrored her small smirk. "Ah, we have more in common than just looking alike. Ben tries to tell me what to do and where to go all the time. I just nod and smile then do whatever the hell I want." She rested her chin on the tips of her laced fingers. "I don't think they can help it. They probably act that way because of their advanced age. I bet it's normal for them to revert to some kind of Neanderthal. So it's up to me to drag Ben into the 21st century." She squinted as she tapped her forefinger against her lips. "And I think you should do the same thing with Pete."

Jena stilled. "What do you mean?"

Her sister dropped her hands and leaned forward with a hard set to her lips. "I mean, look harder. How do you feel about your relationship with Pete? Do you believe his line of crap that what happened between you was just a fling? Or do you think it could be something else?" Her unmoving expression softened, as if she was trying to send a silent message.

Jena's instincts screamed she and Pete had something special. And it had nothing to do with the "stress" of the moment. Her eyes unfocused as she relived those heart-pounding moments when they made love. Pete's sensuality had been all-consuming. A man only interested in getting what he could at the moment didn't react like that.

"So, Jena. What are you going to do? Don't you believe in what the two of you have?" Julienne's eyes narrowed. "You say you won't let others make decisions for you. What, now you're just going to roll over and let Pete call all the shots?" She sat back with her arms crossed.

"Here's one more thing I'd like you to consider. From what I understand, a woman betrayed him a long time ago and broke his heart. How he feels about you probably scared the shit out of him. I bet he's using this bullshit about protecting you as an excuse to run away. Maybe he just needs a little proof you aren't like that at all." Julienne's stare was unwavering. "So, ask yourself this, isn't he someone worth fighting for?"

Jena's face heated. How had her sister narrowed in on the crux of her problem so quickly? Ever since she was small, she went out of her way to please others, afraid of rejection if she didn't. With downcast eyes, she slumped. If she was being honest, she even went to veterinary school to please her mother. While she loved animals, that wasn't her life's passion. She'd rather be a conservationist/forest technician—someone who took care of the habitats of the wild animals to ensure forests were maintained for everyone.

She worried her lower lip and relived the day when her adoptive parents died in a car crash. Until that happened, she'd filled her life with getting her degree and working with her mother in the clinic. She never indulged in a personal life. She was too afraid to disappoint her adoptive parents so she did everything she thought would please them. When they died unexpectedly, she sold her condo and moved back into the family home to become mother and father to Nate and Nick without a second thought. Not that she wouldn't do it all over again, but everything in her life since then revolved around them.

That was why she'd agreed to go to lunch with Claude. He'd been the first attractive man who asked her out in a long time. Then when she bumped into Pete, all else faded away. Being with him was perfect. No matter what the dumbass said. She sighed. Looked like it was up to her to make things right.

She pressed her lips into a hard line. "What can I say? When you're right, you're right. What do you have in mind?"

~Sub-Prince Murduk~

Murduk slouched on the massive gilded throne with his cheek resting on a clenched fist. His other hand lay on the armrest as he tapped his fingers in hard succession on the surface. With narrowed eyes, he watched the small band of warlords as they entered the throne room.

They were silent as they approached the raised dais, each with a ceremonial sword in the scabbard at his side, worn over a flowing traditional robe in their respective house colors. Along with the cloaked entitlement they carried everywhere they went.

Accompanying each warlord were two guards—grim-faced, steel-eyed soldiers used to putting their lives on the line for their master. Not that the imbeciles could do anything to protect their master's life if Murduk ended it. Each enormous column holding up the ceiling had disintegration beams embedded inside. It would only take a mental command to the palace security system using his implanted communications to fire on anyone he wished. But that would be the simple way out. It would be a sheer joy for him to make a personal example of what happened to traitors.

Murduk stopped tapping and straightened. With both hands gripping the armrests tight enough to make his knuckles white, he allowed the silence to blanket the air, waiting for one of them to speak. He didn't have to wait long.

"How dare you call us in without going through the proper protocols!" This came from Warlord Mattaki-Bunu. The middle-aged warrior had been loyal to the throne. Unfortunately he'd been voicing his criticism about Murduk's rule without the proper procedures in place that would declare him absolute monarch of Akurn.

"I insist you tell us what is so important that this couldn't wait until the scheduled assembly." The icy stare from his blue-green eyes matched the rigid cords pulsating in the warlord's thick neck.

A snort came from the elder statesman standing to Mattaki-Bunu's immediate right. "We have no women we want to offer you, Sub-Prince." The last was spat in a condescending sneer.

Ziyatum had never claimed to be an advocate of Murduk's. And the fool didn't have any trouble voicing his opposition regularly. Too bad he wasn't the one Murduk planned to set an example of. Sometimes the universe just didn't allow the luxury of presenting things the way one wanted it to.

With slow deliberation, Murduk rose from his throne and sauntered down the wide steps to stand on the last dais. The ledge would make him taller than the others, giving the impression of authority. With his fists on his hips, he returned the contemptuous sneer to each of the warlords. By the time he glared at each one, there was no question who was in charge. Traditional protocols be damned.

None of the men flinched.

It gave him a sense of pride to know these weren't simple idiots he had to deal with. They were the cream of Akurn society. It would be his greatest pleasure to maintain their obedience and keep them at heel like the dogs they were.

"I have no desire to sample any of the lackluster women in your territory, Ziyatum." Murduk stared as he spoke in a soft tone. "However, now that you've brought it to my attention, it behooves me to demand you send all the females of marriageable age in your household to the palace. I'm sure by now they need a real man to teach them what a true Akurn male expects in a sexual partner." He crossed his arms with a smirk. "Obviously I've been derelict in my duties in this area, and for that I offer my condolences. I'll make sure my staff rectifies this immediately."

A rumble of dissension echoed in the wide chamber.

Murduk raised a palm. "Be still. We are not here today to discuss your females. A matter of grave importance demands immediate action on my part." He uncrossed his arms and raised a hand to direct the warlords' attention to a vid he'd prepared. "Observe."

With a flick of his wrist, a three-dimensional hologram played. While the vision was grainy and out of focus, the audio was quite clear.

"Did he agree?"

This comment came from the image of the well-known traitor, Sychar. Clad head to toe in a gray battle suit fashioned like those worn by the warriors of their traditional past, the male had the ancient symbol, the Dingir, prominent on his breastplate. The eight-pointed star with the tips on the left ending in an inverted pyramid was an ideogram of the ancient God An, the supreme father of the gods. The symbol also proclaimed the man to be a priest of that sect.

"Yes, supreme Sychar. He has wholeheartedly agreed to join the resistance and begs to know what you may need from him. His goal is in alignment with ours to remove the impostor Sub-Prince from the throne."

A collective gasp echoed in the room as the identity of the new speaker became apparent. The image of the warlord Alalngar was clear, even given the poor resolution of the video.

Murduk purposely snapped the video closed.

While the image of Alalngar committing treason sealed his fate, the person they were talking about was still unknown. They didn't need to know that was all the pertinent information he'd received from the vid Damkina gave him the previous day.

Damkina was proving to be more of an asset than he originally considered.

"Alalngar, you stand before us as a traitor to the Akurn populace. Do you have anything to say before I pronounce your sentence?"

The well-respected warlord was around Murduk's age. Young enough to have the fire of his convictions, he should have been old enough to protect those convictions better.

The man took a step forward and clasped his hands behind him, his pale-blue eyes narrowed in contempt. "My only regret is I couldn't do more to replace someone as despicable as you to lead our people. We deserve better than a self-absorbed masochist who is killing the Akurn race." He spat on the floor just in front of Murduk's feet. "You are a coward and a disgrace to our people."

Murduk bared his teeth with a curled lip. Stepping through the spittle on the floor, he stopped in front of Alalngar. "I am no coward. I assure you I have no problem dealing with traitors personally."

Not taking his glare away from the man, he pulled out a small round device from his breast pocket. Another one of his favorite personal weapons. "By the authority vested in me by my father, King Du-Uru, I declare Warlord Alalngar from the house of Rearith, is hereby sentenced to death."

With steely eyes, he addressed the room. "Do I hear any opposition?"

Silence was his answer.

Most of the warlords displayed rigid expressions, though some shook their heads in denial. But no one spoke. The evidence was irrefutable and sealed the traitorous warlord's fate.

He stood mere inches from the traitor who never flinched as he approached. Pinching the tiny proton grenade between his fingers, he brought it up, giving Alalngar the ability to see what he held. When implemented, the weapon was a nasty piece of work that exacted excruciating pain before death.

He stepped closer, so they were touching chest to chest. Murduk leaned to whisper in his ear. "If you confess who Sychar is and where I can find him, I will not only spare your life, I will promote you to my second-in-command." As he spoke the last word, Murduk licked the outside shell of Alalngar's red-tipped ear.

Alalngar flinched and stepped back. "There is nothing you can say or do that would tempt me to work in any capacity with you." He glanced over his shoulder at the line of warlords staring at him. "I'd rather die as my own man than become one of your lackeys." He opened his arms wide and thrust his chest out. "Do what you must. Know this, my death will inflame the resistance. You are a traitor to the Akurn people, and one day you will suffer a worse fate."

Heat blanketed Murduk's face. Without another word, he shoved the proton grenade on the skin of the man's exposed throat.

The bullet shaped device absorbed quickly into his skin. Alalngar's pale-blue eyes widened as he gasped, his arms flinging backward. At first the man gulped as if trying to gather air.

Breathing would soon be the least of the traitor's worries. The primary function of the weapon was to disintegrate the cells in the body at the molecular level.

Within moments, the bones, muscles, and nervous system of the traitor dissolved, and the last image of Alalngar was his wide-eyed expression of pain as a low hiss escaped his open mouth. The man disintegrated into a silty dust, his noble attire falling in a heap on the pile. The long purple cape denoting his house floated and covered the uninhabited clothes.

"Nungal, get somebody in here to clean this vile mess up." Murduk went back to his throne. He slouched in the seat and glared at the rest of the warlords. "And make sure Alalngar's entire family is eliminated and all his holdings become the crown's property."

The satisfactory sound of the warlords' dissension rumbled through the room.

"Yes, Lord." His loyal personal guard murmured acknowledgment in his earpiece.

"Sire," his other personal bodyguard, Uruk, spoke from the other side. "Anbu requests immediate attention."

Murduk nodded. "Let him in."

The contemptuous group of the remaining warlords were silent as they glared with hardened expressions.

He grunted and waved an impatient hand at them. "Be assured, I have eyes everywhere, and I am aware of your every move." He leaned over and pounded his fist on the gilded armrest. "As you can see, I will deal with these vipers swiftly and efficiently. If you value not only your own life but that of your family, you are to inform me immediately if you have any information involving these betrayers. Understood?"

The remaining warlords snapped their heels together as they slapped their arms across their chests with a bow of respect.

"Yes, Majesty." The words echoed throughout the vast luxurious chamber.

"Leave me."

As one, the group filed out.

Rushing through the exiting mass came the captain of his guards, Anbu. "Sire." He bowed before standing at attention. "We have unfortunate news from FarDeep Base. Commander Kud has informed us that the human they had in captivity has disappeared. He awaits your orders."

Why was it every time he turned around, that imbecile on FarDeep Base complicated things? He pinched the bridge of his nose. "Tell that worthless piece of yetu that I want Phase II implemented immediately. He's to activate and stabilize our main power points on planet Earth. Be sure he puts in the safeguards to prevent humans from accessing them. He'd better speed up the financial downfall that was initiated in Phase I as well." Murduk relaxed and crossed an ankle over his opposite thigh. "Tell him he is not to contact me again until he can verify these orders are in motion." He glared at the captain. "It's your responsibility to make sure he does what he's told. If he doesn't, I will take it as a personal affront from you."

Anbu's pale complexion blanched even paler. "Yes, sire. As you command."

~Pete~

Pete followed his brother Michael down the long corridor that led to the secure cell housing the Akurn scientist, Thoth.

To keep the Akurns from finding the man, they'd brought him to the spaceship, CS Zikia. Their parents used this ship to escape when Murduk flooded the planet thousands of years ago.

In one of his more whimsical frames of mind, Pete thought the name was appropriate since it was the ancient word for life of earth and water. The vehicle was refuge to their little family on the wild and untamed planet they called home.

Now, CS Zikia housed his comatose father, Adapa, in stasis.

Pete swallowed the urge to turn around and head to the stasis chamber to sit with his comatose parent. Not that it would do him any good. It wasn't like he could run away from himself. The pained expression on Jena's face when he callously told her she meant nothing to him would haunt him forever.

When this was all over, maybe she'd let him crawl back to her as he begged for forgiveness. His only consolation was she had a better chance to stay alive if she stayed as far away from him as possible. Neither he nor his family had the right to bring her and her sisters into this shitstorm. Next family meeting, he'd make that clear.

It wasn't like she posed a threat to him or his family any longer. The whole reason the Akurns wanted her was to activate her genome to harm him or his brothers. Now that she defused that threat, no telling what the Akurns would do to her if they caught her and found out she was useless to them. He doubted they'd sing "Kumbaya" and let her go.

After all, Uncle Murduk wasn't a touchy-feely kind of guy.

He grunted as he picked up the pace to stay a respectable distance behind his taller brother. His shortest stature among his siblings never seem to cross their self-absorbed, tiny little minds. They always trotted ahead of him, forcing him to go faster or get left behind.

Pete glared at the back of his brother's auburn head. "Man, when are you going to do something about that mat on your head? You look like a troll doll on steroids."

Michael's deep ginger-colored hair reached the middle of his shoulders and was kept tied at the nape of his neck. Several strands floated free as the whole thing threatened to come loose. Unlikely he brushed it before pulling it back.

No answer. Instead, Michael flipped him off.

Pete sighed. His brother obviously wasn't in the mood. "Okay, what have we learned from Thoth at this point? Why haven't you psychically probed him yet? Not that I don't think Zamush got most of the intel from the asshole when he, ah, did his thing." Their second-eldest brother had a tendency to act like the legendary vampire of old, complete with sucking blood while absorbing the person's recent memories.

"No, with everything going on, I hadn't had a chance to yet." Michael looked over his shoulder with a half smile creasing through the red beard surrounding his lips. "That's what you're here for. If things somehow go sideways, I'll need your hulkness to stop it." His brother chuckled. "If nothing else, you're at least good for muscle."

"Bite me."

"Nope. That's Z's job, not mine."

Pete rolled his eyes. One of these days the guy might come up with something better than that tired old cliche. A slither of unease slid down his spine. This brother was a terrible liar on a good day, and Pete would bet one of his favorite classic cars that the man was up to something he wasn't going to like. He frowned.

"Ah, here we are." Michael waved over the indentation in the wall to open the sliding panel.

Growing up and living in the spaceship for most of his younger life, Pete knew every inch of the vessel. So, when they came into the room housing their prisoner, his eyes widened.

What had once been a cargo hanger was now a maximum-security holding cell. The wide expanse had a round security bubble in the middle. The force field waved in a rainbow of iridescent colors, showing the protection was up and running.

Several guard droids shaped like Easter eggs floated around the chamber.

Inside the translucent bubble lay the Akurn scientist in a stasis pod.

Pete crossed his arms and glanced at his brother. "Why do we have this man in double protection cocoons? It's not like he's strong enough to break through the main chamber."

"That's true, but we have to keep him like this so the Akurns can't probe and find him."

"Are you going to wake him up?"

Michael went to a row of controls and waved open a small drawer.

At once the chamber darkened. An emergency red glow replaced the natural lighting as a blistering siren pulsated in and out. "Alert. Alert. Incoming hostile is approaching the outside perimeters." The mechanical sound of the ship's major computer echoed in the chamber.

Shit! Had humans somehow found their high Himalayan retreat? Or worse, could it be the Akurns? Did they have ships on their moon base?

"Come on!" Michael rushed past him out the chamber door.

Pete didn't hesitate; he ran close behind his brother.

They went to the main control chamber where Michael waved and opened up several video displays. He directed his search around the mountain retreat.

There, in the distance, a small dot headed straight for them.

Striding to the exit, Michael grabbed a pair of ocular lenses and a formfitting coat that contained a body regulator.

They used the garment when they had to go outside into the hostile atmosphere of the high elevation of the mountain's peak.

"Are we going outside?" Stupid question, since that's where Michael headed. Pete didn't bother putting on a regulation suit that would maintain his body temperature. The extreme cold wouldn't bother him. All he had to do was regulate his skin to harden against the cold.

Going through a Transkip mirror, he and Michael departed into the blistering winds.

Michael aimed the ocular lens at the dot coming closer.

"Can you tell what it is?" Pete put a hand over his brow to shade his sensitive eyes from the blazing sun. As the dot got bigger, he was certain it couldn't be anything mechanical, like a plane or helicopter. The movement was more like a large animal swimming in the ocean. It was undulating as if riding through deep waves.

"Not sure." Michael thrust the ocular lenses at Pete.

Pete didn't hesitate and put the lenses up to get a closer look. He leaned forward. That couldn't possibly be what he thought it was. "Is that... is that a dragon?"

Instead of answering, Michael clicked something cold and heavy around Pete's neck.

"What the fuck?" Pete fisted the snug metal collar around his throat and glared at his brother. The asshole put what Pete sarcastically called the Band of Eternal Fucking Misery on him. Its official name was something technical his father came up with eons ago. Not that he gave a shit what they called it.

Adapa created the device when Pete went through that dark period in his life, right after Qamra betrayed him. Back then, he'd tried more than once to end his life by shifting and putting himself in the sights of either human hunters or local wildlife. His father made the damn thing to mute his psychic abilities, including shape-shifting or regulating his body.

With his abilities gone, the slicing cold made him suck in a freezing breath.

Michael placed something warm across Pete's shoulders and flipped a hood over his head.

"For once in your life, Pete, shut the hell up and listen to what she has to say. You'd better figure out how to fix this because you know deep inside you belong together. I'm warning you, don't you dare fuck this up." With that last word, Michael vanished.

Asshat. Michael's telekinesis allowed him to teleport short distances with a mere thought.

Pete jerked at a loud screech. The small dot was now a gigantic twenty-foot-long European red dragon of legend. Before he ran, it gripped him in a prison of crystalline claws and lifted into the freezing sky. The ragged peaks of the Annapurna mountain range fell far behind.

Chapter Sixteen

~Pete~

It didn't take Pete long to figure out that the creature who held him in a tight grip was Jena. While he fumed that she'd had the nerve to kidnap him, his heart raced. How in the hell did she turn into a dragon? It's not like they were running around so she could touch one! Even though he sat there and seethed like a whiny little baby, he wore a wide smile that made his face hurt. He loved flying, so here he was grinning like a loon even when pissed off. He gripped the protective coat tighter against the cold.

Michael. Damn rat bastard was in on this. Pete clutched the cold metal of the Eternal Fucking Misery band lodged around his neck. Michael better have given Jena a way to unlock the stupid thing. He grunted. The brick-red scales of the dragon's belly caught his attention. Damn, she'd done a fine job creating this ancient creature. He couldn't remember the last time he'd seen a dragon before they'd ended up extinct.

Caught up in his internal musings, it took him a while to realize they'd gone from the cold air of the Annapurna mountains to a warmer climate. In fact, sweat rolled into his eyes. Blinking and wiping away the moisture, he shrugged the coat off and peered around his cage of red crystalline claws.

If he wasn't mistaken, they were flying over the Mediterranean. His chest tightened as they flew with unwavering determination until the dragon began its descent. As the ground came closer, he barked with laughter. Shit, they were headed to his family's private island off the coast of Italy.

Nestled within the natural vegetation, Château de Starbrook had been rebuilt in the classic mode of the 1940s. Brick-red tile roof, arches, and rough plaster adobe adorned the various balconies and archways that made up the sprawling twenty-room estate.

Instead of taking him to the obvious landing pad the family had installed over seventy-five years ago for helicopters, she landed by a private pool close to the shores of the warm Mediterranean.

Pete's face flushed. Fuckin' Michael knew this was one of the favorite places Pete brought female companions to for some unrestrained private time. Not that he ever brought the same woman here twice. The irony bugged the shit out of him.

He gritted his teeth. She had no right to bring him here. She shouldn't be anywhere near him. Hadn't he made it clear that she needed to stay as far away from him as possible? Who did she think she was, putting herself in danger? He didn't suffer the agony of leaving her, only to have her ignore him.

With steady precision, Jena the dragon landed on her hind legs with her humongous wings flapping. Those wings were a work of art—pale umber with curved talons growing from each end like a giant's scythe. She gently placed the claws holding him on the ground and opened them to let him out.

Heat flushed through him as he threw the coat on the ground.

Jena the Dragon rested her massive body on her forelegs.

With each breath, he tensed and narrowed his eyes at her. "What the fuck do you think you're doing?" He waved a hand to encompass the supposedly serene area. "Enough of this! I demand you take me back right now." He gripped the thick metal around his neck. "Never mind. Just take this damn thing off and I'll save you the trouble."

The dragon stared at him with gentle cinnamon-brown eyes that sat in a scaled, bony skull. A trio of ruby crystal horns sat atop her head between her thick, dog-like ears. Along her jawline, small crystal spikes reflected in the bright sunlight. Matching long fangs poked from each side of her mouth. The outer scales of the dragon were resplendent in the warm Mediterranean sun. They shone in a vast spectrum of red from the palest pink to the deepest bloodred.

Never had there been a more magnificent sight. Again he asked himself how Jena could morph into the legendary creature she'd never seen or touched before. She took his breath away. Her creativity surpassed anything he'd ever come up with when he first started experimenting with the different ways he could change his appearance.

Not that his admiration would save her from the consequences of this dumbass move of bringing him here. The boiling anger in his gut threatened to explode. He clenched his fists around the metal collar choking him. "Jena! How in the hell can you be a dragon? Never mind... You change me back and take this goddamn thing off me!" He jerked on the Band of Eternal Fucking Misery.

The dragon huffed, and a small plume of dark smoke escaped a nostril. She rested her massive triangular head on her forelegs and gave him an unblinking stare.

He stomped to stand in front of her with his fists planted on his hips. He sent her a blistering glare. "I mean it, woman! Let me go right the fuck now!"

At the word woman, Jena blinked eyes as big as he was. Not that he cared. She'd never hurt him, just piss him off. "So, what's the point in bringing me here, huh? My brothers and I are a little busy trying to save the world from an alien invasion, ya know?" His grip on the collar tightened. "Which I can't help with since I've got this fucking thing on!" Buried memories of having the damn thing forced on him made his neck burn. Why not cut his nuts off while she was at it?

He narrowed his eyes. "Is this because I pointed out that you misunderstood what was happening between us?" He gave a self-deprecating laugh. "So what, you turn yourself into a dragon and bring me here so you can salvage your pride? Really? What makes you think I didn't mean what I said?"

With a smoky huff, Jena closed her eyes.

What, he was boring her now? He clenched his teeth so hard, one of his back molars cracked. That's when it happened. Adrenaline rushed hotly as the pounding in his ears obliterated everything around him. His vision narrowed to single pinpoint. He exploded.

Thousands of years of suppressed emotions thundered through. Him not being as psychically strong as his brothers or father. His feeling of worthlessness when his first love Qamra betrayed him to a rival for the promise of perceived riches and power. That she died a violent death at the hands of that man only made the whole damn thing worse.

The frustration that he couldn't help his ailing father or have a bigger role in stopping the Akurn invasion. To top everything off, his cowardly action of throwing away what he found with Jena made his stomach hard. While he might have convinced himself he did it to protect her, he'd never admit he'd done it to protect himself.

He ranted. He raved. Wild hand gestures met punches in air as he paced back and forth. He rambled on and on about how Jena had no right to bring him to the isolated château. Who did she think she was to interfere with the important work he was doing? She needed to stay far away from him as possible. How hard was that for her to understand?

The whole time he carried on, sweat broke out. He couldn't breathe. The weight of the world made him stumble to his knees as he gasped for air.

With head bowed, he trembled with his arms around his waist. He squeezed his eyes shut as he struggled for control.

A subtle spicy aroma enveloped him. It was a spunky blend of black pepper and cinnamon. A shadow blocked out the heat of the sun and soothed his burning skin. A comforting feminine form wrapped around his bent shoulders.

"Has anyone ever told you that you have a tendency to stand in your own way?"

~Jena~

Jena held the trembling man as his emotions played out. He had a lot of anger, hurt, and unresolved issues to struggle through. While she may have been the catalyst to start the avalanche, his frustrations weren't all about her. Unresolved emotions, especially a sense of worthlessness, had to be hard to confront. She would be there for him. She'd show him he was not only worthy but was the most deserving person she'd ever met.

She hugged him from behind and murmured soft words of comfort into his ear. As his trembling lessened, she nuzzled the side of his neck. A small kiss here, a light caress of her lips there. All the while she reveled in his unique scent. It was a fresh earthy flavor that reminded her of leather and black licorice. Her nipples hardened into sharp pebbles. Cream gathered between her thighs in a pool of anticipation.

She moved so she could feather her fingertips along his firm chest muscles. Her wandering hands slid down his trim sides. His muscles spasmed under her touch. When he straightened, she explored the hard landscape of his sinewy back. Even through his clothes, each pass over his hot skin made her breath come out in short pants. With care, she examined his trim waist and stroked with teasing little scratches. The temptation to delve under the waistband of his tight jeans was hard to fight. Instead, she brought her knuckles around to his lower back and kneaded the tight muscles.

"Jena—" He hunched his shoulders. "—why did you bring me here?"

She resisted the urge to let loose a sarcastic snort. "I brought you here because I need you." She nuzzled the side of his neck and breathed the words into his ear. "I brought you here because I want you." She gave the side of his neck a slight lick before whispering into the other ear. "I brought you here because I love you."

"Jena." Her name came out tight and filled with pain. "I thought I made it clear you and I were only a passing fling. What makes you think it was anything different?"

In normal circumstances, if a man had said that to her, she would've backed off and run away as fast as possible. Not this time. This time she knew he was fighting more against himself and his feelings of unworthiness rather than how he felt about her. This was a discussion that had to be face-to-face.

She drifted her hands over his shoulders and swung a leg over to mount his lap. Clasping her hands around his thick neck, she suckled his tender Adam's apple that bobbed with his hard swallow. "Do you really want me to go away?" She couldn't help but grin as her lips encountered the pounding vein in his neck.

He pushed away and stared at her with eyes so wide only a sliver of white surrounding his colorful irises showed. "Holy fuck, woman! You're naked." His pupils dilated even more as he looked her up and down. For a moment, his gaze lingered on her swollen and puckered nipples.

With a small shrug, she rewarded him with a sensual smile. "So? You have something against a naked woman on your lap?" She licked her lips. Time to take this bold seduction to another level. She transformed the fingers on one hand into sharp, thin claws and snipped the collar off his neck. It dropped onto the grass with barely a sound. All the while she brushed her swollen breasts against his clothed chest and gyrated her sensitive groin against the rigid bulge under his jeans. The musk from her soaked pussy perfumed the air. "Or do you just have something against this naked woman being on your lap?" She made her fingers return to normal.

He gripped her hips with a firm hold. His nostrils flared and his alien eyes narrowed.

"Tell me, Pete." She reached between their bodies and boldly stroked his swollen cock. "Are you as uninterested in me as you're trying to make me believe? Or are you brave enough to celebrate what we mean to each other?"

An inhuman growl rumbled deep inside his chest. He pushed her to the grassy knoll, never releasing his hold.

She landed on her back with legs splayed.

He dove in, his trim hips settling between the cradle of her thighs. "Woman—" His heavy tone was barely intelligible. An animal snarl took up most of the air. "—don't push me."

"Push you? Push you to do what?" She gripped the loose strands at the back of his head and pulled his head back to glare into his eyes. No way would she allow any more "misunderstandings" to come between them. "If you're as indifferent to me as you say you are, prove it." She wrapped her legs around him and locked her ankles together.

Dual moans peppered the air as the action made their groins rub together.

"We both know you're powerful enough to get up and walk away. I double-dog dare you to do that." Her vision narrowed. "But if you stay, there'll be no more of this bullshit on how casual this relationship is." She leaned until their faces were mere inches away. "You and I will be in this for the long haul." Her eyes focused on the plump mounds of his lips. She licked hers and breathed in his intoxicating scent. "So, what's it going to be, big boy? You ready to take on the adventure of a lifetime?"

He stared at her. Blazing heat mixed with adoration.

She sucked in a ragged breath and stared back. Heat filled her body as he purposely rotated his hips so his rigid member stroked her sensitive clit that poked out, begging to play. Oh, that delicious weight covering her. Her breasts swelled, making her nipples throb. Her pussy pulsated as precious moisture spilled and slicked her plump sex lips.

"Are you sure this is what you want?"

His ragged whisper made her clench.

"Because if I stay, I'm not going anywhere." His bright, alien eyes narrowed. "And neither are you. We both will face what comes next together." His alluring mouth whispered against hers. "Hmm?"

Fire energized every placed they touched. Eyes wide, she gave him a brief nod with a sultry grin. "Oh... yes." The breathless last word became muffled as she claimed his tempting lips with hers.

Jena whimpered when Pete broke the kiss off.

"I can smell your need." His seductive whisper fanned the tender skin behind her ear. "Luscious and hot. Do you know what being here with you does to me?"

"Wha'?" It was hard to concentrate when he switched their roles to become the dominant one. His amorous exploration between her neck and shoulder caught her off guard. She shivered and her skin pebbled under his touch.

"I'm in complete awe on how you affect me." He pulled back with a half-lidded stare. "And, contrary to how I've acted, I am man enough to admit that being with you is all I think about. How you make me hungry and I'm dying to taste you. How I burn to lick and nibble all this tempting flesh under me." His gaze swept down her body before focusing on her breasts.

"Pete." She weakened at his words. She squirmed on the grassy ground as a gentle wind caressed and added to his sensual onslaught.

"Look at these pretty treats quivering just for me." He rested on an elbow and gripped her straining breast. "With the prettiest little nubbins puckering, beggin' for me." Pete's eyes darkened. "I'd do anything to suck on those beautiful breasts, Jena."

He cupped one mound and squeezed it hard enough to make the tip stiffen to a thick point. His gaze locked with hers as he took the rugged bud into the blistering cavern of his mouth. He nipped with slow deliberation and suckled. Lavish broad strokes from his tongue continued the torture against her ultra-sensitive flesh.

Jena drew a sharp breath. "Oh my God!" She grasped his bulging arms to hang onto as she arched.

He switched sides and feasted on the opposite breast. After his fiery mouth ravished and devoured her, he released her quivering mound with a pop. He smacked his lips with sensual scrutiny. "Sweet Jena. Do you like this, my arammu?"

His swollen lips glistened. Not waiting for an answer, he continued his onslaught.

Each caress from his firm mouth caused a torment of pleasure straight to her core. She was at the precipice of straining lust and wanton need. "So good." She moaned.

"Delectable." A growl as he peppered light kisses over her flushed skin.

It was wild. It was intense. Jena swore she couldn't wait much longer. She craved more. To hell with foreplay. She wanted Pete inside her. Now. She swiveled her head back and forth. "Pete... please."

"Yes, baby. Let's burn together." He scooted to the juncture of her thighs and spread her legs wide. He stared, his gaze filled with glittering intent. A callused hand smoothed up the inside of her thigh before cupping her soaked sex. He stroked a finger up the narrow slit and coated it with her juices. His eyes rose to look into hers. "You're killing me here, Jena. So sweet and hot."

His powerful hands trembled as he placed his mouth on the sensitive skin of her upper thigh. The first lick from the flat of his tongue was easy.

Jena shook with violent pleasure. Her hips jerked as pulsating sensations ricocheted through. "Pete." His name came out in a keening moan. Grasping his thick strands of hair, she hung on.

"Yesss..." He trailed light kisses to her straining clit, swiping through the drenched folds in a slow, firm lick, stormy and wicked.

She nearly came, but he moved away before the detonation could light.

He nipped around the sensitive skin.

A building maelstrom pinched low inside with each pass. "Oh God, yes! Please, oh please!"

His breath seared her soaked sex as he licked every drop of the flowing cream coating between her thighs. "Jena, you possess me. If I had my way, I'd lay between your thighs for an eternity, only surviving on the soft cream that flows from you."

She would have laughed if he hadn't chosen that moment to fuck her with a broad finger into the welcoming depths of her channel. His sinful mouth sucked on her hard bud.

Her hips jumped.

Firm male hands held her down. A strangled scream tore from her as his sinful finger manipulated with unerring precision. Her orgasm was fast approaching as her pussy convulsed. She couldn't keep her senses intact as he pulled away. When she cried out at the emptiness, he replaced his finger with his fiery tongue and plunged into her quaking core.

He ate her like a man starved, as if he craved her like a drug. His mouth suckled as his tongue flicked hard.

Tension spun tight until everything inside let go. Her orgasm exploded, creating stars behind her closed eyelids.

Her responsive nerves quivered as Pete withdrew his tongue and knelt between her legs.

With quick efficiency, he disposed of his clothes until he was as naked as she was. "Jena, pinch your nipples for me. I want to watch you play with yourself while I fuck you."

Heat crept up her neck. "I... you... what?" It was hard to understand him with her brain checked out. She couldn't focus. She'd rather watch his wet, swollen lips move as he spoke.

"Do it for me, please?" He gripped the tip of his swollen cock, swirling the pre-cum over the tip before stroking it against the swollen folds of her sex.

She couldn't deny him any more than she could herself. She grasped both nipples and gave them a slight twist, groaning as a tense zing made her womb spasm.

"Fuck, yeah. Just like that." He pulled his cock free and rubbed it against her clit with a rotating up-and-down motion. After a few swipes, he nestled the crown of his erection inside the folds of her flesh.

She groaned when he rubbed inside. The friction caused her to relax around the hard steel wedge.

"Are you ready, arammu?" He eased out, then in.

Her hungry channel spasmed as his cock smeared with her juices speared her tight tissues. "Yes. Yes, damn it! Why don't you fuck me already!"

His only answer was to invade inch by slow inch. He worked his engorged cock back and forth as loud growls hissed out of his throat.

Never in her wildest dreams did she imagine a man could make her react like this. He conquered with each penetration into her hot, eager channel. Shit, she may not survive, but at this point, who cared?

"Yes, baby." Pete's crooning voice slid through her. "Play with your pretty nipples with one hand and your clit with another. Hurry, arammu. Play with yourself as my cock slides inside your tight pussy."

The explicit directions were intoxicating. She buzzed with pleasure as an oncoming orgasm roared to life with relentless pressure. She obeyed, tweaking a nipple and stroking her straining nub of her clit with circular motions. None too soon, his large member surged into her. Her hands fell away as her core strained around the engorged flesh of his cock.

"Yeah, Jena. Fuck." His eyes squeezed shut. He grabbed her hips and lifted her.

The action caused their groins to rub in frantic ecstasy as her ankles rested on his shoulders.

"Hell, you're so fucking tight I'm going to strangle." With slow, torturous strokes, he picked up the pace.

He was hot and thick inside her, and every stroke against her sensitive channel caused an avalanche of tension to build. She trembled and dug her nails into the ground. She thrust back, taking him in deeper.

He withdrew before slamming into her again, his hard hold on her ankles keeping her in place. "No, baby. Keep touching yourself."

He grunted, groans and growls highlighted by desperate lunges.

He picked up the pace, making it impossible for her to touch herself as he demanded. Pleasure slammed through her as her overly sensitive channel fought to grip and hang on to him. "No, Pete. I can't... you..."

Pure ecstasy burned into her mind. Dark pleasure became everything.

With a final hard thrust, he let loose an agonized growl. Hard hands gripped her hips and held her still as his release surged into her. "Jena, my everlasting love." He collapsed. Minute spasms twitched his slowly thrusting hips as he spilled into her convulsing womb.

~Pete~

Pete's back arched as the last contraction obliterated any higher thinking his brain might have. Everything went numb, except for the amazing sensations surrounding his softening cock. He might as well not exist in those fleeting moments.

He was such a fucking asshole. How could he possibly think leaving her was a good idea? Okay, he was a little pissed off that she kidnapped him. As a dragon, no less. But one glance at her alluring face created a bolt of insight that slapped him upside his thick head. This was what he needed. Someone who wouldn't put up with his self-destructive bullshit. All the while proving her commitment to him and him alone.

How could he possibly confuse Jena with Qamra? It would be the same as comparing the world's smallest lizard, the Jaragua dwarf gecko, to the magnificent red dragon she'd turned herself into. No comparison.

Taking a deep breath, he pulled back without looking at her. Just call him a yellow-bellied chicken. He'd hate to see the look of disgust on her face if she'd changed her mind and now responded like Qamra had all those centuries ago. He couldn't bear to see that expression clouding her beautiful cinnamon eyes.

By the time he drummed up enough courage to turn to her, her eyes fluttered open. Her dilated gaze peered at him with a possessive, sensual smile.

"Ah, there you are." She hummed. "Are we back now?" Her gaze fluttered at the space separating their chests, their groins still connected. "Or do you need more convincing?" She wrapped a strong, slim leg around one of his.

He couldn't help it. The fear and tension he'd carried for so long vanished. His smile had to be wide enough that his cursed dimples were probably black pits. He gave a tentative thrust of his hips and chuckled when she moaned with eyes closed. "I'm not sure. You know, I'm a little slow. Maybe we should explore my learning disability deeper..."

Pete, God dammit! Get back here right now!

The scream of Ben's voice in his head made a blaze of pain shoot between Pete's temples. He jerked in reaction and closed his eyes to focus. *Ben? What's wrong?*

"What's wrong?" Jena gripped his arms.

These idiots on Azadi are threatening to not help us while things on Earth are happening right before our eyes. Come back to Azadi with me and Raiden so we can figure out what to do next. Dammit, no time to explain! Just get your ass back here. Hurry! His brother snipped the connection off.

Pete shook his head and looked into her eyes. "I don't know. It's Ben. He's talking to me mentally and is freaking out about something." His body tensed. He tried to answer his brother, but all he got was silence. "He's never acted like this before. We'd better go back to FarDeep Base."

They both groaned as his semi-hard dick slid out.

"Son of a bitch! I can't believe his bad timing." He muttered under his breath as he pulled away from the embrace of Jena's warmth.

"How are we going to get there?" She stood and waved a hand up and down her flushed, delectable torso. "And I refuse to go around naked all the time."

He raised an eyebrow and gave a low whistle. "I'd love for you to go around naked all the time." He cleared his throat. "But we better get to Ben as soon as we can. Come on, we'll just go into the villa and find us something to wear before we take a Transkip mirror back to Azadi."

With eyes that sparkled, she laughed as she raced with him through the soft grass and over the warm terracotta tiles that led up to the house's entrance.

Without giving her a chance to check the place out, he grabbed her hand and led her to his bedroom on the second floor. He gazed at the wide bed with its white duvet, red accented blankets, and pillows with longing. He'd love nothing more than to throw Jena on the soft mattress and have his wicked way with her. First opportunity, he promised himself.

One of the domestic drones assigned to the house buzzed into the room behind them.

"Do you require assistance?" It kept a respectable distance and spoke in a flat, metallic voice.

"Yes. Provide adequate undergarments, clothing, and shoes for my companion. Be sure they are for rough terrain. Also, have the Transkip mirror in the primary room dialed to reach the hidden city of Azadi that's programmed in the main database."

The front panel on the droid's wide cylindrical body opened, with everything Jena would need folded neatly inside.

"Put those on. Trust me, they'll fit."

He scrambled to his dresser and pulled out a black pair of micro hip briefs and yanked them on. Next came a pair of jeans with a black T-shirt before he put on an open sport shirt from his closet. After donning a pair of socks and boots, he stood. He glanced at Jena to see how far she'd gotten.

Which wasn't much. She stood with her hand over her open mouth as she stared at the interior of the drone.

He smiled at her befuddled expression. "Something wrong?"

She peeked at him before looking back at the drone floating in midair. "Um, no. I guess not? This thing won't shock me or anything when I touch it. Will it?"

Her cheeks flushed the cutest shade of pink.

"Trust me, it's fine. This is one of the domestic drones that maintains our estate. It's able to scan and analyze what would fit you." He rubbed the warm skin between her shoulder blades. "We've got to get going."

She pulled the stack of clothes out and held them as she looked underneath them. "Okay. Is there somewhere I can freshen up first? I promise I won't take long."

Pete took her to the bathroom.

True to her word, she dressed and was ready to go in record time.

He led her out of the room, and they went down the stairway to the main foyer. "One of these days you'll have to tell me how you knew the way to our villa here in the Mediterranean." He chuckled. "Or how you even knew we had a villa here."

She shrugged with a wide smile. "It was your brother Michael's idea. And I'm pretty sure he somehow put the directions in my head. I think he's better than Siri any day of the week."

"Before we go, I have to ask you."

She glanced at him with raised eyebrows.

"How in the hell were you able to turn into a dragon without touching one?"

Her impish grin made him smile with her. "That's easy. I admit being a veterinarian helps to fill in the blanks when it comes to animals. But the main reason I could was because either you've touched one or some ancestor in your past has."

He rubbed his chin. "What the hell does that mean?" While dragons were an animal the Akurns brought to earth when they first started mining gold there, they all died out long ago.

"What it means is I can access your ancestral DNA, human or Akurn. When I experimented with my sister, I've found I don't have to touch anything as long as you or one of your ancestors has." Jena visibly shivered. "Who knows what we can come up with together?"

While turning into long-extinct creatures was something Pete couldn't wait to explore with Jena, now wasn't the time. Pete led Jena through the Transkip mirror to a massive control center in the hidden city of Azadi on Earth's moon. Holding his woman's hand, he spied Raiden and Ben standing with the Azadi co-rulers, Edinni and Damuzi. They were in a round translucent bubble in the middle of an equally round room. Along the walls, manned by a handful of personnel, were various control panels with accompanying monitors displaying floating graphics.

Pete smirked at his younger brother.

A tight-mouthed Ben gestured at Damuzi and spoke in a stern tone, his head tipped. "That's asinine." He clenched a fist. "You can't ignore what will happen to billions of sentient people if the Akurns are successful with their plan." He straightened and crossed his arms and glared. "Besides, where will you get all your supplies if Earth is gone?"

That statement startled Pete. It never occurred to him where the hidden city might get the resources they needed to function. Made sense. They used the Transkip mirrors and small spacecrafts to go back and forth from the moon to Earth.

"My mate didn't say we wouldn't get involved." Edinni placed a hand on Damuzi's arm when he tensed and mirrored Ben's aggressive stance. "As you pointed out, we wouldn't be able to survive without Earth's resources. However, please understand we are a small community that can't afford..."

"I'm afraid it's more dire for you than that." Raiden interjected. With his hands clasped behind his back, he brought a sense of calm into the conversation. "If the Akurns are successful in blowing up the Earth in order to propel them out of our solar system, what do you imagine will happened to the moon itself?"

Damuzi swung his focus to Pete's older brother. "Are you inferring the moon might get destroyed?"

Raiden's chin tilted. "Indeed."

Edinni sucked in a breath. "When we ran our simulations, we did not project that the blast would do anything but kick us out of Earth's orbit and we'd end up captured by Mars' gravitational pull. Once in orbit of that planet, we'll terraform it in order to bring life back to it."

One of Raiden's pale eyebrows rose. "Are you willing to stake your very existence on that scenario? What if the blast radius does not destroy the moon, but flings it too far out to be caught by Mars? How would you sustain yourself then?"

Raiden waved to the round monitor in front of them that showed Earth in a defined holographic image minus the space junk and cloud cover. Simple red dots pulsated on each of the continents. "We've determined that the Akurns have activated their technology on the planet in order to access the Earth's ley lines. Once they've completed the sequence, they'll draw extra energy straight from the earth's molten core." His eyes flickered at Pete as he and Jena approached. "Pete, we're glad you and Jena can join us."

Pete recognized what those dots represented. They indicated several historic pyramids located in Peru, India, and Egypt. "Yeah, so what's the big emergency?" He smirked as he gestured to the rotating image of Earth. "Other than everything, of course."

Jena squeezed his hand.

He looked at her. Her narrow-eyed stare was accompanied by a slight shake of her head, telling him to behave. As if.

"Well." Ben ran a hand through his short blond hair. "Let's see." He ticked off his next words with his fingers. "As you can see, some ancient sites now have a kind of shield around them along with an unknown buildup of power. The global financial collapse has begun, and..." Ben's bland announcement didn't match his rigid stance. "Michael is missing."

A sudden coldness hit Pete's core. "What do you mean missing? That's impossible. No way can mind-boy disappear." He aimed a thumb where Raiden stood with his body and face relaxed. Until Pete looked closer.

There were tight brackets around Raiden's mouth.

He took in a deep breath. It didn't take him long to individualize the myriad of smells in the room and isolate them. Ah, there was Raiden's. The sour taste of worry that bordered with panic dominated his scent. Shit, things must be more dire than he let anyone know.

"Why do you say it's impossible for Michael to be missing?" Jena gave a brief tug on his hand.

Pete brought her hand up to his mouth to give it a slight kiss before he replied. "Because Michael and Raiden are the strongest telepaths in the family. They've always been able to keep in contact with each other on a mental level." He eyed his big brother. "Are you telling me you can't contact him?"

The brackets framing his brother's mouth deepened. "That's correct. While not severed, he's blocked."

"That's where you come in." Ben interjected. Even though his attention swung away from the Azadi co-rulers, he wasn't any less tense. "We're going to call in Z to come up here with Mother to help Raiden coordinate our defenses from here." His attention focused on Damuzi. "If that's okay with you folks."

Edinni nudged him. With a frown, Damuzi gave a brief nod.

"I'll go back to Earth and work with my contacts in the American government. I can help them stem the global financial crises that's started." Ben's arms dropped. "We need you to go back and see if you can't track Michael. Now isn't the time for him to go missing."

"Do you think he's found one of my sisters?" Jena chewed on her plump lower lip.

Pete sucked in a breath. How in the hell did that small action make his cock twitch? Shit, he was so far into her it wasn't funny. He wrapped an arm around her shoulders. Yeah, and wasn't she the best fucking thing that ever happened to him?

"I'm afraid finding the rest of your sisters are the least of our concerns."

Pete appreciated Raiden saying the bad news in a soft tone.

"The chance of one of your sisters following through the Akurn plan to incapacitate us is remote." He nodded at the Azadi couple. "We have it on good authority they've abandoned that plan and are now concentrating their efforts on a bigger scale."

Pete watched the rotating planet with the numerous red dots pulsating. "Okay, Jena and I are in."

She nodded vigorously.

"Where's the last place you know where our bro was? We'll start tracking him from there." He looked down and gave her a sheepish smile. "Wanna try turning into a Goraxag?"

Jena gave him a sultry smile and patted her tummy. "Nah, I think I'll just lay off any more shapeshifting until I find out if it affects the baby or not."

Every cell in Pete's body stilled. He couldn't catch his breath. The vision of his father and the bright starlight was real?

"Baby? What baby?"

~Michael~

Michael jerked awake from a vision-induced sleep. Gasping for breath, he put his hand over his heart and concentrated on taking deep, cleansing breaths. Sitting up in his bed, he swiveled and draped his legs over the sweat-soaked sheets, gripping his thighs as fading images swirled. He hadn't had an intense vision like that in centuries. Whatever he saw woke him up and scared the shit out of him. While the dream images were all a blur, he carried back a feeling of deep helplessness.

One thing for sure, it involved Jordyn Lamont, one of Julienne's sisters he'd become obsessed with. He found her a couple of days ago in Carson City, Nevada, and immediately conducted a thorough background check on her. She worked as a general manager at a small local downtown casino. No immediate family except for an aunt who raised her and lived in the same small city. Apparently, Jordyn and her aunt were quite close and didn't live far from each other.

With reluctance, he made plans to go there. He hated leaving his haven in Napa Valley and loathed travel. He ran a trembling hand through his tousled hair and glanced at the floating vid monitor playing soothing background sounds that also had a small stamp of the current time on the bottom right corner. Son of a bitch, he'd only fallen asleep a half an hour ago. He sighed and took a deep breath, hoping to clear his fuzzy mind.

The one thing that became crystal clear was the image of Jordyn. When he'd joined her in the Dreamwalk, he did his best to keep the interaction light. At first, his only intention was to get a feel for her personality, but all too soon he became fascinated with everything about her. It was a shock when she stated her aunt warned her about aliens coming for her. He couldn't believe he didn't take the time to investigate her aunt Amata. Obviously, this "aunt" wasn't just some human who raised Jordyn. He'd better put that on his ever growing list of things to look into.

But this vision that woke him up was something different. It came across as a warning... about her. It was a brutal warning for him to stay as far away from her as possible. But that didn't make sense. For her to be dangerous to him, the Akurns would have had to have activated her genome. Since he was psychically linked to her now, he should have known if something like that happened. Unless that prediction was that warning.

Exasperated, he ran a hand over his face as a pounding headache bloomed, making him nauseous. The distinct sound of the Transkip mirror whirred in the hallway. Grabbing a loose sheet, he flung it over his naked lap. No need to give his unexpected guest a cheap peep show.

Instead of one of his family members, the unmistakable feline form of a grossly overweight Siamese cat strolled in. It was Bubbas, Jena's so-called pet.

It was a shock to him and his family when the creature introduced himself recently. Especially when Bubbas turned out to be more than a domesticated house cat. Turned out he was a demigod named Maathes, a son of the Egyptian goddess Bastet. In his natural form, he had the physique of a seven-foot human male with the head of a Siamese cat. He and his kind colonized Earth thousands of millennia ago when they'd been assigned as guardians of the planet.

Couldn't be a coincidence Bubbas attached himself to Jena. The woman was an Akurn hybrid mated to his brother Pete. She now had the ability to shapeshift like his brother did. He suspected the couple would soon discover they were going to be parents.

The cat stopped and sat in front of him. He lifted a paw to lick and groom.

"And what brings you here to my abode, oh great one?" Pete wasn't the only brother who could throw out a sarcastic comment now and then.

The cat eyed him as he placed his paw on the floor. The icy blue of his direct stare narrowed. There are a few incidents that have occurred you should be aware of.

The cat whipped his head up and within a blink of an eye morphed from his feline form into his humanoid one.

Towering before Michael was a naked, muscled, broad-chested adult male holding a was scepter, an ancient Egyptian staff.

The flat protrusion at the end of the staff made it look like a golf club, and Michael had to resist the urge to ask what the male's handicap was. "Damn, man. Could you at least put something on besides your armband? You're gonna make me go blind."

The headache throbbed behind his eyes as he flung the sheet away from his lap. With his legs shaking from the pain, he went to his dresser and put on a pair of sweats. "Okay, follow me while I get some coffee. You can hit me with what you got then." He grabbed a hair tie from his dresser and pulled his scraggly shoulder-length hair back and tied it out of his eyes. Taking his time, he headed to the kitchen.

His personal domestic droid, DD-CrowT, a machine he created to resemble the Crow-T Robot from Mystery Science Theater 3000, floated and pointed to the single-cup coffee maker bubbling the last shots of the exotic coffee of dark roast he craved. "Your beverage is ready, oh master man. Ya want anything to eat?"

Michael shuddered. Between his headache and being subjected to the naked form of Maathes first thing in the morning, he'd lost his appetite. "No, thanks. Maybe later."

"Okey, dokey. Shout as usual if you change your mind." The droid lowered to the floor and powered down.

Michael grabbed the lifeline of his steaming cup from the holder and motioned it toward the enormous male. "Can I get you something?"

The demigod shook his head and narrowed his eyes. "No." The word was guttural.

Must be hard to speak through a cat's whiskered snout.

To avoid jostling too much, Michael carefully sat on a chair by his kitchen room table. He put the steaming coffee cup on the solid walnut surface and glanced through the large, open kitchen window. His ripening harvest of burgundy wine grapes swayed in the gentle breeze. Taking a deep breath, he savored the aroma of his growing fields with their musty tang reminiscent of home. He took a sip of his steaming nutty beverage and eyed his uninvited guest. "Suit yourself. Tell me what you've got."

"As requested, I've placed Jena's brothers and the family they were with into one of my people's safe places. I will speak with your family later so they can coordinate with Jena to transfer them to one of your facilities."

Taking another careful sip of the steaming beverage, Michael gave a slight nod. His headache was getting worse. "Sounds good. We thank you for accommodating us in this emergency. I suspect the Akurns would have taken them to force our hand."

"Agreed." Maathes tilted his head. "However, the primary reason I'm here with you is to aid you personally." He leaned over and stared with expanded slitted pupils. "Your latest vision reached out to me."

Michael's eyes widened. "Really, how? Why...?"

"Listen carefully, *Adamou*." The large creature straightened. "They activated the female you seek. You have a limited period to reverse the process before she becomes harmful to you."

The Akurns activated Jordyn's genome? Michael swallowed hard. That meant if he got near her, she could rip his psychic abilities away and use them for herself. He'd either end up comatose or be killed outright. "If she's activated, how can I get near her to..."

Maathes touched the was scepter to the middle of Michael's forehead, the hard surface firm on his skin. His pounding headache receded.

"I will bind your psychic powers for a brief time, except for your ability to Dreamwalk. This will enable you to reach her and take her away from captivity in order to reverse the process."

The daunting task loomed. "Wait! How can I do that if I can't access my powers?"

"Do not fear, Adamou. I assure you, you have all you need for the task. I pray to the Lady of Blessings for her to grant you the strength and wisdom to aid you in your success."

Before Michael could protest, the Egyptian demigod activated the was scepter.

Now that you've finished reading *Alien Legacy: The Shapeshifter*, it'd mean the world to me if you left an honest review on Amazon. Just click here. This type of feedback is an authors lifeblood and helps others find their work. I can't continue writing without you.

Thank you!

Keri Kruspe, award-winning *"Author of Otherworldly Romantic Adventures"* loves nothing more than to write about romances that feature "feisty heroines who are afraid to take a chance on life... or love". Her writing career started when she became irritate that most SciFi Alien Romances had women kidnapped before love found them. Determined to create something different, she turned "the alien kidnapping trope upside down" (Vine Voice) and the **ALIEN EXCHANGE** trilogy was born.

Keri's latest SciFi Romance series, **ANCIENT ALIEN DESCENDATNS**, is taking the Ancient Alien motif and mixes it with a sensual, romantic twist.

A native Nevadan, Keri is a lifelong avid reader who lives in northwestern Michigan with her hubby and the newest member of the family, a Jack Russell Terrier names Hestia. When not immersed in her made-up worlds, she enjoys discovering the fascinating landscape of her new home and pairing red wine with healthy ways to cook while indulging in classic rock. Most of all, she loves finding her next favorite author.

If you want to know when Keri's next book will come out, please visit her at her website where you can sign up for her mailing list. You'll get a FREE copy of the novella, *The Day Behind Tomorrow* that is a prologue to the **ANCIENT ALIEN DESCENDANT SERIES**. Not to mention being kept updated on the life of a dedicated, obsessed author.

Social Media Links:

Facebook

Twitter

Instagram

Alien Legacy: The Vampire

Alien Legacy: The Mage (coming 2022)